Evonne and Vrawg: Bounty Hunters

Jeremy Hayes

ISBN: 0995029709
ISBN-13: 978-0995029705

For Mrs. J. Sneddon, my grade four teacher and former librarian at Edgewood Public School. In grade four we were given a project to make our own book with the help of a local author. From that point on I knew I wanted to keep making books. Thanks Mrs. Sneddon.

Other Books By Jeremy Hayes

The Stonewood Trilogy

Book I: The Thieves of Stonewood

Book II: The Demon of Stonewood

Book III: The King of Stonewood

Tales Most Strange

The Goblin Squad

Even More Tales Most Strange
Coming Soon

The Wizards of Stonewood
Coming Soon

Northlord Publishing

Visit us at: www.northlordpublishing.com for news about
upcoming releases or to contact the author.

Cover Artwork: Joseph Garcia
Cover Color Artist: Roberto Garcia
Map: John R.L. McNabb
Website/Logo: Cody Kotsopoulos www.kotsysdesigns.com

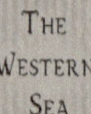

NORTHERN WASTES

THE
WESTERN
SEA

GLASTONBY

DALECANIN
VALLEY

BALVERN

GREY ASH MOUNTAINS

WAYFARE

IRONCLIFFE

PORT
BAYSWATER

TAUROS

TO
TROLLPORT

TO
STONEWOOD

VALDROW

HADFELL HILLS

GOLDFIELD

GUILDBURG

ZALHANDRIA

ZAL~BARON DESERT

PROLOGUE

The rain was coming down with such force that it stung the woman's face. She grimaced uncomfortably and looked to her enormous partner. If the rain was bothering him at all, he did not show it. She imagined that he hardly noticed. His greyish-skin was thicker than hers; thicker than any human, in fact. He was only half ogre but you could not tell it from the sight of him. The ogre blood ran predominantly throughout him and the monstrous brute possessed a pain tolerance like nobody else she had ever encountered.

Evonne shivered. After their long trek through a dark forest in search of a secluded cabin, her clothing was thoroughly soaked. The mismatched pieces of armor she wore chilled her skin. The evening's storm had been relentless thus far. She would have much preferred sitting in a tavern this night, warming her bones beside a fire with a mug of foaming ale. But she and her partner had no choice in the matter; they were forced to endure the miserable storm.

They had received word from a reliable source that the man they sought would be on the move come sunup. They had tracked his location to this remote cabin and knew that he would not be remaining here for long.

Evonne, the former pirate, glanced upwards through squinted eyes in the driving rain. She regarded the full moon and wished it could have been any other night than this one. She tapped Vrawg's heavily-muscled arm and motioned towards the cabin that sat a short distance away. The half-ogre nodded. His face, what she could make of it in the darkness, was all business as usual.

She winced as her gigantic partner exited the cover of the dark forest and crept across an open expanse of land towards the cabin. She cringed with each snap of a twig and from the sucking sound his massive boots made in the thick mud. Vrawg possessed many endearing and valuable qualities and skills but stealth was not one of them. Her only hope was that the sound of the driving rain and the occasional loud clap of thunder would render anyone inside the cabin oblivious to the half-ogre's approach, at least until he was in position.

The cabin was small and simple in design. Squarish in shape with only one door from which to enter and exit. A curtained window faced in every direction and a flickering light source was evident inside. The structure was in a state of disrepair but Evonne had guessed that this cabin was only used as a waypoint and not a permanent residence.

Thankfully, a loud crack of thunder boomed overhead as Vrawg reached the front door and took up position to the right side, opposite the window. The seven-foot tall, grey-skinned bounty hunter, wore mismatched pieces of a variety of different armor types, much like his female companion. His massive war hammer hung across his back and in both hands he held a glittering net which he had just removed from a large sack. The net sparkled from the light of the full moon and was a special invention of Evonne's, designed to hold a certain kind of quarry.

Although Vrawg could not see Evonne within the cover of the forest, he knew she was watching and nodded his head in indication that he was ready. Evonne's heart thumped in her chest as she eased the crossbow off her back and loaded a special kind of bolt into the weapon. Like the net, the bolt was a recent invention by the highly adaptive bounty hunter.

She took careful aim at the cabin's front door and worried about the force of the rain coming down. Evonne was an expert marksman, having honed her skills over years on the bobbing deck of a pirate ship. She just hoped the storm would not affect her accuracy and thus put her partner at risk. Vrawg placed much trust in his petite friend, knowing what she was capable of and how deadly accurate she was with that crossbow.

Evonne steadied her breathing as she watched Vrawg knock on the front door to the cabin. He remained just to the right of the door, his net ready in his hands.

Nothing.

A few moments later he knocked again, more forcibly.

No response.

Evonne lowered her crossbow and considered their next move. That is when she heard it. It was a faint sound at first and could have been easily dismissed as the howl of the wind. Then it grew louder and was most definitely the feral growl of some beast. Evonne cursed inwardly as she guessed at the source. The hunters had become the hunted.

Before she could even turn to look behind her, Evonne was tackled with such force that it stole the breath from her and her crossbow flew from her grasp. She landed hard in the clearing and slid several feet in the slick mud with the beast on top of her.

Instinctually, she managed to free her hands and grab her attacker by the throat. She could feel the thick, coarse hair that covered its humanoid body, and it took all her strength to hold its snarling snout at bay. It growled with anger and its warm breath washed over her face. The coppery-scent of blood was evident and told her the beast had just recently fed.

Her arms trembled and finally gave way; the beast was far too strong for the small woman to resist. Her eyes closed, waiting for the inevitable snap of its jaws upon her face, but it never came. The weight was removed from her chest as the howling beast flew into the side of the cabin, nearly crashing straight through. Evonne smiled, weakly. Vrawg.

The half-ogre arrived just in time to save his friend from a ghoulish fate. He grabbed the war hammer from his back and stalked towards the hairy beast that was now back on its feet and snarling.

"No, you fool. The net. Use the silver net," Evonne attempted to say, but it only came out as a whisper as she still fought to regain her breath.

Vrawg now got a good look at the man-beast that stood before him. He thought that it did not resemble the man they were looking for in the least, aside from the fact that it wore tattered green pants; the same colored pants that they were told Devon Klurk was wearing earlier that same day. Vrawg understood that the full moon had changed the man and all his humanly facial features were replaced with the head of a wolf. He was bare-chested and sported thick brown hair that covered every inch of his body.

The werewolf dove at the half-ogre with inhuman speed. Vrawg was deceptively fast, considering his immense size, but he was not fast enough. He swung his hammer with crushing force but the beast got to him first. The werewolf clung to his right shoulder and sunk its fangs deeply into the bounty hunter's skin.

Vrawg growled and grabbed the beast with his free left hand. He plucked him off like it was a mere child and slammed the werewolf into the ground, splattering mud in all directions. Vrawg's hammer came down swiftly but found only the mud-soaked ground. The werewolf rolled out of the way and then managed to sink its fangs back into the half-ogre's skin, this time his left leg.

Evonne slashed at the beast with her curved sabre, biting into one of its arms. It merely backhanded her with little regard to the wound and sent her flying several feet away. The werewolf was nowhere near the size of the half-ogre but she imagined he was just as strong.

Vrawg jammed the handle of his hammer down into the werewolf's back. The beast let go of his leg and stumbled away. Vrawg roared and struck the stunned monster in the shoulder with his massive hammer and heard the crunch of bones as the werewolf's arm now hung at an odd angle.

The huge bounty hunter's jaw hung open as the werewolf's shoulder popped back into place. An evil smile spread across its face. He realized his partner had been right in her assessment that only silver could do any real damage to this type of creature.

Before it could lunge at the half-ogre again, a silver streak flew past Vrawg and struck the werewolf in that same shoulder. The beast gasped as smoke issued forth from the wound. Evonne quickly reloaded her crossbow with another silver bolt and then shot him in the leg.

Devon Klurk fell to his knees in immense pain. These damned hunters had come prepared, he realized. Then a net, coated entirely with silver, was thrown atop him and stole his strength. He slumped to the muddy ground, whimpering in defeat.

As Evonne approached, Vrawg pointed to his bloody wounds with a worried look upon his face.

"Don't cry. Your ogre's blood makes you immune to his bite. You cannot be infected with the lycanthropy disease. Now, me on the other hand…," her voice trailed off as she considered how close she had come to getting bitten.

They had been sloppy. She should have figured that the werewolf would have sensed their approach. The moon was full and Klurk would have been out on the hunt.

"I don't think he is going to be any more trouble tonight. Come on, you big oaf, let's get him back into town. We are gonna drink heartily tomorrow with the price on his head."

*　　*　　*　　*

The two bounty hunters strolled out of the tavern

with their bellies full. It nearly took the establishment's full store of food to satisfy the giant half-ogre, but they had paid in gold, so the tavern owner was more than happy to supply the two hunters with whatever they desired. They were heroes, after all, having captured the vile werewolf that had been terrorizing the town for the better part of a year.

Evonne was considering their plans for the future when her thoughts were interrupted by an elderly man who addressed them.

"Evonne and Vrawg? Can it really be 'the' Evonne and Vrawg? Tell me my aged eyes do not deceive me."

Evonne quickly studied the frail-looking man and did not consider him any kind of threat. His hair was snow-white and he wore a robe of the same color. Round spectacles sat on the end of a pointy nose and he carried an armful of rolled up scrolls.

"Yeah, yeah, it's us. Now if you don't mind, we will be on our way."

"You do not understand. My name is Hornoglio and I have come here seeking the two of you, all the way from the Ivory Citadel."

Evonne had heard stories of the Ivory Citadel. It sat within the borders of Tauros, though it was independent from the rule of The Purple King. It was a place of scholars and scribes and was said to house the greatest library in the world. The men and women of the Citadel strived to map the known world and document all of its historical events. Wealthy folk paid a pretty coin to study at the Ivory Citadel.

"Why?" she asked. "What does the Ivory Citadel want with us?"

"The two of you are quite famous. Possibly the most famous bounty hunters to walk these lands. And I heard about your capture of the werewolf. Impressive indeed. We at the Ivory Citadel wish to record your exploits. We want to document your lives."

"Why?"

"It is what we do. We record such things. Important events and important people should never be forgotten by future generations. I can ensure that long after the two of you are gone from this world, your legacy and story will live on within the Citadel."

Evonne had to admit that it did sound interesting. She would be lying if she said there was not a small part of her that enjoyed some level of fame. Besides, it could not hurt to have someone paint her in a more favorable light and possibly erase some of her terrible reputation as a feared pirate.

She looked to her giant partner to gauge his opinion. Vrawg just shrugged his shoulders, indicating his indifference to the matter.

"Alright, what do you have in mind?"

"Oh, splendid," the man said, clapping his hands together. "I have a relative that lives on a farm on the outskirts of town. I will give you the directions and perhaps we could meet there tomorrow morning. I will bring plenty of parchment and ink."

Evonne agreed and she and Vrawg made the half-hour trek the following morning to the appointed location. Hornoglio welcomed the bounty hunters and directed them to a smaller guest house where he had a table already set up. Several pots of ink and many sheets of parchment were spread across the table. He held a feathered quill at the ready.

"Please, please, make yourselves comfortable. I have some fresh bread and sweets just over there, with some ale to wash it down with."

Evonne sat at the table across from the scribe while Vrawg attacked the bread.

"So," she wondered. "How do we do this? Where do we start?"

"Why not from the very beginning? Your childhood."

"The very beginning? I thought you wanted to know about our adventures as bounty hunters?"

"And I do. But I think it is important to learn everything there is about the person. What is it that has molded the two of you into the people you are today? What has brought a Taurosian woman to partner with a half-ogre from the Grey Ash Mountains? I feel there is an interesting story here worth hearing. So please, start from the very beginning. Tell me about a young Evonne."

Evonne thought back to the painful memories of her childhood and then to her time as a pirate.

"I don't know if you have enough ale."

CHAPTER 1

Evonne Zyndelbrun was born into a poor family that lived in the port city of Guildburg. She had two older brothers, Jarold and Zack, along with one younger brother, Harlon. Her mother, Amely, was once a barmaid in a seedy tavern but now stayed home to raise her children. Her father worked a variety of odd jobs to earn whatever coin he could, namely using his children as chimney sweeps.

Most folk in Guildburg worked on the docks. It was a city very much dependent on the trade that the ships brought in and they did not care whether the ships were legitimate merchants or pirates selling stolen goods. No questions were asked. Guildburg was part of the great western nation of Tauros, ruled by the iron fist of The Purple King. Some said The Purple King was mad, though they said that quietly, as he was not a forgiving man.

The King was strongly against piracy, at least in the waters around Tauros, though Guildburg was located at the very southern tip of the nation, and did not have the full support of the Taurosian navy to patrol its waters. So pirates came and went with little regard to laws.

Evonne's father, Griff, was a terrible drunk and tended to drink away most of the coins the family could bring in, which was not many. Griff had a habit of blaming life and everyone else around him for his hardships, not willing to admit his own laziness and lack of ambition. He had once worked at the docks, unloading cargo from ships, until his repeated patterns of showing up to work drunk got him fired. Now nobody would hire him.

Griff started his own chimney sweep business, which involved lowering his oldest son, Jarold, down into chimneys to clean them, while Griff sat nearby with a drink. When Jarold grew too big to fit, the job fell to his younger brother, Zack.

Now, too big to be a chimney sweep, Jarold was forced by Griff into a series of jobs which had the boy working nearly twenty hours a day, with less than four hours to sleep. By the age of sixteen, Jarold had reached his wits end and disappeared. A note was left behind that he had gone to join the army of The Purple King.

Griff was furious, and as per usual when he was furious, he took that anger out on his children. He beat them all senseless as a stern warning that they should never repeat the actions of their foolish older brother. Evonne's mother would just watch, fearing what would happen if she ever stepped in.

Evonne always seemed to get it worse than her brothers, as her father's favorite line to her was, "You should have been a boy."

She would never forget the day when her father and Zack returned home early one morning. Zack was now twelve and was shoved roughly into their tiny living room;

his arms scraped and bloody, tears streaming down his face.

"Wonderful, just wonderful," her father roared. "Zack won't fit in the chimneys anymore, will you, you useless little brat? How are we going to eat now, huh? What job are you going to get now?"

Evonne could smell the alcohol on her father already, despite the early hours of the morning. She knew he was not worried about how they were going to eat, he was worried about how he was going to drink.

Then he fixed his gaze on his eight-year-old daughter and she knew trouble was coming. "Well, well, looks like Evonne can finally make herself useful around here instead of just being another filthy mouth to feed. You are the perfect size to replace Zack."

Evonne was tiny, even for her age, so therefore would have no trouble fitting into the chimneys, as that was what her father had in mind. Later that evening, Evonne was having trouble sleeping in the small room she shared with her two brothers.

"Don't worry, sis," Zack whispered. "It won't be so bad. Just be sure you work quickly or father will not be pleased. He likes to fit as many jobs into one day as possible."

"What are you going to be doing now?" she wondered.

"I already have a job at the docks starting tomorrow. I will be helping to unload ships."

"Pirate ships too?"

"Yes, most likely."

Even in the darkness, Evonne could make out Zack's smile and rarely did anyone ever smile in this family. Zack had always been fascinated by the ships that sailed into port and dreamed of adventure at sea. A life away from Guildburg, and more importantly, a life away from their father.

Evonne's life had now drastically changed. She no longer spent the day helping her mother cook or clean or do laundry and spending most of her time alone with her own thoughts. Now, her father dragged her out of bed before the sun had even risen and she spent the entire day being lowered into dark chimneys, endlessly scrubbing until her hands bled. If she was not fast enough, she was hit. If she did not do a thorough job, she was hit. If she cried, she was hit.

Evonne would usually arrive home with her pale skin turned black with soot. She would pass out with exhaustion then start the process all over again in the morning. Most mornings she was not given any time to wash and the soot continued to build. She had almost forgotten the sight of her own skin as it was now replaced with layers of filth. She had earned the name, "Dirty Evonne," from the neighborhood children.

One particular day, Evonne was given a rare break. Her father had spent the entire night drinking and was unable to rise in the morning. When she was absolutely certain that he would not wake, she pulled on her boots with the holes in them and skipped out of the house to find some other children to play games with.

The streets of her neighborhood were narrow and winding with so many ramshackle houses all crammed tightly together. She did not live far from the harbor so the air was invariably salty and smelled of fish. Evonne hated fish as it was part of her daily diet. It was cheap and easy to come by in Guildburg, so each meal consisted of it.

Now, ten years old, Evonne had not seen many of her friends in quite a long time. She turned a familiar corner to a dead end street and found several young girls hopping about on squares they had drawn on the ground with chalk.

Evonne immediately recognized some of their faces. "Hello, Kara. Hello, Vera. Can I play too?"

Five girls in total stopped their game and turned to face Evonne. A few of them wrinkled their faces, and then Vera, who had once been a close friend of Evonne, spoke.

"Eww, it's Dirty Evonne. Don't you ever bathe?"

Evonne frowned, looking to her bare arms. "I tried to this morning but this soot is so hard to get off."

Another girl, who Evonne was not familiar with, snickered. "Don't let her get too close to you, girls. That dirt is going to rub off and will turn your skin a different color."

"No it won't."

"Yes it will," Vera said. "If she touches you it will transfer to your skin, turning it filthy like hers."

The other girls laughed and they took up the chant of "Dirty Evonne. Dirty Evonne."

Evonne fought back tears and stared Vera directly in the eyes. "How about we test your theory?"

The tiny blonde-haired girl marched straight up to the taller girl and punched her right in the nose. Vera fell to the ground in a sitting position, holding her nose which had begun to bleed. The other girls stood staring in shocked amazement.

"Oh, look," Evonne said. "Her skin did not turn grey or black…just red."

As Vera started to cry, Evonne turned and walked back home. She never again sought out friends to play with.

*   *   *   *

Evonne's twelfth birthday had come and gone and life continued as it had for the last several years. She was still small for her age and had hardly grown at all, which made her father quite happy.

"Maybe it is good you were not a boy after all," he said one day. "As long as you don't grow much you can continue to work the chimneys."

Late one night, despite how exhausted she was, a strange noise awakened Evonne from a deep sleep and she sat up straight in fright. As her eyes adjusted to the gloom, she noticed Zack climbing into the room from their open window. They were not allowed out at night and she guessed that it was long after midnight. Zack was smiling.

"Where have you been?" she whispered, ever fearful of waking their father in the next room.

"Working."

"Working? It is night time. We aren't allowed out."

"So what? Father was drinking all night as usual and wouldn't even notice that I was gone."

"What kind of work can you do in the middle of the night?"

"Running errands."

"Errands? For who?"

"Someone."

"Someone who? I am not going to tell."

"Captain Krayne."

"Merchant?"

"No, a pirate captain. He is the captain of a beautiful ship, The Grinning Kraken."

"You shouldn't work for pirates, they are dangerous."

"Says who? We work for father, isn't he dangerous?"

Evonne thought on that. Surely their father was cruel but he was still their father. She could not imagine what other men could be capable of, who did not share the same blood. Even The Purple King hated pirates and whenever they were caught, they were publically hung.

"What kind of errands does Captain Krayne have you do in the middle of the night?"

"None of your business."

"Does he pay you?"

"Of course he does."

"And father doesn't know? You are keeping the coins for yourself?"

"Yes, I am saving them. And if you tell anyone I will make sure you regret it."

"Saving them for what?"

"So I can buy my own sword. Then I can join Captain Krayne's crew and sail away from this dump forever."

"You are going to leave us, like Jarold? Do you remember what father did to us when he found out Jarold had left?"

"That is not my concern, sis. I have to look after myself. There is no future in this house for me."

"I don't want you to leave."

"Tough."

His cold reply upset her. "But we are family."

"And? What does family mean? Father is family and

look what he does? Mother is family and she lets it happen. Jarold was family and he left us. No, sis, it is everyone for themself in this life. Remember that."

*   *   *   *

When Evonne was thirteen she experienced a growth spurt. She was still considered petite for her age but was finding it increasingly difficult to fit into the chimneys. After bleeding from both knees and both elbows she had given up on the chimney she was to clean.

"I-I can't do it no more, father. I think I am too big," she said nervously.

Griff fixed her with an icy stare. "What are you going to do to contribute to this family, then? Huh? What?"

"M-maybe I-I could work at the docks like Zack does."

"Girls don't work at the docks. That's a man's job."

"So? I can do it. Chimney sweeping is a boy's job and I have been doing that."

Evonne received a stiff smack across the face. "Don't you dare talk back to me, you little wretch."

Thankfully, their return home was uneventful and her father said not another word. Unfortunately, though, her little brother Harlon was told the news that starting in the morning, he was the new chimney sweep.

Evonne spent two hours that evening attempting to remove all the soot stains from her skin and nearly rubbed her skin clean off. But she happily endured the pain, knowing that she would never crawl through another chimney for as long as she lived. What came next, she had no idea.

After a thorough cleaning, Evonne examined herself with a small cracked mirror. An attractive young girl had lay hidden under layers of dirt. No more "Dirty Evonne," she mused to herself as she brushed her long blonde hair.

She walked into the room to join the rest of her family sitting by the fire.

"Wow," Harlon said. "You finally look like a girl."

That comment grabbed Griff's attention and he stared at his daughter, an idea forming in his head.

"I will get you a job in a tavern starting tomorrow."

"I would prefer to work at the docks. I can do the work."

Griff rose to his feet and Evonne slinked backwards. "I don't care what you would prefer. You will earn more in a tavern so that is where you are going to work."

"You will be fine, Evonne," her mother commented. "I worked in taverns for years. You are a pretty girl and pretty girls can earn a lot."

"By the way," Griff said, looking out a window. "Where is Zack? He should have been home hours ago."

"Perhaps he is just working late," Amely reasoned.

"He has never been this late before," Griff growled. "I need a drink and he needs to get home with his pay."

Evonne slipped away into the bedroom she shared with her brothers. She knew the loose floorboard where Zack had been hiding the coins he was saving in secret. Sometimes, when she knew Zack was working, she would lift the floorboard and marvel at the sight of the coins. She would never steal from her brother, she just liked to hold them and look at them. Most of the coins were either copper or silver, though in recent months, he was beginning to collect more gold. Evonne loved how the light of the candles reflected off the gold coins. They almost hypnotized her as she would run her fingers over the stamped face of The Purple King.

She lifted the floorboard and her suspicions were correct; all of Zack's coins were gone. "He left," she whispered to herself. "He really left."

Once Griff had come to the realization that Zack was gone, he of course took his anger out on the rest of the family. Evonne's mother and brother took the worst of it, as Evonne had to look presentable to the tavern owners if she was to get hired.

CHAPTER 2

The sound of a screaming infant echoed down the dimly-lit tunnel. Lugnor followed the sound to his sister's chamber and pushed the door open unceremoniously. He found his sister, Gurtha, lying in a bed of furs, rocking the newborn.

She looked up at the arrival of her brother and smiled. "It's a boy."

Lugnor approached and studied the face of the infant, then spat on the ground. "The rumors about you were true. You shame our family."

Gurtha frowned. "He is an ogre boy, just like any other in this mountain."

"No, he is not. He is a cursed half-breed. You mated with a weak human and your son will now be weak and hated."

"He is my son and will be treated as such."

"No, sister, he will not. Save yourself the trouble, save us all the trouble and dispose of him now."

"Dispose?" she could not believe what she was

hearing.

"Yes, throw him off the mountain. Or if you will not, give him to me and I will do it."

"Now it is you who shame me, brother. You would take this baby and cast him off the mountain to his death? Your nephew?"

"I would. That is no nephew of mine. That, in your arms, is not an ogre. Thank Blaggrath that our mother and father are not alive to see this, *thing*," he said, referring to the god of ogres.

"Why do you hate the humans so much? They dominate this world. We need to ally with them for trade at the very least."

"They are small and weak. They do not deserve to dominate this world. This world should belong to the ogres. We are bigger and we are stronger."

"They outnumber us. You think you can defeat all the humans?"

"They cannot be trusted. The barbarians are evil."

"The barbarian tribes fight to protect their land and their families, same as us. We have been fighting them for so long I bet none in these mountains even remember the reason why. Maybe even ogres started this war."

"Careful, sister. Careful what you say. Do not anger Blaggrath any more than you already have by giving birth to this devil."

"If Blaggrath was against this birth, then why did he allow it? Blaggrath must have approved."

"Blasphemy!" roared Lugnor. "Give me the child."

"No," Gurtha replied, holding her infant protectively. "You will have to kill me to take him."

It appeared that Lugnor struggled with that thought

for a moment and then turned to storm out of the room with a growl. "He will never be accepted here."

Once alone again with her child, Gurtha's smile returned to her face as she regarded her beautiful son. "Your uncle is right, Vrawg, life will not be easy here. But you are my son and nobody will take you from me."

*   *   *   *

The Grey Ash Mountains was a vast mountain range that separated the nation of Tauros from the wild lands of the north. Ogre tribes called the mountains their home and had fiercely defended them for thousands of years from humans and trolls and other such threats. There were a handful of human settlements just north of the mountains that did trade with the ogres but the wandering barbarian tribes were not among them. The ogres and barbarians were hated enemies and had warred with each other longer than recorded history. Quite often the ogres would raid barbarian encampments to steal food and furs.

There was no one leader in charge of all the ogres. Three large tribes occupied the mountains, with several smaller splinter-groups, and each acted independently. In rare times of great need, the chieftains of each tribe had come together in agreement for joint ventures in the defense of the mountains.

Vrawg was part of the Drogheim tribe. Ogres did not possess distinct family names and just took on the name of their tribe. As predicted from birth, Vrawg Drogheim found life very difficult. Aside from the obvious fact that Vrawg was slightly smaller than a full-blooded ogre, it would be difficult for anyone else to know that he was only half ogre. The other differences were more subtle, though immediately evident to any ogre eyes.

Ogres possessed dark grey skin, and while Vrawg's skin was grey, it was a paler shade. Vrawg's ears were also more rounded on top, resembling a human's ears, as Ogre's ears were more pointed.

As far as anyone knew, Vrawg was the first child born of an ogre mother and a human father. Ogre males were not above mating with human females during their raids, though, it was said that any subsequent offspring that came as a result were put to death by the humans.

Vrawg's mother, Gurtha, was a trader and traveled often to the human settlements that tolerated the ogres. She had spent many years learning the common language of the humans and was a valued member of the tribe because of it. The humans were ever distrustful of the ogres, which they viewed as evil brutes, but traded with them for the valuable leather of the mountain goats and the iron that was predominant within the mountains.

The fishing town of Glastonby was where Gurtha did most of her business. It was there where she met the wandering mercenary, Drubin Silvershard. He was considered large by human standards, with barbarian blood in his veins, but he was still dwarfed by the seven-and-a-half-foot frame of Gurtha.

Ogres aged differently from humans, and while Gurtha was still considered young at the age of fifty-three, Drubin was considered well past his prime at the age of forty-seven. Drubin lived most of his life as a wandering sellsword but age and several nagging injuries had led the man to seek a place to settle. Glastonby was a quiet town and far from the reach of The Purple King's politics.

Gurtha and Drubin became friends and then more. After the birth of Vrawg, Gurtha was forbidden to travel to Glastonby by Chief Yarg. Yarg was the biggest and strongest of the Drogheim ogres and thus, their chief. Though, Yarg received most of his advice from Zolar, the tribe's shaman and the mouth of Blaggrath. Zolar, like many of the ogres, was not in favor of allowing Vrawg to live, but Gurtha was a favored member of the tribe and respected by Chief Yarg. However, Zolar did convince Yarg that Gurtha should not continue her relationship with the weak human, that Blaggrath disapproved.

Gurtha missed Drubin but did not want to risk the safety of Vrawg and did as she was told. Instead, she focused all of her attention onto her only son. She was never interested in other ogres and found most of her own kind distasteful. There had been many potential mates but she had turned them all away. If it were not for her command of the human's language and her ability to deal successfully with them, Gurtha might have found herself in much trouble. She had the protection of Chief Yarg, though, and other ogres had to respect that.

For the first six years of Vrawg's life, Gurtha kept him away from the others in the tribe, electing to shelter him from disdainful stares and hurtful comments. When Vrawg was old enough, she spent several hours each day teaching him the common language used by the humans. She thought if her son was to have any future within the tribe, he would need to become a valuable asset as she had. He would need to become a trader and ally with the humans.

Vrawg learned quickly to the elation of Gurtha; a testament to his human side. Most ogres were brutes and not the most intelligent. Young ogres generally excelled in activities of strength and battle but learned everything else at a very slow pace. Gurtha did, however, spend time teaching Vrawg about weapons and defense. She knew as he got older, they would also come in handy, most likely from the threat of other ogres. She wished that her brother, Lugnor, who was a valued warrior of the tribe, could teach her son to fight, but Lugnor seldom visited her, wanting nothing to do with the half-breed.

Lugnor received constant whispers from the shaman, Zolar. "Blaggrath disapproves of your nephew's continued existence."

"Do not refer to that devil as my nephew."

"Ah, but he is the son of your sister. He is of your bloodline."

"What does Blaggrath say?"

"Blaggrath says nothing but he shows me much. He shows me signs of his anger."

"Such as?"

"The disease that killed Bolga and Drock, who do you think sent that? Two strong and healthy ogres taken from us so young. And now food is scarce and the barbarians have been staying out of reach of our raids. Blaggrath looks to punish us this winter. I fear as long as Vrawg lives, things will only get worse."

Zolar whispered poison into the ears of any ogre who would listen, and most did, with the exception of Chief Yarg.

"If Blaggrath was angry, he would have sent disease to claim Vrawg's life," the chieftain said to the shaman one morning.

"Not so! Blaggrath wishes us to right this wrong and

will continue to punish the tribe until we do."

"Bah. Leave me."

"Why do you defend this half-human? Why do you value his life so much?"

"I do not value the life of the half-breed. He is inferior and not ogre. But Gurtha has done much for this tribe. It is my respect for her that stays my hand. And will stay yours as well."

Gurtha could not shelter Vrawg forever and as a teen it was time for him to learn more about the tribe and of their god, Blaggrath. Vrawg now mixed with others his own age and received teachings as part of a large group. Other ogres teased him relentlessly and whispered behind his back. To befriend Vrawg was to invite the wrath of others, so Vrawg felt isolated and alone. He was quiet and rarely spoke, even when teased by peers. Gurtha noticed the change in her son as he got older. He would return to their chamber, somber and distant, not willing to converse with his own mother about the day's events.

Soon Vrawg's torments turned from emotional to the physical. It was time for him to train as a warrior and spar with other ogres. The young ogres of the tribe took great pleasure in inflicting beatings on the smaller half-ogre. Vrawg was quite strong, just not as strong as his larger tribesmen. He had to train harder in order to compete. Despite returning to his chamber some evenings in immense pain, Vrawg would continue to train on his own. He would practice his forms and techniques with a variety of weapons and tirelessly work on his strength-conditioning activities, long after another ogre might have collapsed with exhaustion.

Gurtha worried about her son as he grew more

obsessed with training and spoke less and less. He did, however, continue with his language studies and enjoyed sitting quietly and listening to stories of humans, especially of his father and his exploits as a mercenary. Drubin was a highly-skilled warrior and it appeared that Vrawg had inherited some of his father's traits.

That was never more evident, than on the day when a sixteen-year-old Vrawg defeated one of the worst bullies in a sparring match, breaking his jaw with a club and knocking out several teeth. A friend of the defeated ogre stepped over the unconscious body and thought to exact revenge for that humiliation. Vrawg defeated that ogre as well, leaving his face a bloody mess.

The adult in charge of the training had to restrain several other ogres from attacking the half-breed. While Kragnath had never been fond of Vrawg, he had to respect the abilities he had just shown. He yelled at all the other students to stand down and praised Vrawg for his obvious discipline in continuing his training even when class was over.

"Vrawg shows dedication. This is why Vrawg wins," he lectured. "If you cannot show the same level of discipline, you will never be ready to face the evil barbarians."

After regaining consciousness, Feldrog, the first defeated ogre, approached Vrawg as the class was dismissed.

"You got lucky, half-human. I will make you pay for that next time. I will bash in your skull and decorate this cave with your brains."

But that never happened. Despite the anger and determination of every ogre in that class, Vrawg never lost another sparring match again. The part that Kragnath found most surprising was that Vrawg never boasted or gloated over any defeated opponent. He never taunted them or gave any indication that their taunts bothered him in any way. He went about his business, silently, without a word.

CHAPTER 3

It had been a year since Zack left and Evonne had
bounced around from several different taverns after
getting fired for one reason or another. She hated being
harassed by drunken fools. It was as if she was constantly
surrounded by dozens of clones of her father.

This night was no exception as the owner of The
Singing Sailor tavern tossed a few coins at her and told her
not to return. Evonne had told a wealthy merchant several
times to cease groping her and after the fifth time she
bloodied his nose. It took several staff members to keep
the drunken merchant from hanging her from the ceiling.

The teenage girl trudged home slowly; her feet feeling
like blocks of iron. She dreaded the thought of telling her
father she had been fired...again. After the beating, he was
only going to tell her she needed to find another tavern to
work in. She was miserable and would have done any other
job at this point; in fact, she wished that she still fit in
chimneys. At least when she was inside a chimney she was
alone.

Evonne passed by the same shops and the same homes she had done for her entire life and came to the sudden realization, that while the sights and the streets were familiar, nothing felt like home. During her year inside several taverns, she had overheard sailors speaking about grand adventures and battles at sea, but how they had always missed their home and had a longing to return there. The young girl had no concept of that. She possessed no fond memories of this city and could not imagine a reason for her to ever miss it, were she to leave.

And where would she go if she ever found the courage? she wondered. She had not been able to save up any coins like her brother had done, Griff would take them all. She had no skills aside from scrubbing chimneys, carrying trays of drinks or sweeping floors. But Evonne felt she was not meant to be a maid. There was a fire burning deep inside her that craved more out of life but this city, and her father in particular, was doing their best to snuff out those flames.

Evonne turned a corner and glanced down to a poor homeless woman sitting on the street wearing nothing but the filthiest of rags. Beggars were all over Guildburg, especially near the docks, hoping to elicit some spare coins from arriving merchants. The woman looked old, extremely so, far too old to work. She looked up to Evonne as the young girl had stopped and stood in front of her. Evonne almost felt as though she saw a reflection of her own face buried beneath the wrinkles of the much older woman's face.

Was this her fate then? Would that be Evonne one day when she was too old to work and had nowhere to live because her father had taken and drank away every coin she ever earned? Clearly this beggar had no family in her life, or nobody that cared for her at least, much like Evonne.

The young girl sighed and handed the few coins she was just given to the older woman. To the Abyss with her father, she would just say the tavern owner refused to pay her.

"Bless you, child," the woman said. "It is not often I receive such kindness from a visitor to the city."

That stopped Evonne as she had turned to leave. "Visitor? I have lived here my whole life."

"Oh, my apologies. You just don't look like someone who belongs in Guildburg. There is a spark within you that I do not often see among girls here."

"A spark? I am afraid that only emptiness and misery are destined to reside inside of me."

"That is not true. You are destined for great things. I can see it in your eyes."

The poor woman had gone mad, Evonne thought to herself as she bid the beggar a good night and walked away. Her father was not expecting her home for several more hours so Evonne took a slight detour and found a quiet spot to sit by the harbor. She stared out at the sea and thought about the words from the old beggar. How could she be destined for great things while trapped in this city? Then she thought of Zack and wondered where he was at that moment and what he was doing. She wondered if he was truly happy now, having escaped the rule of their father.

As a ship appeared in the distance, heading towards her location in the harbor, Evonne thought it would be a good time to head home. She did not want to be the first person those sailors saw after who knows how long they had been at sea.

She arrived home without incident, took a deep breath, and then entered. Her father was on his feet in an instant.

"What are you doing home already?"

Evonne lowered her gaze. "I was fired."

"What did you just say?"

Evonne's mother and younger brother cringed as they watched the exchange.

"I don't like how those men look at me. And they are always trying to touch me. Maybe I can do some other kind of work?"

"What kind of work do you think you can do, huh?" her father raised his voice. "Maybe if you had been born a boy you could find other work. But you are a useless woman. You are small and weak. You are fortunate to have a face adequate enough to work in a tavern. Where is your pay?"

"I didn't get paid tonight."

"What? Did you do any work?"

"Yes, but I was told to leave and I wasn't paid."

"I know the owner well. I will go over there right now and demand what he owes me."

Before her father could leave, Evonne spoke up. "Wait. He did pay me."

His face went bright red. "You lying little wretch. You were going to keep those coins all to yourself like a selfish brat? Give them to me."

"I-I-I gave them away."

"You did what??"

"There was this old beggar…and…"

Her father had heard enough and did not wait for her to finish her story. He removed his belt and proceeded to beat Evonne in front of the family. Harlon began to cry. Evonne was not sure if it was because he felt sorry for his sister or if he was just worried that he was next. She fought back her own tears not wishing to give her father any satisfaction.

Once finished, he tore her clothes looking for coins that she may have tried to hide from him. When he was positive she had none, he stormed out of the house in search of more to drink. Evonne's mother approached, looking to comfort her distraught daughter.

"Do not come near me!" Evonne shouted.

"Evonne, I am not him, let me hug you."

"You are just like him. You stand there and you watch him do what he does without emotion. You never want to help me then. Why?"

"What can I do?"

"Why don't you speak up? Why don't you step in?"

"Men will do as they please, we have no say in it. You will have to learn to accept that."

"Accept that? Are you mad?"

"Don't you speak to me like that."

"Or else what? What are you going to do? You are a coward."

Evonne took a smack across the face and this time she did cry. She really was alone. "As I said, you are just like him. You deserve each other."

* * * *

Harlon did try to console his sister when they were

alone in their room but Evonne was not in the mood and eventually cried herself to sleep. It was some time after midnight when Evonne awoke to a strange sound coming from their bedroom window. Her heart raced as she sat up straight. A dark form slid into the room from the window and before Evonne could scream in fright, a hand shot over her mouth to stifle any noise.

"Shhh, sis, it's just me," a familiar voice whispered in her ear.

"Zack??"

"It's me," he smiled in the dark.

Evonne could not believe it. "What are you doing here? Have you come back?"

"I am only here for a few days. Our ship is in port unloading some goods. I just wanted to stop by and see how you were doing. How is father?"

"Father is father, he will never be any different."

Evonne risked lighting a candle to look over her brother. He looked different; harder in fact. He had allowed his facial hair to grow longer and wore a red bandana around his head. Two large daggers were strapped to a belt with a shiny silver buckle. He appeared every bit a pirate.

"How have you been, brother?"

"Life is good. Living on a ship takes some getting used to but I am now a respected member of the crew. I have learned so much about sailing."

"So, you are a pirate now?"

"I am a sailor."

"On a pirate ship."

He shrugged. "They do what they need to do in order to survive. As we all must do. Anyways, sister, I must go. I just wanted to say hello to you."

"How long are you staying in Guildburg?"

"Three days only. We leave at first light on the fourth morning."

Without even thinking it through, Evonne blurted, "Take me with you."

"What?"

"Take me with you, please? I can't stay here any longer," she begged.

"Don't be foolish, a ship is no place for a woman."

"I don't care, I have to get away from him."

"Yes, you do. But you need to find your own way. Women are bad luck on ships and believe me, you would not want to be on a ship with these men. Trust me on that."

Zack embraced his sister in a hug and noticed how she winced from the beating she took earlier in the evening. "Get out of here, Evonne. Leave Guildburg. Just please stick to land. Do not let your fate be decided by pirates."

Evonne watched her brother climb out the window and disappear into the night, minus one of his daggers.

*   *   *   *

On the third night after her brother's visit, Evonne crept into the living room of their small house to find her father passed out on the floor next to a slowly dying fire. That night Griff had drank a lot, more so than usual, as Evonne had played the good girl and continually kept his mug full. He drank until he fell from his chair and slept face first on the floor.

Evonne stood there for quite some time, just watching his back rise and fall with each breath of his deep alcohol-induced slumber. With her mind made up, she steeled her courage and then produced the dagger she had stolen from her brother when he had hugged her. She grabbed Griff tightly by his curly hair and pressed the blade against his throat until blood dripped to the floor.

Griff's eyes shot open but he froze in place, realizing the predicament that he was in.

"Who is there?" he slurred.

"It's me, father."

"Drop the blade, girl."

"I don't think so. You are in no position to give me orders. Try to move and I will cut your throat."

"What in the Abyss are you about?"

"You are going to lay here and listen to what I have to say."

Griff attempted to rise and Evonne made good on her promise and dug the blade deeper into his flesh. He relaxed then, knowing that his daughter was serious.

"Now, father," and she said that last word with such venom in her voice. "I am leaving tonight. I will no longer live under your roof or allow you to touch me ever again. In fact, you will not touch anyone else in this family again. You see, I know you can never give up on alcohol. You will always pass out in some drunken stupor. So, if you ever harm anyone again and I find out, I will sneak back in here while the drink has knocked you unconscious and I will cut your throat. I promise you that."

"You will regret…"

Evonne cut him off. "No, you will regret everything you have ever done. Do you hear me? I care nothing for you and it would be my pleasure to kill you. So, please, do me a favor then and give me the excuse. You will never see it coming, you filthy drunk."

Evonne drew a deep line of blood across her father's cheek and then ran from the room. She grabbed a small pack from the floor of her bedroom, kissed her sleeping brother on the forehead, then climbed out the window and left her home behind without a single backward glance. She knew her father would be angry, enraged beyond anything they had previously seen, but he was a coward like most of his kind. Her father preyed on those who could not fight back. Now, someone finally had and Evonne hoped it was enough to stay his hand from future violence. She hoped he fell for her bluff because she had no intentions of remaining in Guildburg and would never know if he had obeyed or not.

Evonne made her way through the twisting streets toward the docks. Once there, she scanned the harbor for a particular ship, The Grinning Kraken. According to her brother, this was the last night the crew would be staying in the city. Evonne knew from experience, that on the last night before setting sail, the entire crew of the ship would be in a tavern somewhere partying and drinking their fill. That left the ship either empty, or with very minimal supervision.

She found the ship she sought and hid behind a wall of wooden crates on the docks, watching the deck for some time. She did notice one dark form walking about but soon disappeared below deck. Satisfied that there was nobody about to notice her, she raced up the gangplank and boarded the ship. She figured if the pirates would not let a woman join their crew, then perhaps she would not provide them with the choice to refuse her. She looked about desperately for a good place to hide.

*   *   *   *

On the night she had boarded The Grinning Kraken, Evonne had been right; only two crew members were left on board. She made her way below deck and found a nice place to hide among some crates and chests within the cargo hold.

Two days had passed since the ship left the harbor at Guildburg and Evonne second-guessed her decision. She overheard conversations from some of the pirate crew and she fast realized that these were not nice men. What had she been thinking? What would these men do to a teenage girl if she was discovered?

Hunger eventually drove Evonne from her hiding spot. Fortunately, the ship's galley was located next to the cargo hold. When she was certain that most of the crew was sleeping, the young girl crept silently into the galley and snatched a half-eaten loaf of bread. She nearly choked on it as a voice from behind had her whirling around to face a stout dwarf with a long braided beard.

"What do we have here?"

CHAPTER 4

The group of ten ogres moved cautiously through the dark tunnels below the complex of the Drogheim tribe. These tunnels stretched far below the mountain and it was the duty of this group to patrol them and keep them clear of any enemies. Trolls were a constant threat in the Grey Ash Mountains, though, wraggoth was the real concern when this deep underground.

The wraggoth were subterranean albino beasts. They were semi-intelligent and lived in their own tribes but the ogres considered them little more than savages. They were tall and spindly, ferocious, but no match for an ogre one on one. Occasionally, the beasts did venture up into the higher tunnels and make raids against ogre tribes. So the ogres were proactive and patrolled the lower tunnels regularly to keep them free of enemies.

Vrawg's skills in the sparring matches had earned him a spot on this particular patrol group. Vrawg was now twenty years old and despite his fighting prowess, he was still not viewed as anything more than an inferior half-human. But he was a half-human that could fight so the tribe was putting him to good use.

Vrawg was not comfortable in these near lightless tunnels. The phosphorescent moss that provided some light in the caverns of his tribe was less prevalent in the deeper passageways. Being only a half-ogre meant his night vision was not as good as a full-blooded ogre. Some of the other ogres took great pleasure in Vrawg's discomfort. Especially Feldrog.

The other ogre was older than Vrawg by a few years only but was a good five inches taller. He hated Vrawg immensely since his humiliations in the sparring matches. Being added to the same patrol group as the half-human only infuriated him more since now he was required to see his ugly face every day.

Voglar, the patrol commander, led the group into a large cavern and used a hand signal to indicate that they would be stopping here for some time. It was a familiar stop for the ogres and often used as a resting point. Several tunnels snaked their way into the cavern but were devoid of any wraggoth activity.

Vrawg found a patch of the glowing moss and sat himself down in a corner by himself, as he generally did. Vrawg had come to despise his fellow tribesmen almost as much as they despised him, so he did not mind being alone. But he did enjoy going on patrol. Vrawg excelled at combat and took every opportunity that he could to practice it. Most of the time these patrols produced nothing but the odd time they did come across a roaming group of wraggoth, or a lone troll, and Vrawg reveled in the battle.

His mother, however, disapproved. She wanted to

spend more time with him, teaching him the language of the humans and about their ways. She felt that was most important to her son. To survive in the ogre clan he would need to be seen as useful, and perhaps the humans would more readily deal with a half-ogre, over a full-blooded ogre.

But Vrawg spent nearly every spare moment of his time training to be a warrior. Honing his skills and practicing techniques. Gurtha knew that Vrawg sought the ability to defeat his bullies, and defeat them he had, but for how long? How long would it be before he was overwhelmed by attackers and unable to defend himself?

Vrawg watched curiously as one of the younger ogres approached him. It was out of the ordinary since he was generally avoided.

The ogre, Ruthgo, looked about as if to determine that the two were alone and spoke in a hushed tone. "Vrawg, a few of us are taking a walk, will you join us?"

Vrawg tilted his head and wore a quizzical look. Why would they be asking him to join them?

Ruthgo understood his expression. "A few of us have discovered a cavern that the others do not know about. It is littered with treasure, left behind by wraggoth who no doubt had little use for it." When Vrawg just stared silently, the ogre continued. "We are certain that wraggoth are close by...and would value your skills in battle in case we encounter them."

Vrawg glanced over in the direction of Voglar and Ruthgo shook his head. "Voglar does not know. We found the cavern so the treasure is ours alone. We trust you to remain silent and would appreciate your spear in case of trouble. You can earn a share of the treasure. We will not be gone long, Voglar will not even notice our absence."

The half-ogre smiled and nodded. His mother believed that learning about the humans was the only way to become important to their tribe but Vrawg knew better. Vrawg knew ogres valued strength and respected fighting ability above all else. He had become a better warrior than any of the ogres close to his age. Now, finally, the others were looking past his half human heritage and were beginning to accept him.

Soon, Vrawg and three others, Feldrog among them, moved away from the patrol group down a winding narrow tunnel. Feldrog cast Vrawg many hateful stares and was overheard whispering to Ruthgo.

"Why did you bring the half-human?"

"He fights like he is possessed of Blaggrath."

Feldrog spat on the ground. He never cared to hide his hatred for Vrawg.

"There could be a wraggoth raiding party nearby. I would like his spear with us if we encounter them."

"I will not split treasure with him."

"Then he can take a share of mine. I feel better with him here."

Feldrog spat again and did not say another word. Vrawg smiled, inwardly. He would be lying if he said he did not take any joy in Feldrog's displeasure.

The four ogres marched for a short time more and then arrived at their desired spot. A very large and thick stone slab leaned against the wall of this particular tunnel, concealing a narrow passageway. Vrawg watched as it took the combined effort of the other three ogres to move the slab aside and reveal the dark passage.

After a few moments to collect their breath and

strength back, Ruthgo spoke. "Who goes first?"

"Taggra, you are the oldest," Feldrog said.

Taggra shook his head. "Oldest and wisest. No, I will not go through there first. It is a tight fit. Blaggrath knows what could be waiting in that cavern. Let Vrawg go first, he is the smallest of us and will have less trouble squeezing through there."

"No!" Feldrog bellowed.

Vrawg smiled and walked past the others, momentarily locking eyes with Feldrog. With spear in hand, the half-ogre turned sideways and slid easily into the narrow passage. The others would fit, he knew, but he did have less trouble being the smallest of the group. If Feldrog did not want him going first, then going first is exactly what he would do.

He could not see very far in front for the blackness of the passage but Vrawg could not hear nor smell any enemies close by. He held is spear out in front and proceeded forward with great caution.

Vrawg paused for a moment, listening behind him for the other ogres. His heart began to race with panic as he heard the unmistakable sound of the stone slab being pushed back into place. He moved as quickly as he was able in the cramped space but as he reached the passage entrance it was too late; the giant slab was firmly in place, effectively trapping him in the passage.

Vrawg knew he was doomed. It took all three ogres to move that slab so there was no chance of him pushing it aside himself. He could hear the three of them laughing, the sound soon fading in the distance. Feldrog had played him for a fool. He had wanted Vrawg to go first all along.

With no other choice, the young half-ogre continued

down the dark passage, hoping that it was not a dead end and would not be his tomb. He cursed his foolishness. He should have known something was amiss the moment Ruthgo approached him for his help.

Vrawg did not have to travel far before the passage opened into a vast cavern with the sound of falling water. Somewhere nearby was a waterfall but the cavern was too big and too dark for the half-ogre to make out any details. No phosphorescent moss grew in this place so Vrawg resorted to an emergency measure, pulling a torch out of the pack he wore strapped to his back. He always carried a torch with him in the event that he became separated from others; an event which had just taken place.

It was a last resort because lighting a torch in the near lightless mountain made you a target to enemies who did not require such things to see. If anything lurked out of sight in the shadows, they would soon be aware of his presence and exact location. But Vrawg simply had no other choice.

Ogres traveled light when patrolling the inside of the mountain. They did not wear armor as it made far too much noise when moving about. Vrawg did wear heavy boots, however, and soon found the ground crunching curiously underfoot. It took several attempts before he could ignite the torch and was relieved to have some much needed light.

His relief was short-lived as he inspected the ground of the cavern more closely and found that it was littered with bones and skulls. Most appeared to be the remains of ogres, though he did recognize some wraggoth skulls and the odd troll. Vrawg could not imagine how all these bodies had come to rest in this macabre graveyard. Crude weapons were strewn all about the floor amongst the bones and some skeletons still wore pieces of armor. The half-ogre found that odd since dead ogres would have always been stripped of anything valuable after their death.

Something curious caught Vrawg's attention and he bent down low to inspect the skeletal remains of a particularly large ogre that was still wearing a steel breastplate. It was not the armor itself that piqued Vrawg's interest, it was the holes in the armor that had him seeking a closer look. The passing of time had not caused the armor to decay; something had punctured the armor and thus led to this ogre's demise.

Vrawg ran his finger around one of two holes and found it round and smooth. It did not appear to have been caused by the head of a spear which had been his initial thought. Like the ogres, wraggoth favored the spear as a weapon but no spearhead that Vrawg had ever seen would have left a hole like that in someone's armor.

He decided to follow the sound of falling water. He figured if water found its way into this cavern then perhaps he could find a way out. Vrawg did his best to avoid stepping on bones in order to make less noise but there was just too many.

Something glittered from the corner of his eye so the half-ogre went to inspect. To his surprise, it was a pile of gold coins. He searched around the immediate area and found many more coins; some gold and some silver. Some of the coins were of ogre make and the rest were from humans. There were more coins here than Vrawg had ever seen. So, the others were not lying about the treasure, he figured. But why would they lock him in this cavern without taking the treasure for themselves first?

He pondered that for a moment before he detected movement from the darkness, just beyond the reach of his torch. At first it was just a feeling, then he heard bones and coins scattering. Suddenly, Vrawg understood why the others had not come to claim the treasure; it already belonged to someone else. And that someone was responsible for the holes punctured in the dead ogre's armor.

Vrawg dropped his torch on the floor and gripped his spear tightly with both hands, spinning in slow circles as he could not pinpoint the location of whatever lived in this cavern. His heart raced. Whatever was here had killed everything that had entered this cavern before, including fully armored ogres, so what chance did he have? he thought to himself.

A hissing sound made his grey skin prickle. Then, to his surprise, a voice came from the darkness; a deep voice that spoke in the common language of the humans.

"Another comess to sssteal my treasure? A lone ogre thiss time? No, not a full ogre, are you?" Whatever it was could be heard sniffing the air. "I sssmell the ssstench of humanss within you as well."

Thanks to his mother's teachings, Vrawg understood every word. He continued to slowly spin as the voice seemed to echo from everywhere all at once.

"Half ogre and half human," it continued. "How interesting. I wonder how you tasste? Humanss have more flavor but ogress have more meat."

"I tricked," Vrawg answered in the human's language. "I go now."

"No, I am afraid you won't be. I am hungry and you are jusst in time for dinner."

Bones crunched directly behind Vrawg and he spun about. The owner of that mysterious voice finally came into view and the half-ogre nearly dropped his spear in fright. Although he had never seen a dragon before, the thing before him matched the descriptions from the tales he had heard. Dragons were said to be extremely rare and yet here it was.

It walked on four legs with such grace and such agility. Its skin was as black as coal, but its yellowish, serpentine eyes, glowed from the reflected torchlight. Two ivory horns jutted from the top of its head and when it smiled, rows and rows of jagged teeth took the half-ogre's breath away. The dragon's ebony wings were folded against its body and its long black tail swayed hypnotically behind it.

Vrawg recalled hearing how gargantuan dragons could be but this one stood only about twice the height of him, making him believe it must have been a young dragon. The other ogres knew the dragon guarded the treasure within this cavern and had led Vrawg to his death.

The dragon stood on its back two legs and inhaled a giant breath of air. Vrawg understood what would follow next. There were various species of dragons and each one possessed the ability to breathe some form of horrible death upon its victims. Some could breathe fire and some could breathe frost. Not knowing what would come out of this dragon's mouth, Vrawg did not wish to wait around to find out.

Vrawg was smaller than a full-blooded ogre and thus much quicker. He dove to his left just as a cloud of black mist flew out from the dragon's mouth. The dragon had not anticipated the speed of the half-ogre and the mist only brushed his leg as Vrawg dove and rolled out of the way before becoming completely enveloped within it.

Vrawg's eyes went wide as his leg tingled and went numb where the dragon's breath had touched him. He imagined that if he had been hit fully by that black cloud his entire body would have been paralyzed, leaving him helpless and an easy meal. He was fortunate that it only grazed his leg and it still supported him as he stood.

Vrawg threw his spear at the dragon with a tremendous grunt, putting every ounce of strength behind it. His jaw nearly hit the floor as his spear skipped harmlessly off the black scales that made up the dragon's skin. Those scales, he realized, were as hard as steel.

The dragon merely laughed and then swept a taloned-claw across Vrawg's chest, tearing open the leather vest he wore and drawing a line of blood across his skin. The half-ogre grunted and stumbled backwards, nearly losing his footing from an ogre's skull. Vrawg glanced around in desperation and then grabbed a shield from the cavern floor, just in time to block the second claw that came at him. The sheer force of it knocked him back several steps but he managed to remain on his feet.

The dragon swiveled its body and its pointed tail dove at Vrawg like a spearhead. He lifted the shield in time to block the deadly strike but the tip of the tail actually penetrated the shield to stop a mere inch from Vrawg's face. With a flick of its tail, the dragon ripped the shield from Vrawg's grasp. The half-ogre ducked and rolled away as the dragon swung its tail, looking to bash the ogre's skull with its newly acquired shield that was stuck to its tail.

The cavern floor was littered with the weapons of the

dragon's previous meals and Vrawg scooped up a large serrated sword. He knew he could not outrun the dragon so spun back to face it as it sped towards him. The dragon reached for him and Vrawg managed to bat aside its claw with a mighty swing of the sword. Looking to capitalize, Vrawg then countered with a strike of his own, slamming the serrated blade into the chest of the dragon. The dragon grunted from the weight of the blow but to Vrawg's dismay, it had not penetrated its hard scales.

With the speed of a viper, the dragon's mouth clamped onto the half-ogre, its razor-sharp fangs sinking deeply into Vrawg's chest and shoulder. Vrawg howled in pain and dropped the sword. The dragon lifted him into the air with its mouth and shook him back and forth, sending waves of pain throughout his body. With little effort, the dragon flung the half-ogre into one of the cavern's walls and Vrawg fell to the floor with a crunch, several bones breaking from the impact.

Every breath sent pain through Vrawg's body as blood flowed from his mouth and the puncture wounds from the dragon's fangs. He watched in horror as the dragon smiled and slowly stalked forward, taking his time on purpose, and reveling in the fear that was written on its victim's face.

Vrawg cursed Feldrog and the others. He also cursed himself for walking freely into the trap that they had laid for him. He thought of his mother then and how she would never know what happened to him.

He would at least die like a warrior, he thought, and grabbed a spear that luckily lay within reach. Vrawg attempted to stand but immense pain forced him back down in a sitting position.

The dragon stood before him and chuckled. "A valiant effort, but it'sss time to die, little half-breed."

The giant fanged-mouth descended once more with great speed and Vrawg held his spear out and closed his eyes, expecting his end was at hand. The dragon gasped as the spear was raised at the last moment, entering its mouth and coming out through the back of its head. Vrawg opened his eyes to notice the dragon's head impaled upon the spear. For a brief moment its eyes flashed with anger and then all life fled from the yellowish orbs. The dragon fell, crashing down onto its side, quite dead.

Vrawg exhaled in relief and lay back on the ground panting, his head resting on the skull of a troll.

CHAPTER 5

Evonne stood as frozen as a statue, her heart thumping and threatening to burst from her chest. A curious-looking fellow stared at her with wonder. She had seen several dwarves in Guildburg before and he definitely was a dwarf, though taller than any of the others she had seen. He could have almost passed for a short human, rather than a tall dwarf.

He had a long black beard which was tied into five braids, a large flat nose, which was distinctive to dwarves, and wore a red bandana tied to what appeared to be a bald head. His white shirt was open and revealed a hairy chest with many scars where skin was visible. As with most dwarves, he was stocky and muscled, and looked as hard as the mountains they were said to dwell in.

Evonne's eyes went to the large dagger that stuck out from the top of his boot but she knew he would not need that to deal with her. But the dwarf made no movement toward her, he just stood and stared.

"Now, where did you come from, lass?" he asked in a

deep gruff voice.

"I-I-I…," she stuttered.

"Oy, Grim, what are doing in there? Baking the bread fresh? Bring that loaf already, will ya!" a voice called from outside the galley.

The dwarf pressed a finger to his lips, indicating for Evonne to be silent. He took the loaf of bread from her hands and guided her back to the cargo hold where she had been previously hiding. Before closing the door, he ripped off a small piece of the bread and handed it to the young girl with a wink, then left the galley to deliver the rest to the grumbling pirate.

As frightened as she was, Evonne stuffed the piece of bread in her mouth; after all, it could be her last meal. She always knew the time would come when the crew aboard The Grinning Kraken would discover her but she had yet to formulate a proper excuse for her being there. She did not count on it being this soon. Evonne was not sure whether she should be wary of the dwarf's actions or not. Was it a kind gesture to keep her away from the crew or did he want her for himself first before passing her along to the others?

She did not have long to wait before his heavy footsteps could be heard approaching the door through the galley. The dwarf entered the cargo hold and shut the door behind him. He eyed Evonne up and down before sitting himself down on top of a crate. The young girl flinched as he pulled the dagger from his boot but the dwarf only laughed. He took an apple from his pocket and began to slice off a piece; his eyes never leaving the blonde stowaway.

"So, little lass, you gonna tell me what you are doing

here? You look Taurosian, where are you from?"

"Guildburg."

"Ah, a recent stowaway then. You came here to die?"

"N-no."

"Well, that's what usually happens to stowaways, especially ones who steal food. Now, in all my years at sea, I have never before seen a female stowaway. You're a pretty little thing so I imagine they won't kill you immediately, though you might wish they had."

"M-my b-brother is a member of the crew."

"Well now, who is your brother?"

"Zack."

"Ah, little Zack. And you think that is enough to save your skin? You think Captain Krayne will give a damn whose sister you are? Or the others on board this ship? Lass, do you have any idea what kind of men you are now surrounded by?"

"Pirates."

"Yes, pirates. And a particularly nasty lot even by pirate standards. The Grinning Kraken isn't feared for no reason."

"I want to be a pirate."

The dwarf laughed, nearly choking on a piece of apple. "You are brave, I will give you that. Or stupid. What is your name?"

"Evonne."

"Well, Evonne, I am Grimbold Gravebeard, though everyone just calls me Grim. Count yourself lucky that it was me who found you and not anyone else. Here is my suggestion. You remain hidden down here until we reach our next port. I will smuggle you out and you can find passage on another ship, not a pirate ship, back to

Guildburg."

"I am never returning to Guildburg."

"Then you can go wherever you like."

"I want to stay here with my brother and become a pirate like him."

"Lass, you haven't been listening to me. Your brother cannot protect you from the nasty men on this ship. I am offering to save your life."

"I would rather take my chances here than to go back to Guildburg. I have no coins and I have never been anywhere outside of Guildburg, so I cannot go anywhere else."

Grim tugged on the braids of his beard in thought. He handed Evonne the last remaining slice of apple and then left her alone again. This time when he returned, he shoved Zack into the cargo hold ahead of him, before closing the door behind them.

"Evonne?? What in the Abyss are you doing here?"

Evonne ran to hug her brother but he pushed her back. "Answer the question."

"I-I could not live at home anymore. You know how father is. You looked so happy to be free of him so I wanted to come and join you here."

"Evonne, this is a pirate ship and you are a girl."

"So what?"

"Pirates believe it is bad luck to have a woman on board the ship that is not a prisoner or slave. If you think it was bad at home, that will soon feel like paradise compared to being a slave here. I can't believe you hid on this ship."

"You listen to your brother," Grim said. "We will drop you off at the next port before anyone realizes you are here."

"I am not going anywhere. I am your sister, Zack, why would anyone harm your sister?"

Zack shook his head in disbelief. "Because these are pirates! I am a nobody on this ship. I have no pull to keep you safe from these men. They won't care who you are related to."

"I'll take my chances here. They can't be any worse than the animals I served drinks to in the taverns."

"Evonne, you have no idea how much worse they are out at sea," her brother replied. "There are no laws out here. There is nothing stopping these men from doing whatever they want."

"We could just hit her over the head and dump her at the next port," Grim suggested. "She will have a headache but she will be alive."

Evonne took a step back. "I will scream if you come near me."

"Your sister is mad."

"Evonne, listen to Grim. I cannot protect you out here."

"I am a survivor, Zack. If father has taught me anything in life, it was how to survive."

Grim looked to Zack with a serious expression. "Fetch the Captain."

*   *   *   *

Captain Krayne stood with his arms folded in front of his chest as he coolly scrutinized the petite girl that was standing in the cargo hold of his ship. Zack and Grim stood silently to each side of their captain.

Nervous sweat formed on Evonne's forehead as she shrank back under the man's penetrating gaze. He was not too tall, nor was he as muscled as the thick dwarf, but the lean pirate captain had an aura about him that struck fear in the young girl. The way he had strolled in, the way he now stood before her, bespoke of a man with extreme confidence in himself. He wore black leather clothing of the finest material, accentuated with earrings, a necklace, and two rings of solid gold. His hair was black and slicked back with a thin, neatly-trimmed black beard. A long curved sword hung from his belt on one side and long dagger hung from the other. The captain appeared to be somewhere in his thirties but his eyes revealed a man wiser than his years.

"This pretty little thing is your sister, you say?" Captain Krayne asked casually.

"Yes, Captain."

"Well, she definitely was blessed with the looks in your family. Looking at your ugly mug, I could hardly tell you were related. Evonne, do you know what I did to the last person that stowed away on this ship?"

"Made him a crew member?"

The captain chuckled. "After I removed both his hands for stealing food, I threw him overboard for the sharks."

"That was your mistake then. You could have added someone else to your crew."

Zack shook his head in disgust and Grim put a hand over his face.

"I don't need useless little runaways as members of my crew. That just makes for another mouth to feed and another way to divide booty. I need fighting men aboard my ship. Men with skills who can serve a purpose. I don't need a little girl who will provide nothing but a distraction to the other members of this crew."

"But I can be valuable. I can work on the ship and learn whatever you need me to do. I am a quick learner. I am small and I don't need much food or take up much space. I can…"

"Silence!" Krayne roared. "I have just told you I don't need a little girl aboard MY ship. Now, Zack has proven himself useful to me, so as a courtesy to your brother I will not feed you to the sharks. But you will leave this ship at the first available opportunity. And you will have to split his share of food until such time. I will also not be responsible for anything that happens to you in the meantime."

"I want to be a pirate."

"I don't care what you want."

"But I…"

With great speed, Captain Krayne lunged forward and grabbed Evonne by the front of her top, hoisting her into the air to stare her in the face. Her feet dangled off the ground and her face went pale.

"I already told you I don't care what it is that you want. Why would I care about some useless little runaway girl?"

Suddenly, Evonne produced the dagger she had stolen from Zack and pressed the tip under the captain's chin. "Because if you do not agree to let me join your crew right now, I will slit your throat."

Grim and Zack both wore similar expressions of shock, which was quickly replaced by a look of fear as both figured they were about to witness the brutal murder of Evonne. But Captain Krayne began to laugh. He was genuinely amused. He laughed for some time before tossing Evonne to the floor.

"She might make a fine pirate after all. Bring her out to meet the crew."

Captain Krayne strolled from the room leaving Evonne alone with Grim and Zack. Evonne's heart still raced long after the departure of Krayne. She gambled everything on the hope that the pirate captain would respect a show of courage and it had paid off. Though, there was still the matter of the other crew members.

Grim pulled the dagger from his boot and walked over to Evonne, grabbing her roughly by her long hair. She struggled as he began to slice off large portions of it.

"What are you doing?"

"Cutting off your hair, what does it look like?"

"Why?"

"Lass, in a few moments we are gonna bring you out on the deck of this ship in front of the crew. I have to make you less attractive in their eyes. The more we can make you appear as a boy the better. Zack, fetch something to dirty her face."

*　　*　　*　　*

"Is it a girl?"

"Looks like a grubby little boy to me."

"What's a girl doing on this ship?"

"If it's a girl, I mean to find out."

"Just throw it overboard."

"Has the Captain lost his mind?"

"Girls are bad luck, mark my words."

"Maybe she can cook better than Daryn, I am sick of the slop he calls food."

"Clean her up good and I am betting she is a tasty little morsel."

Evonne stood trembling on the main deck of The Grinning Kraken. Forty-seven sets of eyes were all on her. Some appeared curious, some appeared angry, and some looks downright frightened her. Grim had cut off most of her hair and Zack had rubbed dirt all over her face and arms so that nearly none of her pale skin could be seen.

"Why is she so filthy? Someone drag her out of a sewer? Does she have some disease?"

"She was a chimney sweep," Grim answered the other crewman. "Spent most of her time scrubbing filthy chimneys. Hard to get that soot off."

A particularly ugly man that was missing several of his teeth took a few steps towards Evonne. "Give her here. I will give her a proper bath and clean her up good."

"No, Mister Lowther, you won't be," Captain Krayne finally spoke up. "Evonne here will be treated like any other member of the crew, for now." He fixed the young girl with an icy stare. "Her and I have an understanding that she is going to work very hard around here. The moment she proves herself useless, well, then I wouldn't want to be her."

Evonne knew she had gained some measure of respect from the captain but that respect only went so far. She believed his threat whole-heartedly as she should have. She was informed by Grim and Zack that Krayne could be fair but was generally a cruel man and was not known for acts of kindness. There was a reason why he and this crew were feared.

And what a crew it was. Evonne gazed at all the men assembled on the deck. It looked as though every corner of the world was represented here. There were black-skinned men with white skulls painted on their faces, bronze-skinned men from the southern nations and golden-haired barbarians from the north. They were all shapes and sizes but every man, every single one of them, looked like someone you would not wish to encounter in a dark alley. Evonne had to second-guess herself if she had made the right choice.

Thankfully, all the crew's attention was pulled from the young girl as a man shouted from the ship's crow's nest while peering through a spyglass. "Ship spotted, Captain!"

"Is it the Black Shark?" Captain Krayne called back.

"Aye, it is."

"Positions, everyone," the captain ordered. "Time to teach those dogs what happens when you cross us."

Every member of the crew began scrambling about the deck to their appointed duties. Some began loading large harpoons into the ballistae that were mounted around the deck. They looked like large crossbows and Evonne could only imagine the damage those could cause to an enemy ship.

She pulled on Grim's shirt before the dwarf could rush away. "What's going on?"

"We are going to attack that ship. The Black Shark hit a merchant vessel that we had been pursuing for days. Captain Krayne considers that stealing from us since we had seen it first. He will make an example of that ship of what happens when you do that to us."

"Can we win?"

"You had better hope we do. You do not want that crew getting their hands on you. Now get below deck, lass, this is going to be no place for you."

Grim shoved Evonne in the direction of the stairs that led below and hurried off to unravel more sails to give their ship added speed. Evonne felt she could relax a little as all the crew's attention was now elsewhere. It was as if she was invisible. Grim told her to go below but curiosity got the better of the young girl. She went to the side of the ship and for the first time gazed out at the rolling waves of the sea. She had never before left the city of Guildburg and it was a strange feeling as she considered how far from there she was now. Just water in every direction she looked; water for as far as her eyes could see.

The wind was in their favor and she felt the ship picking up speed. It was not long before she spotted the sails of the Black Shark in the distance. Her stomach fluttered with nervousness at the sight of the enemy ship. What if they lost this fight? She looked down to the waves crashing against the ship and considered jumping overboard if things went sour. At least the sharks would end her life quickly, she figured.

Evonne learned that chasing a ship in the open sea took much patience. Nearly three hours had passed before she could now make out faces on the deck of the Black Shark. These men looked equally as frightening as the men aboard The Grinning Kraken. Though, she noticed the other ship was slightly smaller and most likely had fewer crew members.

Evonne watched with amazement as Captain Krayne stood near the front of the ship shouting orders and others scrambled about, following every command to the detail.

She watched her brother emerge from below deck carrying an armful of swords and dump them on the deck before disappearing below to fetch more. She sought out Grim and found the dwarf standing behind a loaded ballistae, aiming it towards the Black Shark.

Evonne's eyes went wide as she noticed men aboard the enemy ship pick up bows and soon arrows rained down upon their deck. One unfortunate man dropped to his back with an arrow through his throat.

"Return fire!" shouted Captain Krayne.

Several men drew bowstrings of their own and sent arrows into the ranks of the enemy ship. Evonne ducked just in time as an arrow whizzed overhead. She thought now might be a good time to disappear below and hide but something held her in place. She figured she had already begun a trend of bad decisions, so why stop now?

"Now, Grim! We are in range!" Krayne commanded.

Grim fired the giant ballistae and a long harpoon with a rope attached shot forth and penetrated the hull of the Black Shark. Four other pirates fired as well and all found their mark. Five thick ropes now connected the two ships, effectively making escape impossible. More arrows rained down and a skinny man who had climbed the main mast fell to the deck screaming, an arrow lodged in his back. Evonne watched one of the large northern barbarians rush to the man's aid and snap the arrow off.

Grim and the four other pirates now loaded heavy bolts into the ballistae, ones without any rope attached, and fired at the deck of the Black Shark. Evonne's jaw hung open in horror as she watched a bolt impale a man through the stomach and carry him right off the deck and into the sea. Another bolt found an unfortunate man's head and she gagged in disgust as his head literally exploded. Many times she had witnessed men stabbed with knives or swords during tavern brawls but nothing like this. But at the same time she could not tear herself away from the gruesome spectacle.

Evonne spotted what she figured was the enemy captain. He was heavy man with a protruding stomach and long red beard. He shouted commands to his men much like Captain Krayne. They were close enough now that Evonne could see the panic in his face. A stark contrast from the calm demeanor that Krayne exhibited as he stood like a statue upon the deck, never once ducking from the arrows which still rained down. She could tell how the captains played a critical role in morale. The crew of The Grinning Kraken saw Krayne standing defiant and confident, which in turn gave them confidence. The crew of the Black Shark also saw the fear written on the face of their captain and thus had a negative effect upon them.

The pirates aboard both ships now held swords and daggers as Grim, with the help of a few others, lifted a long wooden plank and dropped it over the side making a bridge between the two ships. As a second plank dropped, the enemy captain ordered his men across first. Evonne figured he knew this was the end so sent his men out first in some last ditch effort to appear brave.

The first several men to cross the planks fell to arrows and crossbow bolts before they ever reached the other side. They tumbled screaming into the sea before being swept away and forever silenced. Soon, sheer numbers won over and the enemy crew spilled onto the deck of the Kraken and Evonne watched the battle with awe. It was bloody and it was brutal but she still could not look away.

The young girl screamed as Zack was slashed across the leg and fell, dropping his own sword. Without thinking, she pulled out her stolen dagger and raced across the deck to her fallen brother. The ship lurched to one side from a large wave that crashed against it and Evonne tumbled to the deck skinning both her knees raw. Ignoring the pain she was up and running. She screamed at an enemy pirate who was about to impale Zack on the end of a curved sword. The pirate glanced at Evonne and with little effort, backhanded the girl and sent her sprawling to the deck, her dagger flying from her hand.

The pirate now turned his attention to her but before he got any closer, an axe cleaved his skull nearly in two. Grim kicked the dead pirate away, freeing his axe blade which had gotten stuck.

"I told you to get below deck."

Evonne sat up dizzily, with blood flowing from her nose. She witnessed Captain Krayne join the fight and several pirates fell to his blade before the deck was finally clear of all enemies. She pulled herself up on unsteady legs and watched Krayne and many others cross to the other ship and kill the remaining crew. The enemy captain threw down his sword and surrendered but Captain Krayne beheaded the man regardless. The battle was over.

Grim approached Evonne and handed her dagger back. "Well, if you plan on staying on this ship, lass, then we had better teach you to fight."

CHAPTER 6

Gurtha's anger was beginning to boil over as she was not getting the answers that she was looking for.

"Where is my son?"

"As I said, he wandered off while we were on patrol and he did not return," Voglar answered. "We did a sweep of the area and there was no sign of Vrawg."

"He would not just wander off. He is smarter than that."

Gurtha scanned the faces in the chieftain's quarters but found no supporters. Her own brother, Lugnor, seemed to also accept the story of the patrol commander.

She turned to face Chieftain Yarg with watery eyes. "Chieftain, you have noticed great promise in my son. Will you not dispatch other patrols to search for him?"

Before Yarg could answer, Zolar, the tribe's shaman, cut him off. "That would be unwise, great Chief. Soon we will be moving against the wretched barbarians and cannot waste valuable warriors in a search for the half-breed.

Blaggrath has blessed the mission against the humans and would be most displeased if there were any disruptions in our plans."

The giant ogre rubbed his chin in deep thought. "I do not take the loss of a tribe member lightly, no matter his heritage. Vrawg has proven himself a great warrior and I would not abandon any of our warriors. I want two patrols to go back and search the area again."

"But, my Chief, we should not…"

Several gasps from the room stopped the shaman in mid-sentence. Zolar spun around to face the entrance to the room, the shrunken skulls that made up his necklace rattling loudly. The sight that awaited his eyes caused him to gasp as well.

Vrawg stood in the entranceway, bleeding from several different wounds. In one hand he held the head of an obsidian dragon by a horn, and in his other he held the head of a wraggoth, its tattooed face revealing that it was a shaman. Vrawg tossed both heads into the room so that they rolled to stop at the feet of Chieftain Yarg and Zolar. Gurtha ran to her son and wrapped him in a tight embrace.

"He killed the Black Bane," Voglar said with wonder, referring to the young dragon that had claimed many ogre lives.

"And that sorcerous wraggoth that has been a constant thorn in our side," one of the ogre guards commented.

"What happened, my son?" Gurtha urged Vrawg. "How did you come to meet the dragon?"

"Yes, young warrior, why did you wander away from your patrol group alone?" wondered Chief Yarg.

Vrawg shrugged his shoulders and remained silent. He survived and that was all that mattered. There was no sense in pointing fingers at Feldrog and the others. He felt only his mother would have believed him anyway. In the end he came out on top and his revenge would be the anger this would stir in Feldrog at his failed plot. Vrawg had slain a dragon, along with a group of wraggoth he had encountered shortly after leaving the dragon's cavern.

Chief Yarg was about to command Vrawg to explain when the young half-ogre collapsed to a knee from pain and exhaustion. Gurtha rushed her son from the chieftain's quarters to get him aid and bind his wounds.

Yarg turned to Voglar. "Vrawg will no longer patrol the mountain tunnels. He will raid the barbarian camps with our older warriors. He will bring much glory to the Drogheim tribe."

"Yes, Chieftain."

Chieftain Yarg dismissed the gathered ogres from his quarters and soon Zolar and Lugnor walked together alone.

"Vrawg's actions will anger Blaggrath, I know it," the shaman said in a hushed tone.

"How so? He has slain a dragon that many great ogre warriors have failed to do. Will he not be a hero in our god's eyes?"

"Yes, the Black Bane had killed many of our tribesmen but he was a necessary evil. The existence of the dragon kept many of our enemies away. He unwittingly protected the western tunnels from intruders. When word spreads of the dragon's death, we will soon find more wraggoth or trolls knocking on our western doors. The tribe is more vulnerable and this will not please Blaggrath as we are his favored tribe."

"What will happen?"

"Who can say? Blaggrath will punish us somehow, this I do not doubt."

"Chief Yarg praises the half-human," Lugnor spat on the ground. "Rewards him even."

"Our Chief may have fallen out of favor with Blaggrath. I must cast the bones to see what I may learn."

*   *   *   *

Thick clouds blotted out the moon and stars, making for a particularly dark night. It was just the kind of night that the ogre raiding party was waiting for as they slipped out of their mountain home into the hills of the Dalecanin Valley. The hilly terrain stretched for many miles north and was a common hunting ground for several wandering barbarian tribes. The ogres had spotted the campfires of one such group and dispatched ten warriors to make a raid.

This was Vrawg's first time leaving the dark caves of the mountains and he found the openness to be a strange sensation. He was accustomed to being surrounded by rock in all directions, which left him feeling very vulnerable. He wondered how anyone could use stealth in this outside world. They chose the dark of night to make their raids because the humans had trouble seeing in the dark; something Vrawg knew all too well as his night vision was never as good as the full-blooded ogres.

Vrawg moved uncomfortably in armor that did not fit him properly. He was fully grown, though still smaller than the average ogre. The armorers simply did not craft anything his size and he could not ask them to make something just for him. Vrawg's chest remained bare and he did his best to find pieces to cover his arms and legs. He carried a wooden shield in his left hand and a spear in his right. The other ogres in the party were all fully armored and carried a variety of weapons such as spears, axes and serrated swords.

These were seasoned warriors that Vrawg now accompanied. Mature adults who had fought the humans many times before. Their party leader, Golgra, a giant scarred ogre, informed Vrawg not to underestimate the small humans. The barbarians were considered large by human standards but were much smaller than even Vrawg. They did, however, possess much strength and speed. The barbarians were fierce fighters who were not afraid to die. In fact, the wretched humans considered it an honor to fall in battle and never retreated, no matter the odds. It was said that Blaggrath rewarded bravery in battle but ogres felt it was better to fight again another day if things turned sour.

Vrawg feared death greatly and was one of the factors that motivated him to train as much as he could. He had no idea what would become of his soul when he died. He was not a true ogre and was certain that Blaggrath would not accept his soul. His mother had told him that the humans worshipped a variety of different gods but Vrawg was not familiar with any of them, and again, he was not truly a human either so did not feel he had a place anywhere in the afterlife.

Gurtha had always told Vrawg that the gods were fickle and not to be trusted anyway. She taught him to believe in himself first, to listen to his inner-voices for guidance and not seek answers from any gods. Vrawg knew his mother was wise and listened to her but he could still not shake the fear that none of the gods would ever accept him.

The raiding party navigated their way as silently as possible through the thick grass of the valley. An ogre scout wearing leather armor was far ahead of the others, choosing the best path for them to reach the barbarian camp unseen.

Despite the uncomfortable and unfamiliar surroundings, Vrawg found his excitement level rising as battle loomed closer. He was also most curious to get his first glimpse of a human, monsters that were said to be more dangerous than trolls or wraggoth. Monsters that were part of his heritage.

A howl from behind a distant hill gave Vrawg a start and he whirled in the direction with his spear held at the ready. The closest ogre to Vrawg chuckled.

"A wolf only, little half-breed. They will not bother us."

Vrawg had heard stories of wolves, four-legged, hairy beasts that roamed the valley in packs. A lone ogre could have cause to worry but a wolf pack was no match for their raiding party. They would howl from a distance but they would come no closer. Vrawg wondered if the call of the wolves would alert the barbarians of their approach but the others seemed to pay the howls no heed.

Not too far ahead, near a lightly-wooded area, the ogre scout gave a hand signal, indicating for the group to move more slowly now, and more cautiously. The glow of campfires could be seen from behind a hill only a hundred yards away. Adrenaline pumped through Vrawg's veins as he watched the scout, only a mere shadow to his eyes, crawl up to the summit of the hill for a peek at their quarry. The rest of the raiding party crouched in the tall grass, awaiting a signal to join the scout on the hill.

Vrawg's eyesight was limited in the dark of night but motion from behind a distant tree grabbed his attention. He squinted for a better look. Something did not feel right; something nagged at the half-ogre that danger was about.

As the scout on the hill yelled, "Trap," Vrawg noticed a shadow emerge from behind the very same tree he had been watching. The shadow hurled something and then with a sickening sound, the ogre closest to Vrawg fell to the ground, quite dead, an axe sunk deep into his forehead. Another ogre howled in pain as a barbarian rose up from the grass, skewering the large brute through the belly with a long sword.

"Fight! Fight!" commanded Golgra, sparks flying as his serrated sword blade clashed with a barbarian blade.

The ogres had no time to consider how they had walked into an ambush. The fight was on in full. Barbarians seemed to appear from nowhere and rushed the ogre party fearlessly. Vrawg barely had time to raise his wooden shield to catch the blade of an axe that bit deep. Too deep, in fact, as the human could not pull his weapon free. Vrawg lunged with his spear and caught the man in the shoulder, forcing him to let go of his axe and backpedal away in great pain.

Vrawg dropped his shield which was now too heavy to use properly because of the embedded axe and faced off against his next opponent. A blonde-haired, heavily-muscled barbarian stood in front of him, a huge sword held tightly with both hands. The man growled and attacked first. Vrawg had momentarily paused at the first real sight of a human and his opponent meant to capitalize. The barbarian, however, was not expecting Vrawg to be as fast as he was and found his attack deflected with the handle of the ogre's spear. The blunt end of the spear then rushed in with great speed to connect with his nose, which exploded with red mist.

Vrawg expected the human to crumble under the strength of that blow but the barbarian took it with a grunt and recovered quickly, swinging his sword with deadly intent once more. The human was fast and Vrawg only half-blocked the blade, taking a stinging slash to his forearm. Before Vrawg could even think to counter, the barbarian reversed the momentum of this attack and drew a line of blood across the half-ogre's belly.

Vrawg swung his spear out wide, not in any attempt to land a blow, but merely to force the barbarian to duck and take a step back, allowing the half-ogre a moment to compose himself. This human fought very differently from the wraggoth and trolls Vrawg was used to. He was much faster.

The young half-ogre allowed himself a momentary glance around him to see how the others in his party fared. Battle raged fiercely all around him and it appeared three ogres were down and not moving. He watched the mighty Golgra nearly chop an enemy in half with a powerful downwards strike of his sword.

Vrawg's attention was drawn back to his own fight as the barbarian charged him once more with a battle cry. He held his spear shaft out to block the attack and the human's sword cut right through it, severing Vrawg's weapon in half and causing him to leap backwards to avoid being cut open. Vrawg threw one end of the spear at the man, distracting him long enough so that he could grab an abandoned sword he spotted in the grass from the corner of his eye.

He brought the sword up just in time and sparks flew as the two blades collided with great force. For a moment, the two combatants were frozen in that pose, blades locked together as they leered at one another; the tall human only a few inches shorter than the half-ogre.

To Vrawg's surprise, the human leaned in closer and sunk his teeth into the half-ogre's arm. Vrawg grunted as the human smiled and spat a chunk of flesh from his mouth. Gurtha had always told him that humans were far more civilized than ogres and generally feared the large brutes, and yet these barbarians were savage and fearless fighters.

With his sword out of position, Vrawg clubbed the human with his free fist. The man stumbled and was dazed enough for Vrawg to land a quick strike to his muscled-shoulder with his blade. The barbarian roared and swung clumsily with his own sword. Vrawg parried it with ease and drove the tip of his blade into the man's abdomen. Vrawg pulled the blade free and turned to find a new opponent when the human roared again and attacked with even more fury. The man should have fallen from his wounds, the half-ogre thought, and yet he still came on, and with even more ferocity.

Vrawg's mistake of assuming the barbarian was defeated was costly. He could not turn his body in time to get his weapon up in defense. The savage human's sword bit deeply into Vrawg's arm, causing him to drop his weapon. He was doomed and he knew it. The barbarian raised his sword for another strike and Vrawg just held out his hands in some pathetic attempt to stop the blow from landing.

Fortunately, the attack never came. Golgra slammed the hilt of his sword into the back of the barbarian's skull, knocking him unconscious. Vrawg blinked in surprise and then surveyed the scene around him. Only Golgra and three other bloodied ogres remained standing. Five ogres had fallen in the attack, along with twelve barbarians. Vrawg's opponent surprisingly still breathed.

"I told you not to underestimate the barbarians," Golgra scolded the half-ogre. "Never turn your back on an opponent until he has ceased breathing. Now, finish him."

Vrawg looked quizzically to his commander.

"Pick up that sword and behead the human. Finish him."

Vrawg was suddenly struck with the desire to speak with this human, if he were to survive his wounds. There were so many things he wanted to ask him. He wondered if this warrior might even know of his father.

"Prisoner?" Vrawg said with a shrug.

Golgra pondered that idea for a moment. The barbarians generally fought to the death so there was rarely an opportunity to take one alive. Perhaps they could get some information out of this one about the rest of their tribe.

The ogre commander nodded. "Your responsibility. You carry him."

CHAPTER 7

For the last month, Evonne was given the most menial of jobs to do aboard The Grinning Kraken, namely, scrubbing the deck. The worst part for her was the leering stares she received from much of the crew, with dark promises evident behind their cruel eyes. They stared and they made comments, but as of yet, not one had attempted to touch her. She could not be sure how long that would last.

Although, spending the amount of time above deck that she had been, she was slowly learning the who's who of the ship, and who got along with whom. Just because they all served on the same ship did not mean that they all got along.

Directly under Captain Krayne was Syd Borsenthal, or Mister Bors as he was more commonly called, the first mate. Mister Bors was a grizzled, old, white-haired man, whose pale skin had long ago turned orange from the sun. He was sailing the seas long before many of the others aboard the ship were even born. Evonne noticed that Syd was respected by everyone and nary was a nasty glance ever shot his way.

The same could not be said for Purciful Tannis, a greasy-looking villain with dark eyes and a thin black moustache. Purcy was lanky, and when he smiled with a most sinister smile, his broken and rotted teeth would make Evonne shudder. The man enjoyed questioning decisions made by Krayne and the two butted heads often. Purcy was not well liked by all of the crew but did have strong support from more than a few of them. Bromm, a dim-witted, red-bearded brute, was never far from Purcy's side. Whenever anyone exchanged any choice words with Purcy, Bromm was there growling, hand inching towards the curved sword that hung from his belt.

The three large northmen, Brak, Torthal and Thrag, tended to stick together and did not often socialize with the other crew members. Perhaps the most frightening-looking of the crew was Jabari, a wide-shouldered, black-skinned man, whose face was painted with a white skull and his teeth filed into fangs. It was rumored the man was a cannibal and enjoyed feasting on the flesh of captured pirates, though, as Evonne soon learned, that was just a tale told to instill fear in enemies. Jabari was actually a very jovial individual who enjoyed singing and dancing around the deck, after having too much to drink. He was always smiling and in a good mood.

Evonne's brother Zack, like a lot of the younger members of the crew, had not really found a place in the hierarchy as of yet. They were largely ignored by other crew members and tried to go about their business quietly and not draw too much attention to themselves. Fortunately for her, Grim was another person who appeared to be widely respected by the crew. Perhaps feared was a better description. Evonne found that Grim was not overly friendly with others and they were careful not to anger the dwarf. Even Purcy, while no friend of Grim's, kept a healthy distance.

When not working, and she spent most of the day working, Evonne would stay in the cargo hold of the ship where the door was generally kept locked. She was lucky that Grim was in charge of keeping inventory aboard the ship and not many others were permitted in the hold without his consent. That had nothing to do with Evonne's presence, but that pirates simply could not be trusted.

Each evening, usually before Grim went to sleep, the dwarf would spend time in the hold teaching Evonne to fight. It did not matter how exhausted the teenage girl felt from her day of chores, she found the energy necessary to train and looked forward to her time with Grim every single day. Each night ended with a new bruise or scrape but Grim was impressed that Evonne never complained once.

The dwarf had given her a curved sabre, a thin and light sword that was the favored weapon of most pirates. Evonne was small, even for a girl her age, and Grim knew that it would take a lot of training before she would ever be ready to join the crew in actual combat.

"You are tiny, lass, and I expect you will never get that much bigger. That just means you have to be smarter in a fight. Your opponents will almost always be bigger than you and stronger than you."

"Like a dwarf."

Grim chuckled. "Not quite. They might be bigger

than me but few are stronger or tougher. You cannot fight like a dwarf. You need to be fast and elusive. Forget about blocking an attack. You must move. You must dodge. You have to get inside quickly, strike, and then get back out of reach. This style is not easy and takes much practice and discipline. But if you expect to live long you had better learn quickly."

And Evonne did learn quickly. Long after Grim was snoring loudly, Evonne would continue to practice her techniques. She slept very little but she did not care. As Grim had told her, her very life depended on this training.

It was not until her second month aboard the ship that she got to witness her second battle. The Grinning Kraken had tirelessly pursued a merchant vessel for two weeks before catching up to her. Grim implored Evonne to stay hiding in the hold but her curiosity was too great. She did, however, stay out of the battle this time and found a safe place to hide which still offered her a view of the action.

The merchant ship was larger with more men on board, but these men were not the seasoned fighters like those of the Kraken. She could see the fear in the other crew plainly worn on their faces. One man, in fact, soiled his pants at the sight of a grinning Jabari, his fangs in view as he taunted the enemy crew with promises to eat every last one of them.

Evonne learned that fear played a great role in battle. The Grinning Kraken was outnumbered but fear had won them the battle before it had even begun. Some of their fears were misplaced, as Jabari had no actual intent on eating anyone, but other fears were genuine. Captain Krayne ordered the entire crew butchered and not one man was left alive.

Evonne again found herself questioning her decision. Was this the life she really wanted? She knew the crew aboard that merchant vessel had done nothing wrong except cross the path of Captain Krayne. They were only trying to make a living and they all died horribly as a result of it. Evonne saw no problem with fighting other pirates, other criminals, but murdering innocent people did not sit well with her.

She sat silently in the hold by herself, digesting her thoughts, when Grim entered along with an odd fellow she had seen around the ship. He was wiry with short dark hair and slanted eyes. A tattoo of a large dragon dominated much of his back and he rarely wore a shirt. Evonne had heard others call him Dragon but had never heard him speak.

"What's wrong with you?" Grim asked, noticing the long face that the teenage girl wore.

"Why did Captain Krayne order all those men killed? Could he have not just taken what he wanted from the ship and let them go?" Evonne responded with her own questions.

"Dead men can't seek revenge, lass."

"Those men were terrified before the battle even started. Do you really think any of them would come back looking for this ship?"

"Why were those men terrified?"

"The reputation of The Grinning Kraken, I would imagine."

"Exactly. Men soil themselves at the sight of our ship. They cannot fight effectively when they are terrified. Now, if the Captain let people go, they would be less terrified."

"It still isn't right."

"Well, you can take that up with the Captain at our next meeting. I am sure he will be very receptive to your idea," the dwarf chuckled.

Evonne glanced over to the other man who sat on a crate at the far end of the hold cleaning a crossbow. "What's with him? He never talks."

"Dragon there is harmless, don't you worry about him."

"What kind of name is Dragon?"

"A nickname really, nobody knows his real name. We call him Dragon because of his tattoo."

"Doesn't he know his real name?"

"I imagine he would."

"Why doesn't he tell you then?"

"Because he has no tongue, lass." Evonne screwed her face up in disgust. "Dragon is from the Far East. They like to deal with criminals a little differently out there. They love cutting things off. You steal, they cut off your hand. You run from the law, they cut off your leg. You are caught spying, they cut out your eyes. You rape someone, well you get the idea. Now, the removal of someone's tongue, I suppose Dragon could have said something he shouldn't have, or perhaps he knew something that someone didn't want him to tell. He cannot read or write, so we don't know anything about the poor lad."

Evonne's attention suddenly shifted to a spider which was crawling up a wooden beam, very close to where she sat. She could not suppress a squeal as she had always found the insects revolting.

Before she could jump up and move away, something whistled past her ear and struck the beam, effectively eliminating the threat of the small spider. Evonne turned to regard Dragon, who sat a fair distance away, holding a crossbow pointed in her direction and smiling widely. She could not imagine he could have even seen the spider from that distance, let alone hit it with the crossbow bolt.

"Oh yeah," Grim said absently, as he looked over the contents of a record book, "Dragon is an expert marksman. There isn't anything he can't hit with a crossbow or throwing knife."

Evonne stared in awe at the spot where the spider had been only moments before. "Can he teach me to shoot?"

*   *   *   *

Evonne now divided what little free time she had between practicing with her sword and practicing with a crossbow and throwing knives. Grim decided it was a good idea after all, since ranged weapons would keep the small girl at a distance from enemies. He was quite impressed with how quickly she learned, but Grim did not truly believe a human female could go very far as a swordswoman, not like a tough dwarven lass.

Evonne found herself very comfortable around Dragon. It was not easy to learn a new skill when your teacher could not speak but the man was very patient with her. Before she was even allowed to fire the crossbow she had to learn every single part of the weapon that made it work. She pulled it apart and put it back together again a hundred times, by her estimation, before Dragon allowed her to fire her first shot. And her first shot was way off mark, as with the many others that followed.

The hardest part about shooting such a weapon on a ship was that the ship was never still. It was not like standing on solid ground, the ship was always moving. During one particular practice session, a storm raged and a large wave crashed against the ship as Evonne pulled the trigger of the crossbow. The bolt went through a crate a mere inch from Grim's head, who sat not too far away, nodding off to sleep. Oh how the dwarf's skin turned a ghostly shade of pale when he inspected the hole in the crate and realized how close he had come to an instant death.

"Drop that silly contraption and grab your sword," he said, wanting there to be no more accidents this evening.

The dwarf grabbed a smaller axe he used when sparring with the teenager and stalked towards her. Evonne retrieved her sword and began dancing around the dwarf. Grim swung the axe towards the top of her head and Evonne easily ducked underneath, then pivoted to the side of the dwarf as she had been taught. She stabbed forward, looking to poke her opponent in his unprotected side, but Grim was too fast and slapped the weapon away with his while turning to face her again.

Again he swung and again she dodged and countered, albeit unsuccessfully. Grim feinted this time, hoping to catch Evonne after she pivoted but the girl surprised him and saw the feint for what it was. She skipped in the other direction, far from the dwarf's next attack. Grim nodded with satisfaction. Dragon clapped his hands, enjoying the match.

Grim had taught Evonne to never match strength with strength and never attempt to block an attack unless she had no other choice. She had learned her lessons well.

He went through another series of attacks and each time the young girl ducked or danced away out of reach. One time she even rolled underneath and came up to stand behind the dwarf. Before she could counter, Grim pulled a crate down behind him and the weight of the object knocked Evonne to the floor. She looked up to find the blade of his axe resting on her forehead.

"You cheated!" she accused.

Grim laughed. "There is no such thing as cheating in a fight, lass. You can die with honor if you like, I prefer to live by any means necessary. Everything around you is a potential weapon. Always pay attention to your surroundings."

Evonne stood, angrily, and indicated that she was ready to continue. Grim smiled and advanced on her, swinging his axe with more conviction this time. He knew that going easy on her could only teach her so much and could potentially provide her with a false sense of ability. He meant to end this session quickly to remind her that she still had a long way to go.

Evonne ducked the first swing and immediately noticed the difference in the dwarf's demeanor. She knew if she had not ducked in time, that attack would have seriously injured her. Grim gave her no time to compose herself before he attacked again and again. Evonne did not even have time to counter; she was too busy trying to avoid being sliced to shreds. One wild swing even tore a hole in her shirt, barely missing the skin underneath.

Remembering well the lesson Grim had just taught her, Evonne rolled under his next attack and came up standing next to a bucket of water. The dwarf turned around to face her just as Evonne kicked the bucket up towards his head. Her aim was true and water splashed into Grim's face, momentarily blinding him. Without wasting a single moment, she slapped the hand that held his axe with the flat side of her sword. The strike was just hard enough to cause the distracted dwarf to drop his weapon. Evonne dove in and poked the tip of her sword into his chest, stopping short of actually penetrating skin.

"Ha ha ha ha!" she laughed. "I beat you! I actually be...""

She never finished her sentence. She watched the dwarf's fist fly towards her face and then everything went black.

*   *   *   *

Grim did feel bad about knocking Evonne unconscious but she had to learn that they were not just playing a game. A mistake in actual battle would mean her life. Although, he was quite proud of her. She had learned that every object was a potential weapon and she had used the bucket of water marvelously. She would have actually skewered him through the heart and he had not been taking it easy on her.

The dwarven pirate chuckled to himself as he was returning to the cargo hold after a late meeting with Captain Krayne. He stopped as he spotted an unsavory individual skulking about by the door to the hold.

"Looking for something?"

The lean man with a bald tattooed head whirled about in surprise, believing the dwarf was still in the captain's quarters.

"Or should I say, looking for someone?"

Reginald growled. "What gives you the right to keep her all to yourself?"

"Keep her? Nobody owns her."

"Seems a funny thing to say when she is hidden away in this hold all night and only you and that stupid mute ever come and go."

"Captain Krayne ordered her to sleep in the hold and I am the master of inventory."

"Give her to me. For an hour only, then you can have her back. I promise," Reginald grinned, wickedly.

Grim always hated Reginald. He was one of Purcy's lackeys and a vile human if ever there was one.

"I have warned you all before. Stay away from the girl."

"Or what, dwarf? You gonna fight us all? How long do you think you can protect her?"

Grim took a menacing step forward. "Get out of me sight before I hang you from the crow's nest by your intestines."

"You wouldn't dare."

Grim drew a dagger from the top of his boot. "I will enjoy this."

Reginald paled and moved away from the door while keeping a healthy distance from the fierce dwarf. "Don't think this is over, fool," the man said, as he quickly vanished in the direction of the crew's quarters.

Grim shook his head and entered the cargo hold, nearly knocking a dizzy Evonne to the floor, as she had been listening to the conversation through the door. The young girl's right eye had blackened and she still held a cloth to a bloodied and most likely broken nose. Grim locked the door behind him and took a seat on a crate, smiling at his young pupil.

"I think you broke my nose," Evonne said.

"Did you learn another lesson?"

"Yeah, dwarves are sore losers."

Grim chuckled. "Just because you have disarmed an opponent, do not assume the fight is done."

"So, I guess I now know why the crew has left me alone," she said, changing the subject. "You have threatened them all."

Grim shrugged his shoulders.

"I heard through the door. Why do you protect me? My own brother has no desire to stick his neck out for me."

"Zack has fallen into Purcy's group and Purcy speaks poison into people's ears. He has a way of manipulating men. Be careful of that one."

"But why do you protect me? The others think you are trying to keep me all to yourself."

"Of course they would think that, they believe there is only one purpose for women in this world. You are hardly me type, lass. Your face is far too smooth."

"Smooth? Why would my face be anything but smooth?"

"A fine dwarven lass has a beard every bit as thick as me own. Grow yourself a beard and I may just consider keeping you for meself," he chuckled.

"Then answer the question. Why do you protect me?"

"You remind me of me own daughter, if you must know."

"Oh, you have a daughter? I didn't know."

"Yes, I have a daughter back home. She was only young when I left and I doubt I will ever see her again.

When I saw you, your eyes reminded me of hers."

"Where is back home?"

"Far to the west, lass. On the western side of the sea."

"I thought the sea stretched to the end of the world."

"End of the world? What fool books have you been reading?"

"I thought if we sailed far enough west, we would fall off the edge of the world and into the Abyss."

Grim shook his head in disbelief. "Silly girl, the world is round. There is no edge of the world."

"Round? Then the people on the bottom would fall off."

"The people on the bottom never know they are on the bottom. It always feels like you are on the top."

"How can that be?"

"Look, lass, I don't know how it all works. The gods decided that we won't fall off so we don't fall off. Simple. If you traveled in a straight line from here, eventually, and it may take a long time, you would return to the spot where you started."

Evonne found the idea very difficult to comprehend.

"Forget trying to understand it. On the western side of the sea is the nation of Vendolen. It is a vast mountainous region where the dwarves have a great kingdom. I lived in the dwarven city of Glorbad, within Mount Grail." Grim stared off into the distance as he imagined his old homeland. "But that feels like another lifetime ago."

"Why are you here?" Evonne wondered. Surely the dwarf was a fearsome fighter but he had been nothing but kind to her. He did not seem to fit in with the rest. "You told me everyone on this ship was a bad person but I don't think you are bad."

Grim snorted. "You don't know anything, lass."

"I read people well. And I see a kind soul beneath your rough exterior."

"Everyone aboard this ship is here for a reason. They are all running from something. Outcasts and criminals, all of them, your brother included. Some of these men are wanted for crimes with large prices on their heads. Some were already imprisoned and had escaped. Oh sure, a few may tell you they are innocent but they are all liars."

"And you, then, are also a liar like the rest?"

"Not me, lass, I am a bad person and I won't tell you otherwise."

"I don't believe you are."

"Tell that to the dwarf I murdered. Do I regret it? Absolutely. But did I do it? Absolutely."

"He must have deserved it."

"No, he didn't. I was foolish in my younger years. He was a good friend of mine and I murdered him out of jealousy. Then, like a coward, I fled me city and me family, leaving it all behind. Now I am hiding here, with other cutthroats and murderers, like meself."

Evonne sat silently, feeling sad for the dwarf. Despite his tale, she knew he was different from the rest, even if he would not admit it.

"You, lass, are the only innocent aboard this ship. And I strongly suggest you reconsider your idea of staying before you truly become one of us."

CHAPTER 8

It took a week before the barbarian prisoner opened his eyes for the first time, and even then, they were not open for long. Vrawg worked tirelessly to save the human's life. Zolar and other shamans in the tribe possessed healing powers granted by Blaggrath, but of course, refused to use such powers on the despised human. So Vrawg had turned to his mother for help in the art of dressing and sewing wounds. The work was far from perfect but the barbarian was alive; for the time being.

The other ogres were eager for the man to wake up so he could be tortured for information about the rest of his tribe. Vrawg was hoping to get his own information out of him before the others got their hands on him.

"Has the human awakened yet?" an ogre guard asked of Vrawg, as the half-ogre attempted to hurry past and enter the small cave used to imprison the captive.

Vrawg shook his head to indicate that he had not and entered the cell, closing a heavy wooden door behind him. He failed to tell the guard that the human had awakened a few days ago, but as of yet, had not spoken.

The barbarian lay on a bed of animal furs, and despite his weakened state, was still shackled to the wall with a chain attached to his right wrist. A torch burned in the cell, providing light to the human who would not have been able to see without it. He glared at Vrawg with a hateful stare and spat at him.

"Kill me, you filthy beast," the barbarian said with a weak voice, using the common language of humans.

Vrawg shook his head and just stared at the man with amazement. He was half human and he felt an odd feeling of kinship with the barbarian before him. A feeling which he did not share with the ogres of his tribe. Vrawg wondered if his father looked similar to this man, who was large and strong by human standards.

The barbarian inspected the bandages and stitching that had prevented him from bleeding to death. "Why have you done this? Why have you not sent me to meet the gods along with my brothers?"

"I save you," Vrawg responded, speaking the language that he had only used with his mother before this moment.

"Why? I deserved to die in that field with my brothers."

"You are human."

"You are a clever one, I see. They must have made you a leader with that keen perception of yours. I am clever too. You are an ogre."

"No. Not ogre. Half ogre."

The barbarian tilted his head and regarded the thing before him more closely. He had been fighting ogres since he was strong enough to swing a sword. He came to realize that there was something off about this ogre but he could not quite say what it was. If he was only half an ogre, the barbarian had to wonder what the other half consisted of.

"And half what? Troll?"

"Human."

The barbarian stared in disbelief. His first instinct was to laugh at the absurdity of that claim. But there was definitely something different about the ogre's eyes, an intelligence, a kindness even, that was missing from his brutish kin. As with Vrawg, questions swirled around in the barbarian's head.

*   *   *   *

"Blaggrath is most displeased."

"What is Blaggrath displeased with this time?" Chief Yarg replied, with a wave of his hand.

Zolar frowned at the obvious dismissal of his statement. The shaman spoke for their god, after all, and even the mighty chieftain should heed his words and take them seriously.

"The continued existence of this Vrawg is an insult to Blaggrath! And now we are tending to the health of a barbarian? Our enemy?"

"We could get information out of the human."

"Nonsense! The barbarian would rather die than talk. He will force you to kill him and will take any chance he gets to take one of us with him."

"He is weak and of no threat to us."

"How soon we forget the ogres who died in that raid, killed by these humans. You dishonor them by keeping the human alive."

"I forget nothing!" Chief Yarg roared, finally having had enough of Zolar's lectures. "I am Chief! I make the decisions! We will torture information out of the barbarian and if he will not talk, then he will die."

"And what of Vrawg?"

"What of Vrawg? By Golgra's account, he fought well in his first fight with the barbarians. He survived while other ogres did not."

"That upsets Blaggrath," the shaman insisted. "Good ogres died while this half-human still draws breath. Blaggrath will punish us, do not doubt."

Yarg stood and walked from the room. His two bodyguards followed but did not share his dismissive attitude towards the shaman's claims. They appeared worried that Blaggrath would be angry with their tribe.

Lugnor, who watched the exchange in silence, finally approached the shaman. "Is there still time to appease Blaggrath? Can we divert disaster?"

"Yes," Zolar answered, with a smile.

"Tell me how."

*　　*　　*　　*

"Vrawg, you need to forget about the barbarian."

Gurtha and her son were alone in their own private quarters and Vrawg's mother was becoming increasingly concerned about his safety.

"You should not have brought him here," she continued. "It would have been better for him to have bled to death out there in the valley."

Vrawg tilted his head.

"Ushan revels in torture. He will take great pleasure in hurting that human before they kill him. And there is already talk about the work you did to save his life. The others believe you sympathize with humans and would even side with them."

"Ogres are stupid," Vrawg replied. "All they want to do is kill."

Gurtha smiled a genuine smile and wrapped an arm around her son. "Bringing the human here was foolish, but I am proud of you, Vrawg. I would have done the very same thing. You have much of your father in you. You think more like a human. They are very different from us, very different. There are evil humans, some even more so than ogres, but they are not all like that. Humans have compassion and help others in need. I have seen those qualities in you from the time you were young. You do not behave like an ogre and that makes me very happy."

"I hate ogres."

"You get that from me. That is why your father was human. But you live here with ogres, Vrawg. There are dangerous ogres here in our tribe so you must be careful with your actions. Zolar in particular you must be careful with. He claims to speak for Blaggrath but I know he only speaks for himself, the fool."

"Maybe I go find father."

"Humans are more tolerable than ogres, well some of them, but that is not a good idea. Humans have traded with us but they would not accept you either. Unfortunately, you are safer here, my son. And I would be too lonely without you."

"We go together."

"The world is a very vast place, but here in these

mountains is the only safe place for ogres. War-loving ogres have made it that way for us. Humans do not trust ogres because we have fought with them for thousands of years. Chief Yarg recognizes your value to this tribe. He is the best ally to have. Tomorrow he makes an announcement. I believe you will have the honor of being chosen for the next raid. I know you may not want to fight the humans but that is our way, so it must be your way."

*   *   *   *

Many ogres gathered in the great cavern hall. Most of the warriors of the Drogheim tribe were itching to strike back at the barbarians who had killed five of their tribesmen in the last ill-fated raid. The very same raid in which the half-ogre, Vrawg, had taken a prisoner rather than slay the wretched human. Then, to make matters worse, he had used the tribe's resources to save the man's life. Chief Yarg, though, had promised the human would reveal valuable information. Information that would be useful in mounting another attack against the barbarians. Now, the mighty leader of their tribe was set to make a speech concerning their next raid.

Vrawg entered the hall and received more than a few angry sneers, so opted to remain near the back of the cavern, closest to the exit. The half-ogre did not have long to wait before Chief Yarg marched into the hall, flanked by his two bodyguards and followed closely behind by Zolar.

Vrawg was conflicted about his future. He had strived for much of his life to become the best warrior he could be. But now those skills were being put to use against the barbarians of the valley. Vrawg had no problem fighting trolls or wraggoth. Both attacked ogres whenever possible and Vrawg saw them to be just as evil as the ogres, and even more savage. Trolls feasted on flesh whether you were dead yet or not.

But the humans never attacked the mountains. They seemed to let the ogres be and only fought to defend themselves. Vrawg had always been taught by other ogres that humans were the evil ones. They had driven the ogres into the mountains and still sought to eliminate them from existence. Only, if that were so, why had there never been a human raid into the mountains since Vrawg had been alive? Gurtha always told her son not to believe everything the elders told him. That in time, he would learn for himself what was true and what was not. He realized the humans were not the evil ones, not the barbarians, anyway. His mother told him there were evil humans but he knew the barbarians fought only to protect themselves. So because of that, Vrawg was unsure about participating in further raids against them. Refusing a spot in the raiding party, though, would mean trouble.

The blast of a horn silenced the gathered ogres as their chief was about to speak.

"Fellow tribesmen, we have suffered a terrible loss recently, when five of our seasoned warriors fell to the blades of those cursed barbarians. Our raiding party walked into an ambush. The time for revenge is upon us." A great cheer erupted. "We are going to send a much larger force this time and make sure the humans pay for the ogre lives that were lost." Again there was enormous cheer. "We will begin…," Chief Yarg coughed, interrupting his sentence. "We will begin making…*cough*…*cough*…*cough*…begin making preparations…*cough*…"

The giant ogre grabbed his throat and began choking. His bodyguards rushed to his side with looks of panic. One of them pounded on the chief's back with his fists, hoping to dislodge whatever the ogre was choking on. Nothing helped. Chief Yarg's grey face turned a shade of blue and he collapsed to his knees.

More than one ogre turned in the direction of Zolar for assistance but the shaman stood his ground and watched the spectacle unfold. Yarg finally fell over onto his back and ceased his choking. He lay very still.

"He is dead!" shouted Tuglam, one of Yarg's bodyguards.

There was a collective gasp amongst the ogres in the cavern. They could not believe what they had just witnessed. Chief Yarg was the biggest and mightiest ogre to ever lead the Drogheim tribe and he had just died in front of them.

The hall erupted into chaos.

"How could this happen?"

"What did he choke on?"

"What do we do now?"

"Who will lead us?"

"Doom is upon us!"

"Yes, doom is upon us," shouted Zolar, whose voice could suddenly be heard above all others. The hall went silent. "Blaggrath has been angry with our tribe. I tried to warn Chief Yarg many times but he would not listen. Now, look! He lies dead before us. Dead by the will of Blaggrath!"

Fear was clearly written upon every face gathered in the hall and Zolar smiled inwardly. Chief Yarg was indeed dead but it was not by the will of their god. It was from the potent poison which had somehow found its way into his drink before the meeting.

"What have we done wrong?" one ogre shouted.

"Why is Blaggrath angry with us?" asked another.

Zolar motioned the ogres to quiet down once more. "Blaggrath has ever been insulted by the continued existence of the half-human. Then he brings another human into our mountain and saves his wretched life? Chief Yarg allowed this and Blaggrath has taken his anger out on him. I cannot say who will be next until something is done about this."

Every ogre in that hall turned to the cavern entrance, where Vrawg had been previously standing, but the half-ogre was gone.

*   *   *   *

Gurtha stood close to the mountain ledge and closed her eyes, enjoying the cool northern breeze on her face. She had not come up here in some time and almost forgot about how breathtaking the view was. It was a cloudy afternoon but she was still afforded a marvelous view of the Dalecanin Valley and she thought she could make out smoke from the chimneys in the distant town of Glastonby.

Her mind wandered then to Drubin and she wondered if her human lover was still alive. Humans did not live as long as ogres and she imagined he would be considered an old man now, even if he still lived. The feeling of sorrow washed over her as she considered her life and her decision to listen to the tribe elders and never return to Glastonby. It upset her even more to know that Vrawg would never have the joy of meeting his father. And Drubin, the former mercenary, would have been quite proud to see the warrior that his son had grown to be.

"You made it," a voice said behind her, interrupting her reflections.

Gurtha turned to regard the arrival of her brother. "I have been here awhile. I had forgotten how pleasant the view is."

"Bah," Lugnor snorted. "A view of the lands of humans is no pleasant view."

"How can you enjoy life when you carry around so much hatred all the time?"

"I will enjoy life and the view when we have wiped the barbarians from these lands and they become ours."

"If the barbarians were all killed, then what, brother? Glastonby? Hornwall? Maybe go south and take over Tauros? When does it stop?"

"It stops when Blaggrath says it stops."

Now it was Gurtha's turn to snort in response. "Blaggrath this, Blaggrath that. I grow weary of hearing about Blaggrath."

"How dare you!"

"Yes, I dare. Do you really think that Zolar speaks for Blaggrath? Or does Zolar just speak for Zolar?"

"I asked you here to see if I could change your mind one last time. I can see that your stubbornness knows no bounds."

"What are you talking about?"

"Your son is an insult to this tribe. You should have allowed me to throw him from this ledge when he was born."

"You insensitive…"

Gurtha's sentence was cut off with a scream as the much larger Lugnor shoved his sister off the rocky ledge. Lugnor stood in silence as he watched her body tumble and break against the sharp rocks of the mountainside.

*　　*　　*　　*

Vrawg rushed into the private quarters he shared with his mother but found another ogre present, in her place.

"You seem to be in a hurry, half-human," Lugnor commented, when the smaller ogre entered the room. "Has something happened?"

Vrawg did not reply and scanned the large room for any sign of his mother. His gut told him that something had gone terribly wrong.

"Looking for someone? Gurtha?" Lugnor taunted. "I don't think your mother will be returning."

Vrawg's eyes flashed with anger and Lugnor smiled with amusement.

"By the will of Blaggrath, your mother was cast off the side of this mountain. His anger will not be diminished until you join her."

Vrawg growled with rage and charged his much larger uncle. Lugnor stood five inches taller and was easily seventy pounds heavier but Vrawg did not care. He did not believe that his uncle was bluffing. He knew in his heart that Lugnor had murdered his mother and had now come for him. Vrawg would avenge his mother or die trying.

Lugnor underestimated Vrawg's speed and the half-ogre crashed into him before he could pull the dagger from the back of his belt. A testament to the smaller ogre's strength, the two fell to the hard floor in a tangle of thrashing limbs.

Vrawg landed the first blow, slamming his fist into Lugnor's jaw, but if the bigger ogre was bothered by it, it was not evident as he shook it off without even a grimace. A second blow landed before Lugnor shoved Vrawg back and got to his feet.

Again Vrawg gave his uncle no time to reach for his weapon as the two collided once more. Lugnor brought his elbow down onto Vrawg's left shoulder with a crunch. The half-ogre grimaced then connected with a wild punch to this uncle's abdomen. This time at least, Vrawg was rewarded with the sound of Lugnor gasping for breath from the cruel blow.

Vrawg followed it up with another punch to Lugnor's forehead and then a third to his jaw. The larger ogre stumbled backwards, momentarily stunned. Vrawg's anger had reached a boiling point and he dove at his uncle, looking to tackle him back to the floor.

As their bodies came together, it was Vrawg's turn to gasp as the blade of Lugnor's dagger found his stomach. Luckily it grazed his side and did not dig in deep. Now Vrawg's strategy quickly changed and he grabbed Lugnor's wrist in an attempt to make him drop the weapon.

The two wrestled for control of the dagger but Lugnor was simply too strong. Lugnor broke Vrawg's hold on his wrist and slashed the half-ogre across the chest, staining his leather vest, red.

Lugnor lunged for a second strike, only Vrawg proved the quicker and backed up out of reach. These were Vrawg's private quarters and he had various weapons spread out around the room that he had used to practice with.

While avoiding another slash of his uncle's blade, Vrawg managed to scoop up a ball and chain. He was off-balance and swung clumsily, but Lugnor stepped back, easily dodging the iron ball. The two slowly circled each other with their eyes locked together. Lugnor smiled while Vrawg growled with anger.

Vrawg bled from two wounds and Lugnor knew he had the edge. By all accounts, Vrawg was a fine warrior but Lugnor was a veteran of many battles, and forty years his senior. Lugnor knew that Vrawg had his doubts about this fight. He knew that the younger ogre was afraid.

Brimming with confidence, the larger ogre charged forward, looking to run his blade through his opponent's throat. But again, and for the final time, Lugnor underestimated Vrawg's quickness and strength. Vrawg swung the ball and chain with every ounce of rage he could muster. The counter attack was timed perfectly and Lugnor's skull exploded on contact. His twitching body lay on the floor, lifeless.

Vrawg knew his time in the Drogheim tribe had ended. It was time to leave. And quickly.

CHAPTER 9

From Evonne's vantage point she could finally see faces aboard the pursuing ship. An unknown, but smaller vessel, had been pursuing The Grinning Kraken for two days. Now, with mysterious speed, the ship was closing the distance rapidly.

"Mister Yarin, turn us around!" Captain Krayne shouted to the ship's navigator. "Get us in a better position!"

"Get below deck, lass," Grim said, as he appeared beside Evonne.

"That doesn't look like a ship from The Purple King's navy," she replied, ignoring his order.

"Because it ain't. Those are pirates."

"But their ship is smaller than ours. What pirates would be fool enough to come after us?"

"We will soon find out. But you get below deck. Now, lass."

"But I have learned so much," the young girl pleaded.

"And if you wanna learn more, get below deck and

stay there," Grim said more forcibly, and shoved Evonne towards the stairs.

Evonne climbed down several steps then stopped, intent on watching what would unfold. For the last year she had been learning the ins and outs of the ship, from top to bottom, along with her nightly training sessions with both Grim and Dragon. She had learned nearly every duty there was aboard the ship and felt as though her place was above deck with the rest of the crew. Even if Grim and Dragon were her only friends.

She was still not largely accepted by the others. Either they ignored her completely, or they continued to leer at her and taunt her with things they planned to do to her. In a year, only two men had actually attempted to lay hands on her. One was now missing his front teeth and the other was short a finger. Both courtesy of Grim. Evonne insisted she could have taken care of them but Grim still advised her to avoid trouble, that she was still a little girl aboard a ship of very mean men.

Even her brother wanted nothing to do with her. Zack spent most of his time with Purcy and his group of followers, and Purcy, above all others, hated Evonne's presence. Zack no doubt was influenced by Purcy's words and believed there was no place for his sister on the ship. He had told her to leave countless times but Evonne was a stubborn one and had nowhere else to go.

During the last year, The Grinning Kraken had been involved in a half-dozen battles, and each time, Evonne was ordered below and to stay out of trouble. Each time she remained hidden above deck to witness the bloody and brutal battles that took place. Evonne watched each of the crew members and studied how each one fought. She was surprised by how many of the men had no real style, whatsoever. It was obvious they never trained and just waded into battle, swinging swords wildly. Her brother was among that group.

She learned that Grim and the barbarians used a fierce offense as their defense. They were powerful men who preferred axes to chop through their enemies. Evonne noticed how enemy pirates or sailors would maneuver themselves away from the dwarf and the northmen to avoid facing them.

The same thing happened with the black-skinned warriors. They utilized a lot of theatrics in battle. Screaming, singing, taunting their enemies with promises of eating their innards. Men did their best to steer clear of them in battle as well.

For having such a big mouth, and being the one who stirred up the most trouble amongst the crew, Evonne found Purcy's tactics in battle to be cowardly. He usually allowed Bromm to lead the way and Purcy finished off wounded men left in Bromm's wake. Or he would use the chaos of battle to slink in and stab men in the back. He avoided a straight up fight whenever possible.

Evonne found Dragon to be the most impressive. The mute was usually positioned up high, either in the crow's nest, or in one of two other lookout spots. He used his crossbow with deadly accuracy to pick off enemy bowmen or men of importance. The ship was never still. It was constantly bobbing and moving and yet Dragon rarely missed a shot. If he was forced down from his perch he used throwing knives with the same deadly effect.

Of all the pirates on board The Grinning Kraken, perhaps Captain Krayne appeared to be the most skilled warrior. And Evonne supposed he had to be. He had to keep all these unruly and evil men in line. He was also the main target of enemy pirates. While some men would move away from Grim or the northmen, other men specifically moved towards Krayne. They felt that killing a pirate captain would make a great notch in their belt and also weaken the moral of a crew who had just lost their leader.

Whatever their motives, Captain Krayne had no shortage of opponents in battle, and to his credit, never shied away from any fight, no matter the size of the enemy he faced. Like Evonne, and many of the pirates, Krayne favored using a curved sabre. Most often he fought with the sabre in his right hand, and a long, thin dagger in his right. Typically, his sword was used to block and parry and then the dagger shot in when an opening presented itself. Men fell by the score to Krayne's blades. Evonne studied his every movement and marveled at his speed. She would even try to mimic some of his tricks when practicing and sparring with Grim.

Now she watched Captain Krayne shouting orders to the crew and they scrambled around to their appointed duties. The divisions amongst the crew vanished during battle. All differences were set aside as everyone focused on one common enemy. She could see the curiosity plainly visible on all the men's faces as they tried to determine who would have had the nerve to chase and attack them.

The Grinning Kraken was certainly not the largest ship that sailed the Western Sea, but had the reputation as one of the most dangerous. They had a long list of hated enemies that included merchants they had robbed, scorned and humiliated pirate captains, and of course, the navy for

The Purple King. They navy routinely patrolled the waters around the Taurosian coast and the Kraken was at the top of their list of wanted pirate ships. If ever captured by the navy, every crew member was sure to hang, and that now included Evonne.

The sound of an explosion had all crew members ducking for cover and diving onto the deck. Evonne's heart nearly leapt out of her chest. Panic swept across the ship as their main sail had caught fire. Evonne knew that many times pirates used flaming arrows to ignite the sails of an enemy ship but she could not spot the arrow in question. An arrow would also not explain the explosion and amount of flames that now engulfed their sail.

A second explosion sounded and this time Evonne was thrown from her hiding spot behind a large barrel. Men ran about the deck screaming as their clothes had caught fire. Captain Krayne pulled himself to his feet after also being thrown to the deck by the force of the explosion. He squinted his eyes to regard the enemy ship and then they went wide.

"Wizard!" Krayne yelled.

Wizard? Had he really said wizard? Evonne had heard many tales of wizards as a child but thought that they had just been tales. She squinted her eyes as well and spotted a black-bearded man wearing black robes, standing in the middle of the enemy ship's deck. He appeared to be chanting with his hands held out in front of him. His eyes opened as his chant finished and ten black streaks shot forth from his fingertips and flew towards the Kraken.

Men shrieked warnings and pointed at the approaching black streaks. As they reached the ship, each streak, which resembled a small black lightning bolt, flew off in different directions to pursue different targets. All ten of the magical bolts struck their targets and men howled in pain. Closest to Evonne, Winston, clutched his leg where smoke poured forth from of a hole in his pants. Herb, who was no more than a teen himself, was forced over the side of the ship as a black bolt struck him dead center in the chest.

Zack and several other men rushed about with pails of water in a poor attempt to put out the flames on their sail. Grim reached one of the loaded ballistae and turned it in the direction of the enemy ship. Before he could aim, a ball of fire flew from the wizard's hand and exploded against the ballistae, destroying it and sending the sturdy dwarf flying several feet away. Grim landed hard on the deck and his hands flailed vigorously against his beard which had ignited with flames.

Another pirate, Evonne thought his name was Pavol, took up a bow and fired an arrow. His aim was off and the arrow did not even reach the enemy ship. In response, enemy arrows fired back. Two bounced harmlessly off the deck, a third caught Pavol in the left thigh and the man went down, rolling in pain.

For the first time since Evonne had come aboard the Kraken, Captain Krayne was speechless. He took cover behind a thick mast and watched the destruction around him. She could see the wheels turning frantically in his mind, but for the moment, Krayne did not know how to proceed. Their main sail was nearly burned away completely so escape was no longer an option. The wizard had his men pinned down and running for cover against the relentless magical barrage.

A second ballistae was blown to pieces before one of

the northmen could reach it. Evonne squealed as a sliver of wood bit into her cheek. The same panic that gripped the rest of the crew had a solid hold on her. She figured this was the end of her pirate career. That wizard would most likely sink the Kraken and then enemy archers could pick off floating survivors with ease, unless sharks got to them first.

The ship was now close enough that Evonne could read the name written on the side. The Sea Viper was not a name she had heard spoken before. The enemy pirates hooted and hollered as more arrows and more black magical bolts swept across the Kraken's deck. Evonne looked to Dragon's usual perches but the deadly mute was not in any of them. A quick scan of the deck revealed that her friend had taken an arrow in the shoulder and was crawling for cover as more shafts rained down. Spotting something else, an idea crossed the young girl's mind.

Believing herself completely mad, Evonne raced across the deck and nearly ended up on her face as the ship lurched to one side. She had developed strong sea legs and managed to keep her balance. She was forced to leap over the bodies of three crewmen who had fallen to arrows and spells.

Evonne dove and slid across the water-soaked deck, just in time, as an arrow whizzed by and would have found her head only a moment before. She picked up Dragon's crossbow that her friend had seemingly abandoned. Unfortunately, his pouch of ammunition was still with him. Evonne frantically looked about and found the one bolt that had been loaded into the crossbow but had fallen loose when Dragon dropped the weapon.

Evonne reloaded the crossbow and ran to the edge of

the deck that was closest to The Sea Viper. She laid the weapon onto the railing and took a deep breath. She held her breath as she took aim at the black-robed wizard. She willed her hands to cease trembling and silently whispered a prayer to Azark, one of the sea gods that pirates called upon in moments of dire need.

For a split second, time seemed to stop around the young pirate. She no longer heard the cries of wounded men or the waves crashing against their ship. All was silent. Her peripheral vision blurred and the only thing she could see was the wizard. Evonne pulled the trigger on the crossbow and focused on the flight of the speeding bolt.

She would swear later that she watched it fly in slow motion. Evonne, who had practiced shooting day in and day out, single-handedly saved The Grinning Kraken that day from annihilation. The bolt entered the wizard's chest, somewhere near the man's heart, and he collapsed to the deck. His spellcasting days were at an end.

The enemy pirates paused in silent shock at the loss of their hired wizard. Their captain, Erol Zan, had a long-standing grudge against the Kraken, and Captain Krayne in particular. The man had spent a small fortune in gold to hire himself a wizard in an attempt to kill Krayne and his crew once and for all. Zan knew he did not have the men or the proper ship to battle Krayne in a fair fight, so the wizard was to shift all the odds in their favor. That wizard was now gone.

Captain Krayne took advantage of the enemy's shock and began shouting orders once again. With the wizard down, hope returned to the crew of the Kraken. Mister Yarin, the helmsman, turned the ship so their remaining ballistae could begin firing. Grim was the first to fire a large bolt with a rope attached. The bolt slammed into the hull of the Viper and now there was no escape for Zan. A second bolt pierced the hull and the two ships were coming closer to together as both sides sent arrows onto the other's deck.

When the ships were close enough, the planks were dropped and the men of The Grinning Kraken began to board the enemy ship. Captain Krayne was one of the first across and he cut a bloody path through the Viper's crew. Evonne allowed herself to exhale and relax as she watched the massacre that now took place. The battle did not last long, and in fact, several of the enemy pirates threw down their swords and surrendered. Zan had refused to surrender and fought Krayne to the death. He was impaled by the captain's sabre. The wizard was apparently still breathing when found but was quickly put to the sword before he could utter any deadly spells.

When the battle had ended, all eyes turned to Evonne.

"She saved us," she heard one man say.

"Evonne took out the wizard," said another.

"One in a million shot, that was."

"Azark smiled on the girl."

Each of the crew nodded to Evonne with respect. Several patted her on the shoulder as they walked by. Captain Krayne locked stares with the young girl and gave her a salute and a nod of his own.

*   *   *   *

The man screamed in agony again from inside the crew's quarters.

"Is Mister Bors going to be alright?" Evonne wondered.

"He will most likely lose his leg," Grim replied.

Mister Bors, the ship's first mate, suffered terrible burns to his right leg from one of the wizard's fireballs. As Grim had just informed Evonne, there was not likely anything that could be done to save his leg.

"Lose his leg? How will he lose it?"

"Well, lass, they will liquor him up as best they can and then saw it off."

Evonne looked horrified. "Won't he bleed to death? Shouldn't we get him to a port somewhere for some real help?"

"They will do their best to stop the bleeding but you are right, we have to get to a port. Mister Bors needs the help of a healer and our ship needs some major repairs."

Evonne could not think of any friendly ports in this area that would allow The Grinning Kraken to dock. "What port?"

"Trollport."

"Trollport?"

"Trollport. A haven for pirates. It lies on a very secluded island which is not the easiest place to find for those who don't know where to look. We will dock there and make all the necessary repairs to the ship, and Mister Bors will get some professional help."

"A haven for pirates? Under what nation's control?"

"None. It is a port for pirates, run by pirates."

"But who keeps them from killing each other?"

"There are rules in Trollport. Pirates do not kill pirates. Swift justice is brought to those who break the rules of Trollport. It is place for goods to be bought and sold, supplies replenished, repairs made, but no killing."

"I cannot imagine an entire port of pirates and nobody gets killed."

"Oh it happens, just not openly. It is not a place for the weak," and Grim gave Evonne a concerned look, "or the young. I advise you to stay on board the ship."

"What happens to the men who surrendered on the Viper?"

"They will be sold in Trollport."

"Sold? To who? For what?"

"Just sold, lass. Focus on your task here and don't ask so many questions."

Grim grimaced as Evonne poked him with the needle. She was sewing up one of the many gashes he received during the battle on The Sea Viper. The young pirate was still learning the art of stitching wounds.

"You always tell me to duck and dodge attacks but you never do. Why don't you just try to avoid someone's sword once in awhile?"

"Bah," the dwarf said, taking another gulp of whiskey.

Whenever Grim did not have a proper answer for Evonne, he just said "bah." That also signified the end of that particular conversation.

"You did well today, lass. I told you to stay below and you disobeyed like you usually do, but, we are thankful that you did."

Grim very rarely complimented Evonne on anything. He used the tough love approach to training her. The life of a pirate was not easy and the dwarf was doing his best to toughen up the young girl.

"I am proud of you." Evonne smiled ear to ear. "Don't let it get to your head now. Your life has just gotten a lot more complicated. With shooting like that, you are gonna be expected on deck for all future fights."

The door to the cargo hold burst open and in staggered Jabari. He smiled widely, showing off all his sharpened teeth. In one hand he held a half-empty bottle of some potent liquor looted from the Viper.

"You are late, girl," he said with his thick islander accent.

"Late?" Evonne replied.

"Late for your toast. Come on, Evonne the Wizard-Slayer, tonight you drink with us."

CHAPTER 10

The barbarian howled as Ushan pressed the heated dagger blade against the bare skin of his chest. The prisoner had attempted to appear unconscious but the ogre torturer decided it was time to wake him up. Ushan excelled at torture and it had been a long time since he had a barbarian prisoner to play with. It was very difficult to capture the ferocious humans alive.

The door to the prison chamber opened and Ushan turned to regard the arrival of Vrawg, who appeared to be out of breath.

"Your pet human is awake," the torturer said, with a wicked grin. "Now I will get answers out of him. Or not. I don't care which."

Without a word, Vrawg swung the ball and chain and it connected against the ogre's jaw with a crunch. Ushan fell to the floor unconscious, his head bouncing viciously upon the hard floor.

The barbarian stared wide-eyed, unable to believe what he had just witnessed. For a moment he wondered if he had been hallucinating due to the severe pain. He watched the ogre who claimed to be half human, retrieve a key from the torturer's belt and unshackle his wrist.

"What are you doing?" the barbarian croaked in a weak voice.

"We go," Vrawg responded, pulling the man to his feet.

The barbarian was extremely weak and nearly fell back the floor. When he finally realized the half-ogre was serious about escaping, hope flooded his body with the energy to stand. He had always expected to die within the mountain but it seemed the gods had heard his prayers.

Vrawg tried to pull the man from the room but the barbarian resisted. Vrawg looked at him curiously, then understood and nodded. The barbarian struggled to bend over and pick up the heated dagger. With tremendous strength, even for a wounded man, the barbarian drove the dagger handle-deep into the ogre's heart. Ushan would never rise again.

* * * *

The pair of escapees made their way as quickly as possible through a labyrinth of tunnels. Vrawg held the human by an arm to help keep him up and to guide him through the pitch-black tunnels. Vrawg would have preferred using a torch but his ogre side still allowed him some limited night vision; enough to see where he was going. The barbarian, however, was extremely uncomfortable, and could not even see his own hand in front of his face. For some reason, though, he trusted this strange ogre. Additionally, he had no other choice.

On two occasions, Vrawg made a wrong turn and the pair had to backtrack to a split in the tunnel. Horns could now be heard echoing through the tunnels which told Vrawg that they were being hunted. By this time, a mob of blood-thirsty ogres would have marched to Vrawg's private quarters and discovered the body of Lugnor. They most likely would have also noticed the missing human and the body of Ushan. Thankfully, the half-ogre and the barbarian had already cleared the secured tunnels of the Drogheim tribe, and now traversed the wild, unclaimed tunnels that Vrawg was somewhat familiar with from his time on patrols.

The only problem now, was the chance of stumbling unexpectedly upon a wraggoth patrol group, or a hungry, hunting troll. Vrawg still carried his ball and chain and the barbarian had kept Ushan's dagger, though, in the lightless tunnels, the human was all but useless in a fight.

Vrawg had to keep forcing thoughts of his mother from his mind and focus on their escape. Each time those thoughts crept back into his consciousness, Vrawg was tempted to turn around and fight every ogre in the tribe. He especially wanted to get his hands around Zolar's throat and squeeze the life from the meddlesome shaman. Vrawg knew that was a death sentence though. Even now, escape was not guaranteed, but turning and fighting was suicide. Right now he needed to escape this mountain and put as much distance between him and the ogres as possible. They could only pursue him so far. But where he planned to go, Vrawg had no idea.

Finally spotting the narrow tunnel he had been looking for, Vrawg turned sideways and pulled the human along behind him. Much time had passed since Vrawg's fight with the obsidian dragon but he remembered being in this cavern like it was only yesterday. As the pair entered the vast cavern, the barbarian nearly tripped on the bones of some long ago meal of the dragon.

"There is debris all over the ground," he commented. "Where are we?"

"Graveyard," was all Vrawg said.

Vrawg guided the human to a large rock to sit on. He fumbled inside a pack he hastily grabbed before leaving and brought out a torch. He knew that wraggoth and trolls avoided this cavern out of fear of the dragon, and with luck, they would still believe the dragon lived. Vrawg risked lighting the torch to aid in his search. It would also allow the barbarian to help him as well. The cavern was littered with the weapons of fallen ogres, along with gold coins. Both of which Vrawg would need in order to survive.

The flames of the torch momentarily stung the human's eyes but they gradually adjusted and he got his first look around. The bones of various creatures were everywhere in his limited field of view.

"You weren't joking about the graveyard comment. Some of these skeletons look different. What happened to everyone in here?"

"Dragon."

The barbarian tensed and gripped his large dagger a little more tightly. Vrawg recognized the man's sudden alarm and shook his head.

"Dragon dead."

The man relaxed slightly but still looked about nervously. "I would hate to run into whatever could kill a dragon."

"I kill dragon," Vrawg said, turning his back on the man and beginning to search the floor.

The barbarian stared at Vrawg's massive back with sudden respect. There was something about this half-ogre that made him believe that claim. Even when the two of them had fought against each other in the valley, the barbarian had noticed something immediately different about his opponent. There was an intelligence behind those eyes that was different from a regular ogre. The half-ogre fought with strategy and skill, and not just with brute strength.

He watched the half-ogre kicking bones around and then scoop up some gold coins, stuffing them into a pouch on his belt. Catching on, he too joined in the search and found several piles of gold coins, along with some wraggoth weapons that were more suited for someone his size. He picked up a crudely-made axe and tested the balance. It was far from perfect but the barbarian decided to hang onto it anyway. His body still ached from his wounds and he would not even be half the fighter in his current state, but he would never fall without a fight.

Vrawg too, found many more coins and a few weapons to his liking. He strapped a large dagger to his leg and now carried a sturdy spear. He briefly considered finding some armor that would fit him but then decided against it. Armor would slow them down and make more noise.

"Why did you come for me?" the barbarian asked. "It is clear to me that you were running from here already. Why risk coming to get me?"

Vrawg stared at the human in silence and made a face that indicated that it was complicated.

Realizing he would get no answer from the half-ogre now, he asked, "What is your name?"

"Vrawg."

"Just Vrawg?"

Vrawg considered adding Drogheim, but repeated, "Vrawg."

"Well, Vrawg, I am Harglund, son of Torglund. My people have fought ogres for as far back as anyone can recall. But if you can get me out of this gods-forsaken mountain, you will have my gratitude."

Vrawg extinguished the torch, casting the cavern into darkness once more. "We go."

*   *   *   *

The driving rain was not making their trek down the steep mountain trail an easy one. Harglund was still weak and relied heavily on Vrawg's support. On an impulse, Vrawg chose to exit the dark mountain tunnels through a path that he was unfamiliar with. He figured it was best to get outside as quickly as possible. This area of the mountain was largely wraggoth controlled and Vrawg preferred to run into them, over a pursuing group of ogres.

At least it was the middle of the day. Despite the thick storm clouds, they could both see properly which made it easier to watch their footing and keep an eye out for any pursuit. They had been lucky thus far. Vrawg could hear ogre patrols back inside the tunnels but they had failed to catch up to the escapees. He could only imagine their frustration and anger. Feldrog, in particular, must have been at the lead of one of the patrols, drooling over the prospect of killing Vrawg. And somewhere behind would be Zolar, prodding them all into a murderous frenzy in the name of Blaggrath. Vrawg was almost certain that Zolar had a hand in Chief Yarg's death. He used Blaggrath to control the usually superstitious ogres into believing anything he said.

"Do you have any idea where we are going?" Harglund asked.

The barbarian was shivering from a combination of the rain and the icy winds and wore only his torn and bloodied pants. It was the summer season but at this altitude, the wind was frigid.

Vrawg just shook his head to indicate he did not know where they were exactly. They were going downwards and that was all that mattered. Down was good.

"This is some escape plan, then. You never thought it through?"

Again Vrawg shook his head.

"Ah, it wasn't planned, was it? Something unexpected happened?"

Vrawg nodded.

"What was it that made your tribe turn on you?"

"Lugnor dead."

"Who is Lugnor?"

For a brief moment an image of Gurtha crept its way back into Vrawg's mind and he recalled Lugnor's words. "Lugnor dead," he just repeated again, shaking his head to clear those thoughts.

"You aren't much of a talker, are you?"

Vrawg ignored the comment and kept his focus on not losing his footing on the steep decline. It would have been dangerous on the best of days and the rain-soaked rocks only made it worse. The barbarian sneezed and Vrawg noticed his shivering was getting worse. The rain was showing no sign of letting up and the wind was relentless.

In the distance, a little bit further down the mountain, Vrawg could make out an opening. He could not tell whether it was a shallow cave or a tunnel leading back into the heart of the mountain. Either way, he figured they should get out of the rain and possibly risk a fire to help the human warm up. He picked up the pace.

*   *   *   *

Zolar stood on a rocky ledge, the wind blowing his necklace of skulls as if they were some macabre wind chimes. The shaman scanned the mountainside, the parts he could see, and grunted with frustration. Vrawg had somehow eluded all the patrols thus far and most likely had exited the mountain by now. The barbarian was missing and that just confirmed what Zolar had thought of the half-ogre all along. He was a human sympathizer just like his pathetic mother. Zolar was positive that eliminating the pair of them once and for all would gain them great favor with Blaggrath.

Of course the ogres would continue to scour the mountain tunnels, as well as all the outside trails, but Zolar had another plan in mind, a much more effective one. The shaman closed his eyes and held up a staff that was carved from the shin bone of a troll. He began chanting in a language that was not native to ogres, in fact, it was not a language from this world at all. It was the infernal language of the Abyss and the ogre shaman was casting a complicated spell of summoning, one he had used a few times in the past.

As his voice rose, a swirling ring of fire appeared in the air before him. Within the ring of fire was pure darkness, as black as pitch. When his chanting ceased, a clawed-hand reached through the darkness to grip the ring of fire. A second hand emerged and Zolar knew his spell had been successful. A bolgrock pulled itself completely free and hovered in front of the shaman with bat-like wings. Bolgrock's were native to the Abyss and stood on average about three feet tall. They resembled large black bats, only their face was more humanoid. A ring of small horns circled their head and their eyes were a sickly-hue of yellow. The bite of a bolgrock was highly poisonous and their claws were razor sharp. Like all creatures of the Abyss, they hated every living thing from Zolar's world. They wanted nothing more than to devour the flesh of any living being.

A cruel smile crossed Zolar's lips and he mentally commanded the creature to fly forth and seek out the fleeing half-ogre. The shaman's spell granted him full control over the bolgrock and kept the vile beast from ripping him to shreds. Now, Zolar thought, the tribe would need a new chieftain. Shamans could not become chieftains, so Zolar would see to it that the new chieftain of Drogheim was an ogre under his control. After all, it was the will of Blaggrath.

CHAPTER 11

It took nearly two weeks after the battle with The Sea
Viper for the wounded Kraken to make its way to
Trollport. The crew had prayed to any sea god that might
have been listening that they would run into no other
enemy ships during that time. They were an easy target but
luck was with them as the port came into view. The sound
of gulls overhead was quite welcoming to the crew.

Scores of pirate ships were docked at the port and
many more were anchored not far away. More than a few
of these ships were the hated enemies of Captain Krayne
and The Grinning Kraken, but they were in neutral waters
now, and as Grim had explained to Evonne, there were
rules to be followed in Trollport.

The island was situated west of Taurosian controlled
waters, so the threat of The Purple King's navy here was
minimal. Same went with the southern nation of
Zalhandria. Their navy was also quite formidable but
Trollport was too far out of the way. The port also boasted
impressive defenses. Giant ballistae ringed the entire island

and could easily sink a ship before it ever got close enough to use weapons of their own. The harbor was full of jagged rocks whose location was only known to the pirate captains who frequented the port. Unknowing enemies could have their hulls ripped open in an attempt to dock.

Trollport was governed by Dran Bellos, a retired pirate captain who was the most feared during his days at sea. His head, along with his ship, The Scythe, had the highest posted bounty that any pirate could ever remember. Many tried to collect but all failed. Dran was quite wealthy and settled onto the island which was now known as Trollport. He built much of the small city using his own fortune and hired some of the world's most ruthless mercenaries to enforce the rules of the port.

Rules were very simple. Do not steal and do not kill. Both carried a death sentence. Trollport was a neutral ground for pirates to conduct all sorts of business and feel relatively safe in doing so. Taverns and brothels made up most of the city but plenty of merchants set up shop here as well to buy and sell stolen goods.

Many of the pirates frequenting Trollport were sworn enemies of each other so tensions were high and fights were not uncommon. Fighting was tolerated, as long as property was not destroyed and nobody was killed as a result. Grim had warned Evonne about going into Trollport and advised her several times that it would be best for her to remain aboard their ship. The majority of women in the port worked in the brothels or taverns; a female pirate was virtually unheard of.

But Evonne could now call herself a pirate. Following the incident with the wizard, Evonne was largely accepted by the crew. For the last two weeks she had been invited to drink and gamble with the rest of the men, being treated, for the most part, as just one of the guys. Only twice was she forced to bloody the nose of an overly-amorous drunk crewman. She was also the victim of a bloody nose and a swollen lip, after winning her first large pot while playing cards. Naturally, Evonne was excited and gloated over the win. She quickly found out that barbarians, like dwarves, were sore losers and took one of Brak's fists to her face. Grim told her not to take it personally, that Brak would have hit any member of the crew after that game, and in fact had, on many occasions. It just meant that Evonne was one of them.

Not all of the crew shared the same sentiment, however. Purcy continued to leer at her and refused to speak with her. As a result, all of those close to Purcy also continued to make her feel unwelcome. Her brother wore a mask of jealousy each time he gazed upon his sister. With one pull of a crossbow trigger, Evonne had elevated her status far above Zack's, who had been aboard the ship for far longer. Zack just did not excel at any one thing and had not yet proven himself as highly useful to the Kraken. He was just another set of hands on the deck and another swinging sword in battle. Evonne did feel sad that she could not be close to her brother, her only true family. She tried to speak with him on many occasions but he was always short with her, and cold.

Night had fallen as The Grinning Kraken pulled into the harbor and finished docking. The moment the gangplank was dropped, pirates rushed excitedly across in search of drink and women.

"I am telling you, lass, this is no place for a young woman who is not working here," Grim said again.

The dwarf stood beside Evonne and Dragon on the deck of their ship, as the trio gazed out into the city of pirates. The port really came alive at night and the sounds of singing and fighting poured out of several nearby taverns.

"I can take care of myself, I will be fine," Evonne replied.

Grim looked to Dragon for support but the mute pirate just shrugged his indifference. He was quite impressed with Evonne's skills at shooting and fighting and believed her claim.

"Bah," Grim said, starting for the gangplank.

Evonne smiled and quickly caught up.

"Don't leave my sight then, lass. In little time I may be too drunk to remember you are there, so just stay close."

"Hold it right there, Miss Evonne," an all too familiar voice said sternly.

Evonne turned to regard Captain Krayne.

"Where are you off to?"

"Ah, well, I was going to join Grim and Dragon ashore, Captain."

Krayne nodded and tossed a pouch of coins to the young woman.

"What's this?" she inquired.

"A little well-deserved bonus for shooting the wizard. Don't spend it all in one tavern and don't come back to this ship without buying yourself your own crossbow. Make sure it's a good one."

Evonne's smile nearly swallowed her face. She looked to Grim and then to Dragon. "Come on, boys, the first drink is on me."

Evonne and Vrawg: Bounty Hunters

The dwarf grumbled all the way across the gangplank but Evonne could see the hint of a smile hidden within his beard. The only thing Grim liked more than a good fight was a free drink.

*   *   *   *

Evonne, Grim and Dragon, joined up with several others at a large table within an overly-crowded tavern. Different ships usually had their favorite hangouts and the Dark Mistress was the favored haunt for the crew of the Kraken. Purcy, along with his group of followers, Zack included, also occupied a table within the tavern, though, chose not to socialize with the others.

Evonne took in the sights of the crowded room and noticed, similar to their crew, every nation around the world must have been represented. Pirates of all shapes and sizes and colors filled the tavern, and each of them looked dangerous. Evonne found it curious that two large women, dressed in light armor, stood near the inside of door as the tavern's security. They were the biggest women Evonne had ever seen and they were certainly not intimidated by any of the pirates around them. For the most part, the men tended to ignore them, as if they were not even there, though, the same could not be said for Evonne. She received curious and hungry stares from almost every patron. Despite the ever-present danger around her, Evonne felt oddly safe while in the company of her crew.

"Long time no see, cute face. You couldn't even come over and say hello?"

Evonne watched a petite woman with short, jet-black

hair, playfully tease the braids of Grim's beard with her fingers. She had beautiful round eyes with lips painted as black as her hair. The young woman wore a low-cut, black, sleeveless top, which showed off a multitude of tattoos along both arms and her chest. Two intertwined snakes wound their way up her right arm, while a spider was inked onto her left forearm. The head and wings of a bat poked up from the top of her shirt on her chest, between two large stars. While the artwork was quite impressive, Evonne could imagine far better tattoos to have than spiders and bats.

"Why do you hate me so much?" the woman continued to tease, putting on a mock pout.

"Bah," Grim replied, swatting her hand away from his beard and pouring more ale into his mouth. "Grow a beard like a proper lass."

"Seriously, I have missed you boys. Life's been good?" The tattooed woman turned her attention to Evonne and her eyes dropped to the sword the young girl wore on her belt. "Since when did you start arming your prisoners?"

"I am no prisoner," Evonne answered, slightly offended. "I am a member of the crew."

"Well, now," the dark-haired woman chuckled.

"Evonne, I present to you the Dark Mistress, the owner of this fine establishment," said Jabari, who was also seated at the table. "And Mistress, this is Evonne, a member of our crew."

"Isn't this interesting. It's about time you lot learned the value of a good woman. It's a pleasure to meet you, Evonne. I hope these men have been behaving themselves."

"Sometimes."

Someone slapped the tattooed woman on the behind and her smile turned into a scowl. Purcy leaned over from the next table and smelled as if he had been bathing in alcohol.

"Never mind her. Come over here with the real men. Sit on my lap, girl."

"Ah, Purcy, still alive and well I see."

"That's right and I have gold to spend. Now, sit down here and loosen my coin belt."

Purcy grabbed the woman by the arm and attempted to pull her onto his lap. One of the large women near the door began to move forward but the tavern's owner shook her head. In the blink of an eye, the Dark Mistress suddenly appeared a few inches to the right, and while Purcy had a firm grip on her arm a moment earlier, now his hand was empty. Evonne blinked, wondering if she had already drank too much.

"What's wrong, girl, you don't know a real man when you see one?" Purcy slurred, angrily.

"I am going to forgive your rudeness, this time, since you are clearly quite drunk. I am the owner of this tavern, and you are but a lowly pirate, come back and talk to me when you captain your own ship one day."

"You little brat."

The woman sighed. "As much as I am enjoying the company here boys, I have other business to attend. Evonne, it was a pleasure. I look forward to talking with you more another time."

Evonne nodded and watched the curious tattooed woman disappear into the crowd. She could not understand how a woman who was not much taller than her, could run a business in a place like this, surrounded constantly by evil men. How did she survive? As big as the two women were who stood guard near the door, even they could not stop a gang of drunk and determined pirates, she was sure of it. Whatever her secret was, Evonne admired her strength and courage.

"Alright, Evonne, tell us what you thought of the Dark Mistress," asked Tomar, a skinny pirate who lisped through missing teeth.

"She seems nice."

"No, I mean, how did she look?"

Evonne wore a confused expression. "Ahh, well she was beautiful. Stunning eyes."

"See, see," Tomar said to the others at the table. "Pay up."

"No, no, no," Jabari cut in and pointed to a heavily-muscled man standing near the bar without a shirt. "What do you think of him? Be honest."

Evonne shrugged. "He is very handsome."

"Well that solves nothing at all," Franklan added.

That was when Evonne caught on. "You sneaky dogs. What were you doing, betting on which one I preferred?"

"You are a mystery, girl," Tomar admitted. "You look like a woman but you act like one of us."

Before Evonne could respond to that comment, another patron walked by the table and elbowed Grim in the head, forcing the dwarf to spill some of his drink.

"Watch where you are going," Grim growled.

"Watch where you keep that fat head of yours," the intoxicated pirate replied.

Dragon put a hand over his face and shook his head

as Grim rose from his seat. The dwarf did not even say another word. Grim grabbed the pirate by the shirt and pulled his face down to his level, then smashed his forehead into the man's nose.

"I keep my fat head wherever I want."

The pirate's nose exploded with blood and he fell to his knees. A friend of the drunken pirate witnessed what happened and dove out of nowhere to tackle Grim. He had not heard the stories of how sturdy dwarves were on their feet. The man collided with the dwarf but Grim did not budge. Grim slammed the man into the floor stealing his breath away.

A chair broke apart over Dragon's head and suddenly their whole table was on their feet. Fists and mugs of ale began flying as a full-fledged brawl broke out. Evonne ducked to avoid a bottle that narrowly missed her head and she dove under their table. The young woman did not lack courage but had no desire to fistfight any of these men. She crawled across the floor between brawling and wrestling pirates, looking for the back exit.

* * * *

Evonne breathed in the cool and salty air while leaning against a wall in a dark alley behind the tavern. The sounds of the brawl were soon silenced as she fell into deep thought of how similar this alley was to those in Guildburg. It had been a long time since she allowed her mind to wander back to her home city and she thought of her family. She wondered how Harlon was doing and imagined that her poor brother would have been cleaning chimneys and the sole focus of Griff's wrath now. Not for the first time, Evonne considered her decision to let her father live and thought that maybe her family would have been better off if she had just slit his throat. She was mad when Jarold ran away and left them all behind. Then she was mad when Zack had done the very same thing. She ended up following their example, running away and leaving Harlon behind. Ah well, she thought, he would have to grow up and fend for himself, just as she had done.

"Nice night, huh?" a voice from behind made Evonne jump and she reached for her sword.

She relaxed when she noticed it was the tattooed woman who owned the tavern. "It was a little chaotic in there, I had to get out."

"I don't blame you at all. I came out to wait until they all settle down, as well."

"Aren't you worried they will ruin your tavern?"

"This is common in Trollport. When the brawl is over, the pirates will leave tips to pay for any damage they have caused."

"What if they don't?"

"They will," she grinned. "They know better."

Evonne wondered what she meant by that but the mysterious woman offered nothing more on the subject.

"How is it that you became a pirate? Not to be rude, but you just don't look like pirate material."

"My brother ran away from home and joined the crew on The Grinning Kraken. I ended up doing the same thing."

"Where was home?"

"Guildburg. A small port city on the southern tip of Tauros. Where are you from? I can't place your accent."

"I am from a small town far to the south of Tauros. It was in the middle of nowhere."

"How did you end up here, of all places?"

"How I got here is a long story but I wouldn't want to be anywhere else. I do very well here, Evonne. Pirates come to Trollport to spend all their booty and have a good time. You can imagine the amount of gold that comes through here on a nightly basis."

"No doubt."

"Do you know what you are doing, Evonne?"

"What do you mean?"

"Becoming a pirate. Have you thought this through? You are beautiful and you seem intelligent. Why risk everything aboard a ship of criminals? There is a reason not very many women are pirates."

"I have nowhere else to go."

"There is always somewhere else to go. These men will eat you alive."

"They haven't yet. I can take care of myself."

"Don't fool yourself, Evonne. I have known Captain Krayne before he was a captain. He is a bad man. Those men on his ship are bad men."

"What about you?"

"What about me?"

"You live here, in Trollport. There must be thousands of bad men here at any one time. You aren't much bigger than me and I don't see you wearing any weapons."

"I don't need a sword to take care of myself."

"Well, well, well, just who I was looking for."

A man entered the alley from the street and the smell of sweat and alcohol assaulted the women's nostrils.

Evonne recognized the man's voice immediately. Reginald was a vile man and one of Purcy's followers. The man never hid his offensive thoughts of Evonne and taunted her whenever possible. Now, he licked his lips and swaggered forward.

"Where is your dwarf friend now, huh? Busy fighting inside the tavern? He won't even hear you scream."

Evonne stepped protectively in front of the tattooed woman. "Run back to Purcy before you regret anything."

"The only thing I regret is not doing this sooner."

"Back off, pirate." the Dark Mistress demanded.

"Wait your turn, little girl. I will deal with you after."

"I am not little."

For a man who was drunk, Reginald moved quite quickly and seized Evonne by her shoulders. She did not have room to use her sword and pulled a dagger from her boot. She slashed the pirate across the chest, drawing blood. An angry Reginald looked to the wound and then backhanded Evonne to the ground, bloodying her nose and causing her to drop her weapon. She was suddenly afraid as she realized the man was right, Grim would not hear her scream. Nobody would.

The tattooed woman calmly stepped over Evonne to stand between her and Reginald. Evonne did not want the woman getting hurt trying to protect her.

"Alright, fine," Reginald said, with a grin. "You wanna go first?"

"Funny," was all she said.

The woman held out her left arm and touched the tattoo of the spider. Evonne's eyes nearly bulged from her head and her jaw dropped in awe as the spider tattoo grew in size, then leaped off the woman's arm. The spider, which was now the size of a small dog, landed on Reginald's chest and knocked the pirate to the ground. It scurried up to his head and sunk its fangs into his face. Reginald screamed in pain and horror, but as he himself had said earlier, nobody heard him scream, or nobody cared.

The pirate thrashed about on the ground with the spider latched firmly to his face for several moments before his body went still. Evonne sat there in stunned silence. She regarded the other tattoos the woman wore, the snakes, the bat, and figured those too could come to life if the mysterious woman so wished it.

Reading her thoughts, the Dark Mistress pulled up her black pants to reveal the tattoo of a hideously ugly troll inked on her right calf. "He is particularly effective," she said with a wink.

Evonne now understood how this woman survived and thrived in Trollport. She was some kind of sorceress that anyone would be fool to cross.

"My thanks, ah, do I just call you Dark Mistress?"

"Everyone does, but my name is Nagar."

"Thank you, Nagar," Evonne looked to her bloody dagger and panic washed over her. "Killing is not allowed here. We are in big trouble. If Captain Krayne finds out that…"

Nagar cut her off and motioned to the spider. "Don't worry, Ingrid here will see to it that nothing is left of this pirate to find. He will just be another man who went missing in Trollport. He is not the first and will not be the last."

Evonne nodded.

"Evonne, you can stay here in Trollport if you wish.

You can work here with me. I could use a woman with your bravery."

"I appreciate the offer, I really do, but I am a pirate now. I am not afraid of these men."

"You should be. This can't end well."

CHAPTER 12

Vrawg and Harglund huddled around a small fire within a dark cave. Vrawg was pleased that it was only a cave with one entrance and exit, and not a tunnel leading back into the mountain. There had just been one problem, the cave had belonged to a large troll. This particular troll stood as tall as Vrawg but was quite skinny. Trolls possessed razor-sharp claws and delivered a very nasty bite. The half-ogre and barbarian considered themselves lucky to have come away from the fight with only minor injuries. Vrawg had broken his spear, though, and was not pleased about that.

"We hardly ever see any trolls," Harglund commented. "They rarely leave the mountains, unlike your kin. Fortunately for us, they are solitary creatures."

The warmth from the fire had put a stop to the barbarian's shivering. Normal color was returning to his skin. Vrawg sat across from the human and stared into the fire, considering their next move. He knew that they should not linger long within the cave. The troll may be dead but the ogres, especially Zolar, would still be searching for them. Vrawg figured once they reached the Dalecanin Valley they would be safe. He did not believe the ogres would risk pursuing them too far into the region that was largely controlled by the barbarian tribes.

Hypnotized by the dancing flames of the fire, Vrawg finally succumbed to exhaustion and closed his eyes.

*   *   *   *

Vrawg's eyes shot open as a strange buzzing noise echoed loudly off the walls of the cave. He could not be sure how long he had slept but could see that it was bright again outside. The fire had burned itself out but the light from the cave entrance was enough for Vrawg to locate the source of the buzzing noise.

Hovering above Vrawg's head, sporting a wicked, fang-filled smile, was a large, grotesque, bat-like creature with yellow eyes. Vrawg would have just assumed it was some overly-large bat, if it were not for its strangely humanoid face. He had never seen such a creature before and wondered if it also lived in this cave with the troll.

Those thoughts were cast aside the moment the creature opened its mouth and spoke with a voice that Vrawg was all too familiar with.

"Time to die, you wretched half-human," it said with the voice of Zolar, the tribe's shaman.

Vrawg realized that it was no accident that this creature stumbled upon them in this cave. This was the doing of Zolar. The shaman must have used some foul magic to conjure the ugly beast. Somehow it spoke with Zolar's voice and Vrawg was willing to bet the shaman was also looking through its eyes, which meant the ogres knew they were here.

Vrawg did not have any more time to ponder the implications of the creature's arrival as it dove towards his face with a skin-shivering screech. Vrawg held up his hands in defense and the bolgrock raked his skin with its claws.

The noise was enough to wake Harglund who had been in a very deep sleep. "By Yarwulf! What is that?" he shouted, invoking the name of a barbarian god.

Vrawg had no answer, nor any time to answer, as he attempted to swat the thing away from his face. It continued to cackle with Zolar's awful laugh and shred the half-ogre's skin like it was butter. Vrawg was doing his best to keep the bolgrock away from his eyes while attempting to locate the ball and chain he had left somewhere on the cave floor.

The half-ogre was given a moment's reprieve as a wraggoth-made axe hurled past his head, striking the bolgrock and sending it spinning away with an angry hiss. Vrawg scooped up his ball and chain just as the bolgrock regained its senses and dove at him again. He swung at it but the flying creature deftly avoided the attack with another cackle and then sunk its fangs into Vrawg's shoulder. Unknown to Vrawg, abyssal poison was now flowing into his bloodstream.

He grabbed the bolgrock by one of its dangling legs and pulled it off his shoulder, tearing open an awful wound where its teeth had latched on. Vrawg swung the creature, smashing its head into the wall of the cave. Surprisingly, the thing only blinked, shook its head, and then broke free of Vrawg's grasp. It flew past him, raking a line of blood across the half-ogre's bald head.

Harglund had retrieved his axe and reached for the bolgrock but missed. A clawed-hand shot down and ripped open the barbarian's forearm. Grunting, Harglund swung again and this time planted the stone axe directly into the bolgrock's chest. The wraggoth weapon was poorly constructed, so it was unable to penetrate the abyssal creature's tough leathery skin.

With strength that did not seem possible from the small beast, the bolgrock pulled the axe from the barbarian's grasp and threw it to the back of the cave. It smiled and then dove towards the man's face. Harglund held up his hands in a feeble attempt to defend himself but the attack never came.

Vrawg grabbed the creature by both its wings and slammed it into the cave floor, dropping his full weight upon it. The bolgrock gasped for air and lost its smile. Vrawg understood that this creature was not from this world and their poorly-made weapons would have little effect. So he thought a different approach was necessary.

"Where do you think you can hide, that the eyes of Blaggrath cannot find you?" the thing taunted, with Zolar's voice.

Vrawg said nothing and dug both his thumbs into the sickly-yellow eyes of the dazed creature. A wave of dizziness washed over the half-ogre and he felt his arms growing heavy. He cursed inwardly, realizing the creature's bite must have been venomous. He was determined to take Zolar's conjured horror into the afterlife with him. He sunk both of his large thumbs deeper into its eye sockets, blinding the screeching monster.

*   *   *   *

Somewhere, higher up in the mountain, Zolar screamed and dropped to his knees. He looked about, frantically, but could not see. Blood streamed down from his ruined eye sockets. He cursed the name of Vrawg. He cursed Blaggrath for allowing the hated half-human to destroy the bolgrock. The blind shaman collapsed to the ground and cursed the world.

* * * *

Harglund allowed himself a smile as the rocky ground of the mountain soon gave way to the tall grass of the Dalecanin Valley.

"We made it, Vrawg," he said, but the half-ogre did not hear him.

The barbarian did not know how the half-ogre even made it this far. It was clear to him that Vrawg had been poisoned by the bite of the bat-like creature. The half-ogre was delirious and could barely stand on his own. It took all of Harglund's strength and determination to help Vrawg remain on his feet while navigating the rest of the way down the mountain.

Harglund was not sure if Vrawg was aware of their surroundings but it was now that the half-ogre slumped unconscious to the grass, finally unable to go any further. The skin around the wound where Vrawg was bitten had turned black. With so many venomous creatures making the Valley their home, the barbarian was very familiar with poisons and their effects. Although the bat-like creature was like nothing Harglund had ever seen before, he imagined its venom worked in a similar way.

There were natural remedies to fight poison. The

barbarians were well versed in natural healing methods as their people shunned any form of magic. Harglund considered what he would need to treat the wound but then wondered if his duty to Vrawg was ended. Harglund was certain that if he left now, alone, he could reunite with his tribe before any ogre search parties could locate him.

Vrawg had saved him from a horrible death at the hands of the ogre torturer but had he not done his duty by sticking by the half-ogre this long and getting him his far? Harglund could have left Vrawg behind in the cave when he first showed signs of delirium but did not. Surely any delay here now could mean doom for them both. Why should they both die when one could easily escape? Harglund hated ogres above all else but he did know that Vrawg was different; that he was not a full-blooded ogre.

Harglund let out a very loud audible sigh as his mind was made. He set off in search of the herbs that he would need to fight the poison.

* * * *

Vrawg awoke from a terrible nightmare. He was young again, very small, and his mother was teaching him the language of humans. Lugnor had appeared behind her and began to strangle her. Vrawg was helpless to do anything.

Vrawg sat up straight, dizzy and completely disoriented. He glanced around to find that he was sitting on the ground in the tall grass of the Valley. Behind him loomed his mountain home and the sun was just beginning to disappear behind a tall peak. He licked his parched lips and tried to piece together how he had gotten here. The last thing he remembered was bashing open the skull of the strange creature in the cave. Recalling that awful bite, he inspected his shoulder to find the wound covered in some sticky, paste-like substance.

"You have awakened, it is about time," a voice said to the side.

Vrawg saw Harglund approaching.

"I wasn't sure if you were going to make it. You are a resilient one."

Vrawg pointed to his shoulder.

"A herbal paste to fight that demon's poison. You are fortunate we reached the Valley and the necessary ingredients were readily available to me. You are still going to feel weak for several days but I am confident that the poison's effect has been negated."

Vrawg looked back up to the mountain and scratched his head. Harglund guessed what the half-ogre was thinking.

"Don't think it was easy getting you this far. You must weigh more than two great ice bears. I would have liked to get us further from the mountain and into the cover of those trees over there, but alas, I could not move you in my weakened state. I fear even at full health I could not have dragged you."

"Thank you."

The barbarian waved it away. "We are even. You saved me from being tortured to death and I saved you from the poison. Now, if you can stand, let's find some cover."

With help from Harglund, Vrawg managed to get to his feet and the pair entered a wooded area nearby. Harglund handed Vrawg some large mushrooms he had been collecting just before the half-ogre woke up.

"Eat these, they are safe. And there is a stream about an hour's walk to the north-west. I would suggest you make your way over there when you are ready to leave."

Vrawg looked at the human curiously, thinking about the man's choice of words. Harglund caught on.

"I am going north."

"We go north," Vrawg corrected.

Harglund shook his head. "Where I go, you cannot follow. My people will kill you on sight. There is nothing I could say to stop them. Just as there was nothing you could say to stop your kin from torturing and killing me."

Vrawg thought that humans were more understanding than his evil kin. "We friends."

Harglund smiled and slapped the half-ogre on his good arm. "Yes, Vrawg, we are friends. But ogres have killed so many of my people. They will never forget or forgive. I am sorry, but you will find no warm welcome in the Valley."

Vrawg frowned. He was deeply saddened at the thought of parting ways with the barbarian and being completely on his own.

"You can't go north into the Valley and you can't go back south to the mountains. West towards the coast or east are your only options. In your feverish state, you mumbled the name Drubin and the town of Glastonby several times. I do not know who this Drubin is but Glastonby is about two days walk to the west. I know the town occasionally trades with your kin so you might find some acceptance there. I am sorry I can't be of any further help."

Vrawg nodded. He understood the barbarian and

cursed the ways of ogres. Vrawg would have liked to travel home with Harglund and see how they lived. He felt he could have connected with a race of fierce warrior humans. But that was not to be. He would travel to Glastonby and seek out his father, Drubin.

Harglund motioned to the mushrooms. "Come, my friend, eat up. Let us share a meal before we part ways."

CHAPTER 13

Over the next two years, Evonne really settled into her role as a pirate. She participated in every battle, whether she was perched high above, raining down death with her crossbow, or whether she was on the deck, dazzling all with her sword skills. She continued to practice and train every single night before falling asleep and it certainly showed. Other members of the crew actually felt safer with her around.

She still had her haters, of course, and had very little contact with her own brother. He would not even look at her if they passed each other by. Over time she found that she no longer cared. She had real friends now, like Grim, Dragon, Jabari, and several others. It would have been nice to have a friendly relationship with her brother, but if he could not get past his jealousy, then so be it. She also thought little of Guildburg and the life she left behind. That was all over.

Each day, Evonne was growing more and more into an attractive young woman. She now wore her blonde hair long and tied it back into a ponytail. She favored sleeveless vests that showed off her toned arms and shoulders. She was not ignorant to the looks that the other pirates still sent her way from time to time. Most were respectful of her, or rather, fearful of her. Now, it was not just the fear of Grim who had protected her from the start. Now, other crew members feared Evonne, wishing to never find themselves in the sights of her crossbow, or on the opposite end of her deadly sabre.

While Evonne was enjoying her new life, there were aspects of it which she still struggled with. Not all of the ships they attacked were pirates. Most were merchant vessels only trying to transport goods from one city to another. Grim tried to convince Evonne that none of these men were innocent. The crew aboard The Grinning Kraken was trying to make a living and these men stood in their way. Although, even when men surrendered it did them no good. Captain Krayne still put them to the sword or sold them to others in port.

He had a vicious reputation and it was all for good reason. The man simply had no conscience. Evonne often wondered what Krayne's story was. What made him so angry at the world and so capable of evil deeds without even a second thought? But Krayne's life was a mystery. He rarely ate or drank with the rest of the crew and when he did, he never said much. The others knew very little about him. They just knew not to cross him.

"Mister Ohmra, what can you tell me about that ship?" Captain Krayne asked.

The bronze-skinned pirate sat in the crow's nest looking through a spy glass. "Her name is The White Wolf and she's a Zalhandrian longnose. Appears to be flying the flag of the City of Seven Towers."

Evonne stood next to Grim on the deck of the Kraken, watching the distant ship in anticipation of what it might be.

"The City of Seven Towers? That's not a Zalhandrian port that I am aware of," Evonne commented.

"You're right, it's not a port city," Grim replied. "The City of Seven Towers is deeper into Zalhandria. It's actually somewhere within the great Zal-Baron desert."

"Why fly that flag then? Why wouldn't it just fly the flag of whatever port the ship belongs to?"

"For fear, lass. The City of Seven Towers is ruled by seven wizards, each with their own tower. They fly that flag to ward off pirates, no doubt, who do not wish to anger the wizards of that city."

"So, there would be a wizard on board that ship?"

"It's possible."

"Wonderful."

"What are your orders, Captain?" shouted Yarin, the ship's navigator.

"Stay on course. Pursue that ship."

Several pirates turned concerned looks to Captain Krayne but only one dared to speak, which did not come as a surprise to anyone.

"A Zalhandrian longnose is small and built for speed, as you are aware, Captain," Purcy remarked. "We would waste much time and resources in catching that ship for little payoff. There will hardly be any cargo aboard that ship."

"I am interested in the human cargo, Purcy. The longnose is an expensive ship. I am willing to wager there is someone of importance being transported on that ship,"

Krayne replied, angrily.

Mister Bors hobbled over to stand next to the captain. The first mate had a broomstick attached to his leg to replace the one he lost years ago in the battle with the hired wizard. Other crew members took to calling him "Peg Leg."

"Begging your pardon, Captain, but she is flying the flag of Seven Towers. There might be a wizard or two aboard that ship."

Krayne shrugged indifference. "We have Evonne the Wizard-Slayer aboard ours. Mister Yarin, catch that ship."

*　　*　　*　　*

A beautiful, dark-haired woman was dragged unceremoniously across the gangplank and thrown to the deck in front of Captain Krayne. She was the last surviving person aboard The White Wolf. As others had suspected, the smaller and faster ship was not an easy target. The Grinning Kraken was already due to find a port to replenish food and water stores as they were running drastically low. The pursuit of The White Wolf had taken them a week off schedule and required every trick available to the resourceful pirates in order to catch the ship. Then they learned that catching up to the ship was the easy part.

Their worst fears were realized as there were two capable wizards on board. The Grinning Kraken prevailed in the end but not without sustaining damage to the ship and losing nine good men in the battle. A battle that hardly seemed worth the trouble of capturing one woman. There was nothing else of value aboard the ship.

Evonne watched the woman tremble in absolute fear

as Krayne looked her over.

"My father will have your heads for this," the woman dared to say, in a southern accent.

"Who is your father?" Krayne asked.

"Dargladden the Blue, one of the Seven."

"If your father is truly one of the Seven, then he will surely have the coin required to buy you back. Mister Yarin, get us to Trollport."

"Aye, Captain."

Krayne grabbed the woman by her frilly top and began dragging her towards his quarters. Other pirates laughed and drooled over the sight of their attractive prisoner. Evonne did not need magic to know their minds. Krayne closed the door to his private quarters and the woman screamed from inside. Evonne burst her way.

"Bad timing, Evonne. Get out," the captain roared, already having torn the woman's top.

"What are you doing?" Evonne asked.

"I am going to enjoy the spoils of this hard fought battle."

"I thought you planned to ransom her back to her father?"

"Yes, I mean to. But she only needs to be alive. I have said nothing about her being unspoiled."

"She should come with me and stay in the cargo hold, away from everyone else."

"She is staying here with me. Now unless you plan to join us, get out. That is your last warning."

Evonne stood defiantly. "It is in our best interest to keep her in good health. She will be worth more that way," she attempted to play on Krayne's greed.

Captain Krayne shoved the weeping woman to the

floor and casually strolled over to stand in front of Evonne. Too quick for Evonne to react, Krayne planted a fist on the end of the woman's nose. Evonne's nose exploded with blood and the room went dark as she found herself seated on the floor, without even realizing she had fallen. Before her vision returned, she was struck again and again. She was only semi-conscious when she felt Krayne grab her by the hair and slam her head into the floor repeatedly. Then she knew no more.

* * * *

It took days before Evonne awoke in the cargo hold with the greatest headache she had ever known. Both eyes were black and swollen, and her nose appeared broken, again. Grim and Dragon had done their best to patch her up and make her as comfortable as could be. Grim asked her many times to explain what madness had come over her but she remained silent. In fact, she spoke not a word for the rest of the journey back to Trollport.

The men could not scramble off the ship fast enough when it docked, as many of them had not eaten for two days. The delay in capturing the woman had caused their food supply to run dry. The crew quietly grumbled and questioned Krayne's decision to chase The White Wolf but the Captain assured them of a great bounty when they ransomed their prisoner.

On the second night in port, Grim gave up on trying to convince Evonne to join him and left the woman alone in the hold. Some voices in the galley drew her attention. She figured most of the crew would have been ashore, drinking and eating their fill in a tavern, so she crept over and pressed her ear to the door out of curiosity. It was Captain Krayne and Mister Bors having a conversation.

"Captain, the men are not happy about recent events. And many do not have enough coins to properly enjoy themselves in port."

"They will have plenty to spend when we unload that raven-haired wench. Have you spoken with Bargold?"

"About that, the wizard no longer resides in Trollport. Getting a ransom demand to the woman's father will now take much longer than you had planned. Much, much longer."

She heard Krayne growl in frustration. "Change of plans then. We will just sell her to Zarax for half of what I was originally thinking, which is still enough coin to satisfy the men."

"Zarax? She is a person of importance in Seven Towers. Personally, I don't think she deserves to be chained up in that madman's brothel. Perhaps we..."

"I am not interested in what you personally believe, Mister Bors. Who else is going to pay us the coins that Zarax has at his disposal?"

"Apologies, Captain, I was only..."

"Watch the ship. I am going to visit Zarax myself and broker this deal."

*   *   *   *

Leaving her boots behind, Evonne padded her way silently through the ship to the upper deck. A skeleton crew was left to look after the ship but most had fallen asleep. It was a cloudy night and extremely dark. The normal nightly raucous could be heard from many of

Trollport's taverns located closest to the docks. Luckily, nobody was watching the door to Captain Krayne's quarters.

Evonne crouched near the door and pulled out two pieces of wire from a belt pouch. Most of the treasure chests that the pirates looted from other ships were locked. Dragon had taught Evonne the skill of picking these locks. She now put that skill to a different use, defeating the lock on Krayne's door and slipping inside without being noticed.

She had waited for Krayne to leave the ship in search of Zarax, the wealthiest brothel owner in Trollport. Most of the brothels here operated with willing women, to some degree. Zarax specialized in acquiring unwilling women and charged more than usual for the chance to spend time with them. Evonne found the man and his practices repulsive, and on more than one occasion, had fantasized about placing a crossbow bolt in the man's forehead. But Trollport was full of repulsive people and Evonne was powerless to do anything about them.

Although, she was not about to let this prisoner of theirs fall into the hands of Zarax. Evonne had watched the crew of the Kraken sell prisoners before, and while the act bothered her, she shrugged it off, thinking that at least those men were still alive. But now that it was a female prisoner, Evonne found that she felt completely different. She could not just shrug this one off and pretend the woman was better off being sold than killed. Evonne, herself, would prefer death over falling into the sleazy clutches of Zarax. So now she was doing the unthinkable. She was going to free the prisoner.

The female prisoner scrambled over to the wall she

was chained to when she realized someone had entered the dark quarters. She feared that Captain Krayne had returned already. What little light trickled in through the windows was enough for Evonne to see the sad state of the prisoner. Her eyes were blackened and her body covered with cuts and bruises. She appeared…defeated.

Evonne quickly got to work on the lock that held the shackle to the woman's left wrist. The prisoner looked on, confused, wondering if she was dreaming. In no time at all, Evonne tossed the shackle aside and presented the woman with some clothes and a dark cloak.

"Why are you…?"

"Be quiet. Put these on and do not speak."

The prisoner did not need to be told twice. She quickly dressed and threw on the cloak, placing the hood over her head.

Evonne peered out through the door and when she was satisfied that it was clear, she motioned to the woman to follow. "Not a word," she emphasized again.

The pair crept out of Krayne's quarters and Evonne locked the door behind her. They approached the gangplank to the docks and Dalen, who was supposed to be on watch, sat up in his chair and did his best to appear completely awake.

"Dragon and I are going for drinks," Evonne said to the pirate.

"Raise a mug for me," Dalen replied, sitting back down and closing his eyes once more.

Evonne pulled the woman along the dark and winding streets of Trollport. They passed many drunken pirates but Evonne's reputation as a fighter extended to the port city and fortunately the pair was left alone. She headed straight for the Dark Mistress tavern and entered through a back door which she had been given exclusive access to use. They met with Nagar, the owner and now friend to Evonne, and Evonne convinced the sorceress to hide the woman in the tavern's cellar.

The pirate handed Nagar a pouch of gold, every coin she owned, to see to it that the sorceress would get the prisoner safe passage back to a Zalhandrian port. Nagar agreed and Evonne knew she could trust the tattooed woman.

"You are safe now," Evonne told the woman. "Stay here with Nagar. She will find you a ship to get you back home."

"I cannot thank you enough," the woman said, with tears of joy streaming down her cheeks. "My father will give you…"

"I don't want a reward or a ransom. I didn't free you for that."

"Will you return to that ship?"

"Yes."

"Why? I can see you are not like them. If the Captain finds out what you did…"

"He won't. And I am not worried about him. Farewell."

Evonne left the woman in the cellar without even asking her name. She did not care to know, she had more pressing matters on her mind. After a quick discussion with Nagar over the details of the night's events, the sorceress told Evonne not to worry.

The Dark Mistress strolled out into the tavern's main taproom and mouthed the words to a spell. She whispered into the ears of the Kraken's crew members that they had seen Evonne enter the tavern with Dragon, much earlier in the evening, and Evonne had been drinking with them the entire night. The magical suggestion took hold in each of the pirate's minds and they firmly believed the story to be true.

Evonne thanked her friend and then sat down with the rest of the crew for a drink. She tried to convince herself that she had done the right thing. She knew that freeing the woman was necessary, but in so doing, she had defied Captain Krayne. Curse him, she thought. Their relationship had changed the moment he struck her.

*   *   *   *

Upon returning to the Kraken in the wee hours of the morning, several members of the crew, Evonne included, found Dalen hanging from the crow's nest. He was quite dead. Captain Krayne had turned the ship upside down in search of the missing prisoner, with obviously unsatisfactory results. Evonne felt no remorse for the fate of Dalen. He was a bad man and a rapist himself, and one of Purcy's followers.

Just by pure coincidence, one of the newest members of the crew, Pallo, discovered that pirating was not the life for him, and disappeared in Trollport with no intention of returning to the Kraken. All suspicion shifted to him and Krayne put a hefty bounty on the man's head. Evonne was in the clear.

Once the necessary repairs were finished on the ship, they set sail again and left Trollport behind. Most of the crew was broke and angry, and they needed to find a merchant vessel fat with bounty soon. Receiving a tip before leaving port, Captain Krayne knew just where to find such a ship. He just did not know that tip came from Evonne, by way of a man in the employ of Nagar.

*   *   *   *

Several nights later, while sitting in the cargo hold with Grim and Dragon, Evonne finally had enough of the weird stares she was receiving from the dwarf.

"What is it? Speak your mind."

"Did she offer you a reward?"

"Did who offer me a reward?"

"The prisoner you set free."

"I did no such…"

"Save me the story, lass. Did you really think that tavern witch's spell would have any effect on a dwarf?"

Evonne's face went red. "She would have offered me a reward but I didn't want one. I never even found out her name."

Grim stood, his eyes locked on Evonne's. "Do you have any idea how angry the Captain is? Do you know what he would do if he finds out what you did?"

"I…I…"

Grim walked over to where Evonne was sitting and placed a hand on her shoulder. "You did good, lass. I am proud of you. You have not become like the rest of us."

The dwarf left for the galley and Evonne looked to Dragon, who now knew the truth of what happened. He smiled and nodded, agreeing with Grim.

*   *   *   *

Two weeks at sea had produced no merchant vessel like Captain Krayne had been expecting. He was positive he had the correct location yet the ship he received the tip about was nowhere to be found. The crew was grumbling, yet again.

In desperation to find a ship, any ship worth attacking, Krayne ordered the Kraken dangerously close to the largest port city in Tauros. Port Bayswater was rich with merchant traffic but was also heavily patrolled by the Taurosian navy.

"Captain, is this wise?" questioned Purcy.

"Shut up. We will hit the first merchant ship we see and be out of here before anyone notices."

"But we have already wasted so much time for nothing. This is a very large gamble we are taking by being this close to Bayswater."

"Shut up or I will shut you up."

Several hours later a shout from the crow's nest had all the crew scrambling about the deck. A ship was sighted. Krayne had the Kraken turn around and begin pursuit. It did not take long, though, before they realized the other ship was not about to run away, and was sailing straight for them.

"Ahhh, Captain?"

"Yes, Mister Bors?"

"That's the Lady Jean."

Evonne heard many of the crew gasp and noticed a strange look on Krayne's face…fear? Krayne snatched the spyglass from his first mate's hand and took a look for himself. He put it down and then looked again, as if he had to confirm what he had already seen.

"Mister Yarin, get us out of here. Now!"

Evonne learned that the Lady Jean was the largest warship in the Taurosian navy and its captain, Captain Mikhael, was an avid pirate hunter. The Grinning Kraken stood no chance in a fight, so they fled.

The Lady Jean was not about to give up so easily and the Kraken was forced to flee deep into largely uncharted waters. The further west they sailed, the further they were from any available port. After a week and a half, the Lady Jean had finally vanished from sight, but the Kraken was in the middle of nowhere, with almost no chance of finding any ship to attack. The crew's frustration was growing rapidly and Evonne was overhearing the first ill words spoken aloud about Captain Krayne.

CHAPTER 14

A hungry and exhausted Vrawg lay on a hill overlooking
the town of Glastonby. He had spent the last few hours
just looking upon the town, attempting to build up the
courage to enter. He had arrived while it was still quite
dark and now that the sun had risen, he finally got a good
look at the first human settlement he had ever seen.

Vrawg's mother had described what the town looked
like to him but seeing it with his own eyes was a marvelous
sight. All Vrawg had ever known was the inside of
mountains and a portion of the Dalecanin Valley. Ogres
preferred living within the natural caverns of the
mountains but did tunnel when necessary. So Glastonby
was something the half-ogre was completely unfamiliar
with.

He gazed at the multi-story buildings with awe.
Gurtha had told him that humans built structures to live
within and built shops in order to sell and trade goods.
Vrawg could see many folk already up and going about
their morning routines, pulling wagons full of food or

other goods.

The river that Vrawg had followed to reach Glastonby continued through the town and went further west, where it eventually met the sea. He watched as several humans sat near the river holding long sticks with string that dropped down into the water. He remembered his mother called this practice "fishing." While there were bodies of water located within the mountains, ogres used spears in order to catch the delicious fish that made the underground lakes their home.

Vrawg thought the town looked quite big but had been told that Glastonby was considered a small town by human standards. There was no protective wall that surrounded the town but Vrawg could see many armored men, carrying bows and spears, patrolling the perimeter.

At one time, Gurtha made several trips to the town each year to trade goods. Most often she made the trek alone, but on some occasions, when there were many things to deliver or bring back, she brought some extra help. Ogres had been tolerated, to some degree. While the ogres and barbarians warred with each other, the ogres had always left Glastonby alone. That did not mean that the people of the town fully trusted the ogres, as they still kept a wary eye upon them.

Vrawg was much larger than any of the humans but he still felt vulnerable without a proper weapon. His spear had been broken and Harglund had not retrieved his ball and chain when the pair left the troll's cave. But he remembered that his mother had said the people of Glastonby were reasonably friendly. He figured walking into the town with a weapon may just invoke the wrong first impression.

With a deep sigh, Vrawg stood and descended down the hill towards a rocky road that led straight into town. He was feeling quite nervous. A feeling that he was not very familiar with. With his gigantic frame, it did not take long for a patrolling guard to notice that this was no normal traveler approaching. The man grabbed the attention of his fellow guardsmen and pointed to the half-ogre. Another guard blew a horn and then the three of them trotted towards Vrawg, spears at the ready. Another two guards appeared suddenly from behind a small home and joined with the others.

Vrawg noticed that the five armored men were visibly unnerved. They appeared fairly young and had most likely never seen an actual ogre before. When Vrawg got within a few feet of the men, he stopped and held out his hands, indicating that he held no weapons. The five guards each held their spears tightly and formed a wall between Vrawg and the town, barring his way.

A guard with a long black beard, the leader of this group, Vrawg figured, spoke first. "W-what are you doing here? What business have you in Glastonby?"

"Food," Vrawg replied.

"There are no free handouts to be had here, ogre. Turn back the way you came."

Vrawg thought to correct the man that he was only half an ogre but figured to their eyes he looked every bit an ogre. Instead, he jingled a pouch full of the coins he had taken from the dragon's cavern.

"I pay."

"I hope you did not steal those coins from an honest traveler? Still, this is a human town. Ogres have not been seen here in decades. You should head back to the mountains."

Vrawg was not expecting to be turned away and was unsure of what to say next. Hearing the horn blast, five more guards approached and this group was led by a man with a white beard. He wore the same armor with the white and blue emblem of the town, only his shoulder plates were bright blue, setting him apart from the others. Vrawg guessed this was a man of importance among the guards. This man stared at Vrawg silently for a few moments before speaking.

"Been at least twenty years since I have seen one of your kind around these parts," the white-bearded man said. "Looks like you have seen battle?"

Vrawg realized he must have looked a mess. His pants were torn, along with his leather vest. The wounds that he had received from the troll and the bolgrock were still visible. He nodded his head.

"What tribe are you from?"

"Drogheim."

"Drogheim, huh? You know Gurtha Drogheim?"

"My mother."

The man, who had known Gurtha for many years, looked Vrawg over more carefully this time. He could definitely see some similarities in the half-ogre's features. The man also wondered then if the rumors were true about Gurtha and Drubin Silvershard. There was something different about this ogre, he thought, something about his eyes.

"How is Gurtha doing? It's been a long time."

"She dead. I leave Drogheim."

The guard captain was not overly fond of ogres in general but had come to know Gurtha and had found her surprisingly charming. The news that she was dead sent a pang of sorrow through the man.

"I am sorry to hear that. Follow me and we shall see about getting you something to eat."

*　　*　　*　　*

Vrawg stood at the bar within a tavern called Cale's. He did not dare sit on a stool for fear of breaking it. The tavern was sparsely populated at this hour of the morning, though the few folk that were present ignored their breakfast and stared at the giant stranger.

Captain Sewl, the white-bearded guard that allowed Vrawg to enter the town, guided the half-ogre to the tavern and told Vrawg he would return promptly to speak with him. The large man in the greasy apron, that stood behind the bar, soon placed a plate of steaming eggs and vegetables, with a compliment of fresh bread, in front of the half-ogre. Cale had served ogres in the past but that was quite some time ago.

"Ahh, you have coins to pay for that, I was told?" the man said, somewhat nervously.

Vrawg opened his pouch and pulled out two gold coins. He looked to the tavern owner with a quizzical expression worn upon his face. Realizing that this ogre had no idea what a meal would cost, Cale's face lit up.

"Ah, do you have one more of those coins? Yeah, three will cover your meal and a mug of ale."

Not knowing any better, Vrawg handed the man three gold coins, more than quadruple what the meal should have cost, then dug in and devoured everything on the plate in mere moments. He downed a full mug of ale in one gulp.

"You should have slowed down and enjoyed that meal," said a voice from behind.

Vrawg turned to watch Captain Sewl enter the tavern and approach the bar. Before the door closed behind him, Vrawg noticed several guards posted just outside. He did not blame the humans for being cautious.

"So, what is the son of Gurtha Drogheim doing here in Glastonby? I noticed you have not brought anything with you to trade, as your mother always did."

"Nowhere to go," Vrawg answered.

The man, again, regarded the many wounds that were visible on Vrawg's body. "Are you running from something?"

Vrawg nodded.

"Your tribe?"

Vrawg nodded.

"Did you do something bad?"

"Ogre kill Gurtha. I kill ogre."

"Ah, tragic. I knew your mother, so this saddens me. She was a peaceful ogre and always a pleasure to do business with."

Vrawg nodded and was pleased to hear good things said about her from this human. He knew that she preferred the company of humans over ogres and would have stayed in Glastonby if she could have.

"What brings you here, specifically?"

"Drubin."

"Ah, I have often wondered about Drubin and Gurtha. Is Drubin your…?"

Vrawg nodded, knowing what the man was going to ask. "Drubin here?"

"You could say that. Come, let me take you to him."

*   *   *   *

Vrawg stood in a field, staring at a stone marker that was stuck in the ground, but he did not understand why. All around him were stone markers, hundreds in fact, varying in sizes. Symbols were etched on the markers but Vrawg could not read the language of humans. Gurtha never had the chance to teach him.

He turned to Captain Sewl and shook his head. "Where Drubin?"

"Right in front of you. Or rather, below you, I should say."

"No understand."

"Your father is dead, son. I am sorry. Drubin is buried here. His body is in the ground beneath you."

"How? When?"

"Well, it happened nearly twenty years ago. Some northmen from Valhorn killed him. Valhorn is a barbarian town north of here. Some northmen were passing through Glastonby and heard rumors that Drubin Silvershard had a relationship with a female ogre, and a baby had come as a result. Barbarians hate ogres, as I am sure you are well aware, and these men took out their anger on Drubin. Murder is still murder and we attempted to apprehend the northmen but they fled before we could. Your father was a respected member of this town, despite any of the rumors against him. Many mourned his death."

Vrawg did not know what to say. He always knew there was a chance that Drubin was dead by now, even by old age. But he clung to the hope that his father was alive and he would have the chance to see him and speak with him. Maybe even live here with him. Now those hopes were dashed and Vrawg did not know where he would go from here. Now he was truly alone. There was no sense in traveling to Valhorn to exact some long-overdue revenge. Those men could be dead by now as well and Vrawg could not blame them for their hatred of ogres, he knew his kin were evil. That did not justify their actions in murdering his father but revenge would accomplish nothing now.

A distant blast of a horn pulled Vrawg from his thoughts and he turned to the guard captain. Captain Sewl wore a concerned expression. Two horn blasts in the same day. The guards did not blow their horns unless they required backup from a potential threat. Sewl thought of Vrawg and the half-ogre's story, and figured he just might know what this threat could be.

Captain Sewl pointed to an old shed that sat inside the graveyard. "Vrawg, go to that shed over there and stay inside until I come back for you. Do you understand?"

Vrawg nodded.

*　　*　　*　　*

Vrawg did not like the look that the guard captain had worn and did not remain inside the shed for very long. The half-ogre crept out and made his way back into town, following the path that Captain Sewl had taken. Upon hearing the horn, the residents of Glastonby were trained to find immediate shelter, until the possible threat could be investigated. So Vrawg did not encounter anyone as he took cover behind a house. He was near the road into town where he first met Captain Sewl.

Vrawg sucked in his breath at the sight before him. Five armored ogres stood on the road in a heated exchange with Captain Sewl and twelve other guards from the town. Everyone was on edge and spears were leveled in the direction of the gigantic ogres. From this distance, Vrawg could not make out any of the conversation but he knew the ogres were here for him. Either they had tracked him to Glastonby or guessed that it was a possible destination.

Feldrog was among the group and Vrawg could only imagine how badly he wanted to catch and kill the half-ogre who had humiliated him time and again. Vrawg only carried a dagger and he knew that he was no match for the five ogres. He also figured the twelve men of Glastonby were no match for the ogres either, if the situation deteriorated. These humans were much smaller than the barbarians of the Dalecanin Valley and many of them looked too young to have ever seen battle.

Vrawg worried that his presence here would doom these innocent townsfolk. It appeared that Captain Sewl was denying any knowledge of Vrawg's whereabouts but Grak did not seem convinced. Grak was a veteran patrol commander and experienced hunter. Many were the stories of Grak's savageness in battle.

The large ogre was pointing a finger at the face of Captain Sewl and shouting. The men of Glastonby edged closer to the ogre group, clearly unsure of their chances in a fight. The sudden arrival of ten more armored guards aided in bolstering their confidence. Vrawg knew that Grak would not be so easily intimidated but the ogre commander exercised caution and backed away. He said something else to Sewl and then he and the other ogres took their leave. The guards of Glastonby did not relax until the ogres had disappeared behind a distant hill.

*   *   *   *

Vrawg, again, stood in Cale's tavern and downed another expensive mug of ale while waiting for the return of Captain Sewl. More patrons filled the room now as word spread quickly of a fugitive ogre hiding in their town. The townsfolk were curious, but kept a healthy distance from Vrawg, and did not engage him in any conversation. Even the man behind the bar did not say much. He only stared.

Vrawg worried that Grak would return with a larger force and turn the town upside down in search of him. The ogres had always left Glastonby alone, but he did not underestimate the ogre's hatred of him, and their desire to bring him to their warped sense of justice. If they had traveled this far in pursuit, then they were not prepared to so readily allow him to escape. He knew Feldrog, more than any of the others, would be itching to find him.

Vrawg sighed again and cursed his kin for their ways. So deep in thought was the half-ogre that he had not noticed the arrival of Captain Sewl until the man was tapping him on the shoulder.

"The ogres clearly were not sure that you were here. They were guessing. That does not mean that they will not return, though, or keep an eye on the town."

Vrawg nodded.

The captain then sighed. "The mayor has asked that you leave town. He fears what your kin may do if they find out that you are indeed here. I can see that you are different from the others. You are definitely the son of Gurtha. But I am sorry, you will not be able to remain here."

Vrawg nodded. He understood. He did not wish anyone to get hurt because of him. He had no idea what a mayor was but from the context of the conversation he figured it was the leader of this town.

"I have convinced the mayor to allow you to stay two days at least but you will have to remain in the guard barracks. I will see to it that you will be given food and water and a weapon. I will also see what I can do about getting you some clothes made that will fit. I don't like the idea of turning away anyone in need but the mayor is concerned with the safety of our town, of course."

Vrawg nodded and placed a hand on the man's shoulder. "Thank you, friend."

*   *   *   *

Exactly two days later, at the crack of dawn, Vrawg and Captain Sewl exchanged nods of respect, and the half-ogre followed the road west out of Glastonby. True to his word, Sewl had a change of clothes and a new leather vest made that would fit Vrawg's giant frame. He was given a backpack with some food and water; enough to last several days. Vrawg also felt more comfortable now that he had a new spear in hand.

Vrawg really had no plan of where to go. The ogres had gone back east, so he would continue to travel west until he reached the sea. Captain Sewl informed him there was a small fishing village located where the river met the sea, but not to expect any warm welcome there. Vrawg did not wish to visit the village anyway, unless to replenish supplies, so as not to put them in any danger either. His options were extremely limited. He could not go north towards Valhorn. Sewl had told Vrawg that he could navigate the western-most edge of the Grey Ash Mountains and head south towards the nation of Tauros. He thought that Vrawg could possibly find a safe haven there, far from his tribe, and maybe some work for someone of his size and strength.

Despite his sadness at being alone, Vrawg was looking forward to gazing upon the Western Sea. His mother had described it to him as an endless expanse of water. That it stretched on for as far as the eye could see. He found it hard to believe that so much water could exist but there was a lot for him to learn about this vast new world.

CHAPTER 15

Evonne kneeled breathless on the deck of the Kraken. Blood stained the deck all around her and she winced as she reached up to touch her neck. The bolt from an enemy crossbow had drawn a line of blood across her skin. Another inch to the right and she would have been dead.

Others had not been as fortunate. Her eyes glazed over as she took in the sight of Jabari, or what was left of the black-skinned pirate. A huge ballistae bolt had torn the man in half. Torthal, one of the northmen, had taken an arrow in the shoulder, sending him overboard. He was left behind. Several other bodies of fellow crewmen lay strewn about the deck in a bloody mess.

She noticed Grim sitting down and also breathing heavy. A chunk of someone's scalp was still stuck to the bloody blade of his axe. Evonne was surprised at how relieved she felt when she saw that Zack still lived and walked about the ship, surveying the damage.

Krayne's recklessness had nearly been the end of them. Luck had not been with him over the last several months. Either ships had gotten away or they had proven to be too much work for so little a reward. Desperate, Captain Krayne had sent the Kraken after two ships. He firmly believed they could disable the smaller ship before the other could turn and help. He thought to fight each, one at a time. But things had gone horribly wrong and the Kraken ended up sandwiched between both ships, taking heavy fire from bows, crossbows, and the much larger ballistae.

The only bit of luck they had received in months allowed them to escape. The smaller ship made the mistake of getting close enough to send men aboard the Kraken. They were slaughtered to the man. Some fancy maneuvering by Mister Yarin caused the smaller ship to collide with the larger ship, giving the Kraken the chance it needed to pull away and put distance between their enemies. Thankfully, there had been no pursuit and now the remaining crew of the Kraken could catch their breath and finally relax.

"What were you thinking, you madman?" shouted a heavily-tattooed pirate.

"Careful, Aron," Krayne replied, pointing a finger in the man's direction. "Do not try my patience. Not now."

"Look around you," Aron continued. "You did this. Your foolishness is the cause of all this mess."

"Shup up."

"You were warned against attacking those ships. We never had a chance."

Captain Krayne casually walked over to the other pirate and swung his sword. Aron was quick to block it, expecting the attack. Krayne was the far superior swordsman, though, and a moment later he disarmed Aron and ran his sword through the man's belly.

"Anyone else have something they would like to say?" Krayne asked of all the crew on the deck.

He was met with only silence.

"That's what I thought. Today's events were unfortunate. We will bounce back, we always do. Mister Bors? I want a full damage report. Mister Bors?"

Krayne looked about for his ever-present first mate but he was nowhere in sight.

"Ah, Captain?" a scrawny young pirate called.

"What is it, Korlin?"

"Mister Bors is over here, sir, and…ah…he is dead, sir."

Krayne walked over to where Korlin was standing and saw his most loyal friend lying on the deck with puncture wounds in his chest. Bors had fallen to enemy blades when the Kraken was boarded. Evonne watched the captain storm off the deck and disappear into his quarters.

*   *   *   *

Evonne sat on the railing of the ship, her feet dangling over the side. The cool mist of the crashing waves sent a refreshing shower over her skin. All of the Kraken's sails were unfurled and the ship was traveling at a good speed, forcing Evonne to keep a strong grip on the rails. She could see almost nothing in the dark of the night but found some peace on her quiet perch.

She glanced several times to the door of Krayne's quarters. It had remained closed for the last two days. Krayne had ordered them to make for Trollport, then disappeared back into his cabin and had not emerged since.

"Careful you don't fall, lass," a familiar, gruff voice said.

"I am always careful, Grim. How is the mood below deck?"

"Same as usual. Lots of grumbling and cursing."

"Purcy leading the charge, I imagine."

"Of course."

"He loves stirring the pot, that one. First to argue, last to the battle."

Grim chuckled.

"What will happen? Could Krayne be voted out as captain?"

"That's not how it works here, lass. Someone would have to kill him."

"Eh?"

"To replace a captain, the man, er…or woman, pardon me, who wishes to replace him, would have to challenge him to single combat, to the death. If victorious, the challenger becomes the new captain."

"Well, we know Purcy would never have the courage to do that. Bromm, perhaps? At Purcy's insistence?" Evonne wondered.

"I doubt it. Bromm would not beat Captain Krayne in a fair fight and Purcy would not want to lose his trusted bodyguard. Truth is, nobody has the courage to challenge Krayne."

"You? You aren't afraid of anyone."

"Bah, I have no desire to be a captain. Too many headaches, that is."

"Ah well, they should cease their grumbling then, if

they are too cowardly to do anything about it. When will Krayne choose a new first mate?"

"Probably when we reach Trollport."

"You are the best candidate, by far. Everyone respects you."

"Purcy hates me."

"So what? Krayne respects you and that's all that matters. He is still the captain of this ship."

"Bah, who knows his mind now? The man is going mad."

*　　*　　*　　*

"Ah, Captain, is that such a good idea?"

"Question me again, Arval, and you will be next."

Evonne joined the gathering crowd above deck to see what all the commotion was about. She spotted two men up in the crow's nest and one of them wore a noose around his neck. Most of the crew stood below, wearing concerned looks, with a few pleading with Captain Krayne to show reason. Apparently, Ven, the man wearing the noose, had been the next one to question Krayne's orders.

"Mister Larsan, send Ven to meet the gods of the sea," commanded Krayne.

Larsan, the other man standing in the crow's nest, hesitated and looked to the other faces gathered below. Ven was a good fighter and respected by the others.

"If I have to come up there and do it myself…"

Krayne did not have to finish his threat. Larsan had nothing against Ven but feared Krayne above all else. The lanky pirate swallowed hard and then shoved the other man over the railing of the crow's nest. Everyone heard

Ven's neck snap. His lifeless body swayed in the breeze.

Captain Krayne turned and marched back towards his quarters. As he passed Evonne, he grabbed her right arm and shoved her in front of him. The man reeked of alcohol.

Evonne broke free of his grasp. "What is this all about?"

Krayne again shoved her with such force that the young woman fell to the deck and skidded in the direction of his cabin door.

"Hey!"

Before she could stand, he grabbed her by her ponytail and began to drag her along. "We are several days away from port and I need the company of a woman," he said. "I had never given you much consideration before but you are quite attractive."

Evonne struggled to get free. "I am not your plaything."

"You will be whatever it is that I want you to be."

Evonne pulled a dagger from the top of her boot and dared to slash Krayne's arm, forcing him to let go.

"You wench!" he roared with anger.

He attempted to kick the insubordinate woman but Evonne proved quicker and rolled to the side, then jumped to her feet.

"Get in my quarters, now, and I will consider letting you live afterwards."

"I don't think so," Evonne stated, defiantly.

"You don't think so? I am the Captain!" Krayne shouted.

"Not anymore, you ain't."

"Pardon me?"

"I challenge you, Krayne," Evonne spat, purposely leaving out the title of captain. "I believe I will make a much better captain for this ship."

A collective gasp reverberated around the deck from all of those present. Mouths hung open in shock. Those who grew to like and respect Evonne stood dumbfounded by her apparent madness. Only Purcy smiled widely, anticipating a horrible ending for the mouthy little woman.

Krayne laughed a maniacal laugh. He had commanded The Grinning Kraken for twelve years, after killing the previous captain with a similar challenge, and in all that time, nobody had ever dared challenge him. Purcy was an ever-present thorn in his side but even Purcy knew his limitations and when to back off in order to preserve his life.

"It is a shame that I will have to carve up that pretty face of yours." Krayne stopped laughing and wore an expression of dead seriousness. "I am gonna display your carcass on the bow of the ship for all to see as we pull into Trollport."

"Tough talk, from a dead man," Evonne taunted.

Krayne growled and drew his weapons. A sabre in his right hand, a dagger in his left. Grim broke through the astonished crowd and grabbed Evonne by the shoulder.

"What is wrong with you, lass?"

"Nothing is wrong with me. I am about to rid this ship of a blight."

"You are about to throw your life away."

"I would rather be dead than somebody's slave and plaything."

"Captain," Grim pleaded. "The girl didn't know what she was saying."

"The challenge has been made," Krayne smiled, wickedly. "And accepted. Now, out of the way, dwarf."

"Do as he says, Grim. It will be the last command you ever take from this madman."

"No!" Grim shouted.

At the insistence of Purcy, several pirates, Bromm included, grabbed the struggling dwarf to pull him away.

"You know the rules, dwarf," Purcy said. "The challenge has been made and we must stand aside and see what the gods have in store for us. Will we have a new captain? Or shall we continue under the wise leadership of our current captain? We cannot interfere."

Grim was one of the strongest among the crew but could not resist the five men that held him in place. He spat curses and even bit one of them, but they did not let him go.

Nearby, Zack looked on with mixed emotions. He would never have admitted it but he was jealous of Evonne. He could not bear that his younger sister, a woman, had developed into such a fine fighter and sailor. Better than he had. Zack was just another set of hands aboard the ship, while Evonne's skills were highly valued by most. His jealousy prevented him from maintaining any relationship with her, but now that she was about to die, he felt torn. A part of him was shocked that he thought his life aboard the Kraken would be better without her. He was tired of hearing comments like, "If you can't do it, maybe your sister can," and, "Why don't you take some lessons from your sister."

Captain Krayne patiently waited while Dragon retrieved Evonne's sabre from below deck. As much as he wanted to strike her down right now and wipe that smirk from her face, a formal challenge had been made and he would respect the rules of the sea. But by Azark's beard, he was going to enjoy cutting her to pieces.

Dragon returned and handed Evonne her sword. He paused for a moment and gave her a worried look. Evonne smiled at her mute friend and he nodded to her, then backed away.

It was a perfectly clear, cloudless afternoon. There was very little wind this day and the sea was surprisingly calm. Captain Krayne and Evonne casually circled each other, their eyes locked in an intense stare. Evonne would be lying if she said she was not nervous. It had all just happened so fast. She never entertained any previous notion of challenging Krayne for his captaincy. She grew to dislike the man but never thought to fight him. Now, there was no backing out. She had spoken without thinking first but she did not regret her decision. If she died today, then so be it.

There was one advantage that Evonne held. She had spent years studying Krayne in battle. She knew his favored attacks. She knew his defenses. She knew his feints. She had watched him closely in every battle since joining the crew and she felt that she knew what Krayne would do even before he did it.

Like right now. Evonne had watched Krayne circle opponents before. He attempted to defeat them before the battle even started with his calm demeanor and intimidation. She also knew that he always led with a forward jab of his sword, looking to impale his opponent immediately.

That jab came much quicker than Evonne would have thought from a man who smelled as if he had drank an entire keg of ale. But she was expecting it and danced back just out of reach. She also expected his next feint with his dagger and side-stepped the real attack when it came. The other pirates watched in stunned silence. Many of them expected the young woman to already be dead. They knew Evonne was skilled with a sword but placed Captain Krayne in a whole different league. Evonne, herself, would not deny this either, but she felt she was smarter. Grim had always taught her to fight clever. That she would always be smaller than and not as strong as her opponents, so she needed to rely on her brains and a good strategy to overcome those obstacles. Evonne had been a great student.

Krayne advanced with a series of quick strikes, followed by a slash of his dagger. Evonne knew his pattern. Three strikes with the sabre, one with the dagger. She parried the first, side-stepped the second and rolled under the third. She leaped back, sucking in her stomach to avoid the dagger. Krayne growled.

"Stand still, wench. Stop fighting like a coward."

"Fine."

Evonne knew that Krayne always blocked a forward jab with a downward arc of his sabre. He would knock his opponent's weapon down so that it would be useless to defend against the counter-attack from his dagger. The young woman feinted with a jab and as she expected, he swung his sabre downwards. She reversed her feint quickly and slashed Krayne against his defending arm, drawing first blood.

The crew gasped but Evonne heard not a thing. She was so focused on Krayne that she heard nothing and saw nothing, aside from him.

Angered, Captain Krayne launched a fury of attacks. Evonne expected that reaction and went on the defensive, dancing and skipping away out of reach. Each attack met with only air. He continued to pursue the younger pirate and was finally rewarded when he opened a gash on Evonne's left shoulder. She bit back from making any sound, refusing to give him the satisfaction. Instead, she smiled and shrugged, as if it made no difference at all.

Krayne appeared to back away slowly and then suddenly charged forward instead. Evonne was taken by surprise and pure reflexes alone, allowed her to bring her sword up just in time to block a chopping attack towards her head. She grunted from the impact of their two swords meeting but managed to hold the pose, their blades locked together.

Krayne leaned in closer and smashed his elbow into Evonne's nose, sending her to the deck, dazed. She blinked the stars from her eyes and spat out blood that poured from her nose and into her mouth. Grim renewed his struggle with his restrainers but was unsuccessful.

The pirate captain possessed the upper hand but circled Evonne with a smile. She also knew that he loved to taunt opponents; play with them, cruelly, like a cat would with a mouse. It was as if he drank in the fear of others, savoring every little drop.

"Get up. Die on your feet, at least, with dignity."

Evonne attempted to stand but collapsed momentarily on an elbow. She blinked slowly and then attempted to rise again. She got to her feet and swayed, dizzily, the tip of her sword touching the deck as she was unable to even raise the weapon in front of her.

Krayne nodded to Evonne, a final display that he

respected her for standing. She knew that when the man had someone stunned and defeated, he spun with a backhanded slash to remove an opponent's head. It was flashy and impressive to those who witnessed it, and sent a message to any other potential opponents.

As predicted, Krayne attempted just that. Evonne had cleared the cobwebs from her head before she had gotten to her feet, but continued with the act of still being dazed. Krayne spun and his sword arced towards Evonne's neck. At the last possible moment, she ducked underneath the blade and drove her own sword into the pirate captain's belly. Evonne did not stop until her blade went hilt-deep and the tip came out through the man's back.

Krayne grunted and staggered backwards, dropping both his weapons. Evonne placed a boot on the man's chest and kicked him, pulling her sword free as he sprawled to the deck. Everyone stood silent, rooted in place. Even Grim had ceased his struggling, unable to believe his own eyes.

Evonne loomed over Krayne and placed her bloodied blade against his throat. He looked up but said nothing as he coughed and choked on his own blood.

"Send my regards to Azark," she said, and then ended the reign of the one of the most feared pirates of the Western Sea.

It took quite some time before someone spoke. "Ahh, by the will of the sea gods, Captain Evonne it is, then."

*　　*　　*　　*

Later that same day, one of the worst storms in recent

memory raged and battered The Grinning Kraken. Most of the crew huddled in their quarters, attempting to drown their fears with drink. Many did not know what to think of the day's events. Krayne had been a good captain but recently had become unhinged. He had killed a few good men which did not sit well with the others. But now, what of Evonne? None could deny that she had killed Krayne fairly in the challenge and therefore was now the legitimate captain, but was she seasoned enough to run a successful ship? Could she keep Purcy and his followers in line?

As the ship rocked violently in the storm, Purcy seethed with anger. He hated Evonne, always had. The mouthy little wench had done him a big favor in eliminating Krayne but he could not or would not accept her as his captain. A woman! He considered the storm and its timing. The sea gods were angry with this turn of events and was sending a clear message that a woman should not be the captain of a pirate ship.

CHAPTER 16

Vrawg was among the bandits before they even realized he was there. They were so focused on the merchant and his family they were attacking, that they had not noticed the approach of the enormous half-ogre.

Holding a thick tree branch like a club, Vrawg knocked the first bandit unconscious with one swing. As the second bandit turned to face Vrawg, the much smaller human took the makeshift weapon in the chest and flew right off the dirt road to land in a ditch.

A third bandit, who carried a crossbow, took in the sight of Vrawg and threw his weapon aside, abandoning the fight. He figured shooting the ogre would only make it angrier. Three other bandits also had no desire to face an ogre and fled into a wooded area near the base of the closest mountain.

Vrawg smiled at the merchant and his family. The man sat in a wagon pulled by two horses, trembling as he held his wife and two teenage sons. They slowly and cautiously climbed down from the wagon, never taking their eyes off Vrawg. Once on the ground, they turned and ran back the way they had come. Back south towards Tauros.

Vrawg held his hands out in surprise. He had saved these humans from the bandits but they appeared more horrified of him than by their attackers. His shoulders slumped as they soon disappeared from sight. He was not looking for their gratitude; he had saved them because it was the right thing to do.

Vrawg sat near the wagon all through that night and into the next morning. He was hoping the merchant would come back for it and he did not want the bandits to get ahold of it first. The merchant never returned. At some point during the night, the man Vrawg had knocked unconscious, regained his senses and slipped away. Vrawg let him go.

Once Vrawg determined that the merchant was not coming back, he fed the horses some apples from the wagon, then unhitched them and sent them running back to the south. Not wanting to leave any of the goods for bandits, he took everything from within the wagon back to the cave where he had been living. It took several trips but the cave was not too far from the road that connected Tauros with the lands north of the Grey Ash Mountains.

The last few years had not been kind to Vrawg. As Sewl had advised him, he received no warm welcome in Balvern, the fishing village overlooking the sea. He was allowed to purchase some supplies but his presence had everyone on edge.

Leaving there, Vrawg had followed the road south into Tauros, a land that was controlled by a man referred to as The Purple King. Vrawg entered the northernmost town of Wayfare but met with a similar reception. The Purple King commanded a large army so the ogres of the Grey Ash Mountains never ventured into the southern lands. The people there knew of the ogre's existence but most had never seen one in the flesh. Of course, to Vrawg's dismay, the stories people heard about ogres were not complimentary, so once again, Vrawg was viewed with cautious eyes.

When Vrawg had decided to leave Wayfare, he encountered a group of men on the road outside of the town. One of the men was a hunter and was bent on adding an ogre's skull to his collection. Five men died that day and Vrawg was forced to head back north as Taurosian troops were dispatched to find him.

With nowhere else to go, Vrawg claimed a cave on the westernmost side of the Grey Ash Mountains, facing the Western Sea. To Vrawg's knowledge, ogre and wraggoth tribes did not reside in this region of the mountains. He did, however, have to compete for food and water with several trolls who lived in the area. Human bandits operated on the road between the mountains and the sea. They never bothered Vrawg and the half-ogre only involved himself with them if he witnessed any attacks, like the one on the merchant and his family.

For the most part, Vrawg was alone. He rarely crossed paths with anyone. Even the trolls had learned to give the half-ogre a wide berth and only occasionally they met at a nearby stream that was the only source of fresh water in the immediate area. During the first few months, Vrawg was forced to kill three trolls. Since then, the others avoided him as best they could. Trolls could never be accused of being intelligent but they were smart enough to realize the half-ogre was dangerous.

Boredom was the biggest strain on Vrawg's sanity. He loved his view of the sea, and even enjoyed venturing down to walk in the icy water, but that was not enough to occupy his long days alone. The cave he claimed as his own connected to deep tunnels within the mountain. Vrawg had explored many of the tunnels but found nothing of interest. Some days he almost wished he would encounter a wraggoth patrol group but none made these tunnels their home.

Most of the time Vrawg sat at the cave entrance and just watched the rolling waves of the sea. They could hypnotize him and hold him captivated for hours. He wondered how deep the sea could be and where it ended. He envisioned a gigantic waterfall at the edge of the world where the waters of the sea fell into…well his mind could not fathom where all the water would go at the end of the world.

Periodically, he would watch boats travel across the rough waters. Some were as small as a rowboat and others were enormous ships, propelled by the wind with the use of large sails. Vrawg could not understand how the large ships stayed afloat. Surely something so big and heavy should sink to the bottom. He also wondered if the men on those ships ever feared sailing off the end of the world.

Vrawg had plenty of time to think and ponder life's mysteries. More than once he doubted the existence of the gods. If his life was the result of Blaggrath, then why had the god hated him so much? He considered the power and influence that Zolar had over the other ogres in the tribe, simply by saying that he knew the will of Blaggrath. They blindly followed the words of Zolar with no actual proof that he spoke for the ogre god. Vrawg figured it was just a clever ploy from the ambitious shaman. And how could there be so many gods? His mother had told him that the humans had countless gods they worshipped. Which god you chose only depended on which region of the world you lived.

Vrawg's head spun from the complexities of life. He only wished to live simply; surrounded by others he could call friends. Right now he would settle for just one friend, aside from the furry rodents that he fed scraps to in his cave.

*   *   *   *

It was the middle of summer and Vrawg walked along a rocky ledge, only a few feet above the sea. It was a particularly windy day and the water was rough. Waves crashed against the rocks and refreshed the half-ogre with a cool mist. It had been weeks since he had seen anyone at all. Lately, his only enjoyment was spotting travelers on the road or fishermen in boats. Vrawg would wonder who they were and where they came from. Where were they going? Did they have families? Friends? For that brief moment in time, he did not feel so alone. Once they vanished from sight, though, the loneliness crept back.

This day Vrawg left the cave and headed down to the sea. He planned to walk for hours, hoping to spot someone, anyone at all. He brought his spear in case an opportunity arose to catch any fish. He was growing tired of eating the moss and mushrooms that grew deep inside his cave.

His sanity was slipping away. He had not heard the

sound of his own voice for about a year. Or was it two? He had lost track of all time. Days blurred into weeks and weeks became months. He could not even accurately tell how long ago it was that he fled his tribe.

In desperation, he even attempted to share a meal with a troll. He wondered, if like himself, that not all trolls were bad. Vrawg's bite wound had still not fully healed. At first he considered himself lucky that the wound had not become infected, but lately, darker thoughts crept their way into his mind. Not for the first time, he questioned why he was fighting so hard to survive. What was the purpose? Living alone in a cave was not really living at all. It was just survival and nothing more. He existed but his existence did not matter. If he perished in these mountains nobody would even know and nobody would care.

His mixed heritage had him caught between two worlds, with neither accepting him. Ogres viewed his human side as a weakness. He was smaller than they were and ultimately viewed as flawed and inferior. Humans did not recognize his human side. To them he was a monster. Humans that dwelled near the Grey Ash Mountains knew the reputation of ogres well, even if they had never crossed paths with one. Stories were told around fires to frighten children. Never venture near the mountains or the ogres will get you. Even though trolls were the ones who most often preyed on humans, ogres were feared more. They lived in groups and were more intelligent, and thus, viewed as more of a threat.

Vrawg was strolling along the rocks, wallowing in misery, when a shout pulled him from his thoughts. It came from the direction of the sea and he scanned the water for its source. Then he spotted it about a hundred yards out. A small rowboat had flipped over and a bearded human was struggling to cling to the side and remain afloat in the rough water. Without even a second thought, Vrawg dropped his spear and leaped into the icy water of the sea, swimming towards the man.

The half-ogre was not a strong swimmer but over the course of several years he had ventured into the water many times to try and learn. He always kept his mouth firmly shut as he detested the taste of the salty water. When he first arrived at the sea, Vrawg was quite thirsty from his travels and thought to quench his thirst with a nice cool drink. He never did that again.

Powerful arms quickly brought Vrawg to the struggling human. The man shrieked in terror at the sight of the half-ogre reaching for him. He believed some sea monster had risen up from the depths to claim him as its next meal. Vrawg clamped a mighty hand on one of the man's flailing arms and then did his best to swim back to shore while dragging the resisting human along with him.

Vrawg coughed and spat out the disgusting water that had found its way into his mouth. He eventually found the water shallow enough that he could stand and carried the man the rest of the way, then placed him on a rock at the shore. For quite some time, the fisherman lay frozen in fear, not sure of the large monster's intentions. He had never seen anything like it in all his years.

The half-ogre thought to break the uncomfortable silence. "Vrawg," he said, pointing to his own chest.

The man screamed and found the courage to stand, then turned and ran for the road north. Vrawg sighed and sat on the same rock, facing the sea. In his mind, he envisioned the man being grateful for his rescue. He imagined the man inviting him back to his village where Vrawg was hailed as a hero and asked to stay and live among them. It was a silly thought, he knew now. Humans disliked him almost as much as the ogres did.

Vrawg watched the capsized rowboat bob among the waves. The waves were actually pushing the small boat closer towards the shore. He wondered if the fisherman would return to look for his boat but then he thought back to the merchant and the wagon. The merchant abandoned his wagon of goods, along with two fine horses, for fear of running into the giant ogre again. So, Vrawg figured the fisherman would do the same and consider himself lucky for escaping from the monster with his life.

Vrawg had reached his wits' end and as the boat moved ever closer, he was struck with a dark idea. He would claim the boat as his, and if it supported his immense body, he would row the boat off the end of the world. He figured he could solve two problems at once. Firstly, would finally discover the mystery of where the water went after flowing over the world's edge. And secondly, he would put an end to his miserable, lonely existence.

With his mind made, Vrawg jumped back into the sea and waded out to the rowboat. He flipped the boat over and pulled it back closer to shore where he attempted to climb inside. It was made of wood and solidly built. He expected the boat to sink once he climbed inside but was pleasantly surprised that it did in fact support his weight.

He had watched fishermen use these types of boats before so it did not take him long to figure out how the oars worked. Soon, Vrawg was rowing farther and farther away from the shore. The rough water made things more difficult but the half-ogre was determined. He would not stop until he reached the end of the world.

CHAPTER 17

Evonne sat at the beautifully-carved desk in her new quarters with her feet propped up, while she took a swig from a bottle of some potent liquor. That is when Grim finally decided to burst in. She wondered what had taken him so long.

"Have you lost your mind, lass?"

"Come in and close the door behind you. You are letting in all the rain."

The dwarf, who was soaking wet from the storm outside, grumbled to himself but did close the door behind him.

"Share a drink with me, Grim. Krayne had a nice little stash of all the good stuff."

"Do you realize what you have done?"

"Started without you? My deepest apologies, but you were late for the party."

"What do you know about being the captain of a ship? A pirate ship, no less."

"Well, I have lived on this ship for several years now.

I would say I know how things work around here. And the things I don't know, well, I have you here for that. You are my new first mate."

Grim shook his head in disbelief, the braids of his beard flapping around. "How long before someone challenges you? You do realize these men will not like taking orders from a woman?"

"Let them challenge me. They will fall like Krayne. You have taught me well, my friend."

"You think you can fight this entire ship?"

"I won't have to. I can't see many of them being brave enough to challenge me after what they just witnessed. Purcy wouldn't dare, the coward."

"If anyone challenges you, I cannot help you. That is the code. You are on your own."

"I know."

"You have gone mad."

Now it was Evonne's turn to get angry. She stood and walked over to the dwarf, her face deadly serious. "What should I have done? Let that madman rape me? Is that what you are saying? Because that wasn't an option."

Grim nodded, he understood. "There could have been another way around it."

"No, there wasn't. Krayne was intent on having me. I had to fight him, Grim, I had no choice."

Grim pulled the girl into a tight hug and held her like a child. "I know, lass, I know. You fought so well, you made me proud. But you are in over your head now."

"We will get through this together, Grim. I can be a good captain, I know it."

"Just don't think you can boss me around now. You hear me?"

Evonne laughed.

* * * *

The majority of the Kraken's crew elected to wait out the storm while thoroughly intoxicated below deck. Any excuse to drink and do nothing was good enough for them. Their somewhat good mood, however, was shattered as a man ran into the crew's quarters, shouting frantically.

"Calm down, Eryck, what's wrong?" one pirate inquired.

Eryck paused for a moment to catch his breath. "It's Leo…he…well…Leo went overboard."

"What?" a few men all said in unison, jumping to their feet.

"A big wave hit the deck…washed Leo right over the side. I couldn't see him…he is gone."

"Oh, bloody hell," another man said. "He was a good man."

"Was like a brother to me."

"Poor Leo."

"A man doesn't deserve to go like that."

"When Azark says it's your time, it's your time."

Then a louder voice was heard over the others. "It would seem Azark is sending a message. That much is clear."

"What are you saying, Purcy?" Oslo asked. "What do you know?"

"Isn't it obvious?" Purcy continued, having grabbed the attention of the entire room. "When have we known a storm this strong? Its timing is not lost on me."

"Timing?"

"Azark is angry with us, gentlemen. We all know the code of the sea. Women that are not prisoners or paid passengers aboard a ship are bad luck. And now we call one Captain?"

"Captain Evonne won the challenge fairly," Rory commented. "If Azark was displeased then why did he allow her to kill Captain Krayne?"

"Because that is not how Azark operates. This is our ship and we must deal with our own affairs in accordance to the rules of the sea. We pirates have a code that we follow. Our first mistake was allowing that wench to remain on board and join this crew. Mark my words, gentlemen, Azark is angry and Leo will not be the last of us to suffer because of this."

*   *   *   *

As the thunder outside took a moment's pause, Evonne heard a knock upon her door. She knew it could not have been Grim as the dwarf would not have knocked.

"You may enter," Evonne smiled to herself. It felt good to say that.

To Evonne's surprise, Zack entered, his clothes thoroughly drenched.

"What do you think you are doing, Evonne?"

"That's Captain Evonne, and why is everyone asking me this? I thought the crew was not supposed to question the captain?"

"I can't call you, Captain. You are my little sister."

"Not so little anymore, wouldn't you say?"

Zack screwed his face up in frustration but held back

his next remark. "Leo is gone."

"What do you mean, Leo is gone?"

"Washed overboard. I just figured since you are the captain, you should know."

"Oh well, Leo was a fool anyways. Another one of Purcy's lackeys."

"You should be careful about what you say about who, sis."

"I am the captain, Zack, I will say whatever I want about whoever I want. Your friend Purcy can take that up with me personally, if he so wishes."

"Oh you just talk so tough all the time."

"That's because I am tough. I wasn't just satisfied with sitting on my ass and drinking every night. I wanted to make something of myself. You could have done the same, you just chose not to. And now you are jealous of me because of it."

"Me, jealous of you? You are a little girl."

Evonne fixed her brother with a serious stare. "As I said, not so little anymore."

"You command this ship now. Why not sail it to Guildburg? You can get off there and go teach father a lesson with all your tough talk. You can look after mother and Harlon, too."

"I already taught father a lesson before I left. I feel bad about Harlon but mother is where she belongs. She deserves Griff. So no, dear brother, we will not be sailing to Guildburg. I suppose you are stuck with me."

"The crew won't tolerate you for long. As your brother, I am giving you a friendly warning."

"And I am not going anywhere. I am the captain of this ship and everyone had better get used to that, or, as I said, they can come to me personally with their displeasures."

"Careful what you wish for."

*　　*　　*　　*

"Captain Evonne, these are the men who surrendered."

A group of bloodied crewmen from the Kraken escorted six prisoners across the gangplank from the enemy ship. The recent storm had let up just long enough for the Kraken to make a move on a ship that had, unfortunately for them, crossed the Kraken's path. Under normal circumstances the pirates would not have taken the risk with the highly unpredictable weather but Evonne knew the men needed this badly.

The nasty storm had taken her ship way off course and so far to the west that they were in largely uncharted waters. A few islands were said to populate this region of the sea but they were generally avoided. Some pirates had met with tragic ends exploring the islands and the stories traveled quickly. Spotting a ship in these waters caught the crew off guard but Evonne ordered an immediate pursuit, hoping to lift their spirits and morale.

The Black Sorrow was a smaller ship and appeared to have taken some damage from the same storm that had battered the Kraken. The battle went well and the Kraken did not lose a single man. Six men surrendered, rather than being butchered aboard their ship, and now stood solemnly in front of Evonne. The rain had stopped for now but the skies were black and the storm threatened to return at any moment.

"Kneel before the Captain!" shouted Orwald.

Five of the prisoners did exactly that and quickly kneeled, not wanting to anger their captors. One, however, did not. A wiry, well-dressed man, stood defiantly, eyeing Evonne with a smirk.

"A woman?" he said. "Your captain is a woman?"

"Kneel," Orwald growled, pointing the tip of his sword towards the man.

"Varun kneels before no man, and certainly, no woman."

Another pirate walked up behind the insolent prisoner and slammed the hilt of his sword into the back of the man's head. He stumbled and did fall to his knees.

"A fine score, Captain!" someone yelled, excitedly, from the Black Sorrow. "Five large chests of gold!"

The wiry man shook the dizziness from his head. "That gold does not belong to you. If you let me go now we can forget about this little unfortunate incident."

The crew of Kraken laughed.

Evonne smiled. "Bring the gold aboard quickly and let's get out of here before that storm decides to start again."

Varun angrily rose to his feet. "You have no idea who owns that gold. You sign a death warrant by taking it."

Orwald grabbed the man by his shirt and tore it from his body in an attempt to force him back to his knees. A few of Kraken's crew gasped upon viewing the strange tattoo the man wore on his heart. Two black serpents formed two "S's". Evonne had never seen the tattoo before and thus it meant nothing to her.

"Take the gold and then escort these men back aboard their ship and cut us loose," she ordered.

"You are letting them go?" a familiar, and quite annoying voice, questioned.

"Yes, Purcy," Evonne replied. "They surrendered. We have no need to kill them and don't have the rations to keep them aboard as prisoners."

"An unwise decision, Captain," he said. "You want word to spread that The Grinning Kraken has gone soft?"

Before Evonne could answer, Grim grabbed her by the arm and pulled her aside, lowering his voice. "This time, Purcy is right. You cannot let these men live."

"Why? They are no threat now."

"You see the tattoo on that man's chest?"

"Yes. So what?"

"That is the symbol of the Sundered Sons," Grim said, as if that should be explanation enough.

"Who are the Sundered Sons?"

"I thought you were from Tauros?"

"Well, I did come aboard this ship at a young age, my friend. I have never heard of the Sundered Sons."

"They are a vast and far-reaching criminal organization. Based in Tauros but with agents everywhere. Their membership is kept secret and guarded closely. They generally wear plain white masks to hide their identity. Thieves and assassins, all of them."

"So?"

"So, letting that man go will make us a target in any coastal port. They are not a forgiving lot and not an enemy you want to make."

"You sound fearful? Perhaps we should give them their gold back and apologize?"

Grim shook his head. "I am not saying that. That gold is ours. But we need to kill them and eliminate any link to us. Dead men don't tell tales."

"I am surprised at you, Grim. This is The Grinning Kraken and we do not fear anyone. I will not slaughter men who have surrendered, I am not Krayne. Nor will we ever sell men as slaves."

Evonne turned back to face the rest of the crew. "As I said, take the gold and escort these men back to their ship. Petro, Galin, Darvin, cut us loose."

*   *   *   *

That night the storm returned with a renewed fury. The Kraken rocked violently and Evonne found it difficult to even drink, having spilled alcohol all over herself several times. Sadly, within the first hour, she had lost two more crewmen. Randall, a teenage boy, went overboard and vanished, then Darvin was struck by lightning and died instantly.

Evonne was not having an easy time as the new captain of the ship. The gold they had taken from the Sundered Sons had raised spirits among the crew but they would never get to spend a coin if this storm sent the Kraken to the bottom of the sea.

She gave up on drinking and attempted to get some sleep. When that was unsuccessful, she decided to pace around her quarters, formulating plans for the future. A knock at the door caused her heart to sink. She was expecting more bad news.

"Enter."

Kennyth entered and had trouble closing the door behind him due to the strong wind that assaulted the ship.

"Who died this time?" she wondered.

"Ah, nobody, Captain."

"Then what do you want?"

"Well, ah, the crew was wondering if you wanted to come join us for some drinks. We are celebrating the great haul we got today and you haven't really come down with us since you killed Captain Krayne. It would mean a lot to everyone if you joined us."

"Isn't it a little late?"

"Nobody can sleep with this storm. And as expected, everyone is excited with the amount of gold we took today."

Evonne nodded. She needed the distraction and she had always enjoyed sharing drinks and gambling with the others. She followed Kennyth down to the crew's quarters and a loud cheer erupted as she entered. Several toasts were made in her honor, and despite the storm, they partied long into the next day.

Evonne was thoroughly intoxicated and required help back to her quarters. She blacked out before she reached her bed. The next time her eyes opened it was dark outside but she drifted back to sleep. She awoke with the sun in her eyes the following day, only something prevented her from moving. It was nothing physical, she just felt paralyzed. She could not focus on anything within her quarters and sleep claimed her once more. She had a terrible nightmare.

*　　*　　*　　*

Evonne finally bolted upright as ice-cold water splashed onto her face. Before she could orient herself, someone grabbed her roughly and dragged her out of her bed. She hit the floor hard, skinning her knee.

"What in the Abyss is going on?" she groggily yelled.

"Judgement day, wench," a man answered.

Evonne clumsily fumbled around for her weapons but had none. She had been stripped down to only what she would sleep in. The large and very strong pirate dragged her across the floor of her quarters as another opened the door. Enough of Evonne's faculties returned that she recognized that Bromm was the man dragging her. Her head felt so cloudy and disoriented, like nothing she had ever experienced before.

Bromm pulled a struggling Evonne out of her quarters and unceremoniously tossed her in the middle of the gathered crewmen. Her eyes stung from the bright light of the sun. Not a cloud was in the sky; the storm was long over. The cry of gulls immediately caught her attention. They were near land. How long had she been asleep? she had to wonder.

A furious Evonne finally stood. "What is the meaning of this? Someone is going to pay dearly."

She was not surprised when Purcy emerged from the group. "Oh, someone is going to pay, alright, but it will be you."

"How dare you! I am the captain!"

"Not anymore, you mouthy little brat. Not anymore."

Evonne laughed. "Why? Are you going to challenge me you cowardly weasel?"

"There is not going to be any challenge today. This isn't some personal grudge I have against you. This goes beyond both of us. It is the will of the gods."

"Oh please. What is this nonsense you are talking about?"

"There has been a vote, missy, and the crew has voted you out. The sea gods never approved of your presence here and these recent storms were all the proof we needed. Keeping you in command of this ship would have meant the death of us all. Strange how once the vote was tallied to remove you from command, the skies cleared and the sun had come out to bear witness to this occasion."

"You really are a fool if you think the gods have anything to do with the weather. Sometimes it rains and sometimes it doesn't. Big deal."

"The crew has decided. Time to go, wench."

Panic then hit Evonne as she realized this was not a dream or some silly joke. "Grim? Where is Grim?"

"Even the dwarf knew this was the right decision, he just didn't have the stomach to watch," Purcy remarked.

Evonne scanned the faces of the crew. She could tell that some were not in favor of this decision but were outnumbered. She found Dragon and the man wore the longest of faces. He mouthed the word, *sorry*. She knew in her heart that Dragon would have done something to help her if it was within his power. But he was only one man against the crew. She could not find Grim anywhere on the deck of the ship. Nothing happened aboard the Kraken without the dwarf's knowledge. Evonne felt heartbroken that her dearest of friends might have turned his back on her. Was he angry with her?

Bromm grabbed Evonne once more in an iron grip and pulled her to the edge of the ship. The now, former captain, could see the beach of a large island in the distance. It was not an island she was familiar with.

"What are you doing?"

"Well, the crew agreed unanimously that you had to go, but a second vote went in favor of keeping you alive. So this island is your new home."

Bromm pulled Evonne right passed Zack and for a moment they locked stares. Zack wore an expression of indifference and Evonne was surprised by how much that hurt. She was shoved up onto the plank and ordered to walk to the end at sword point. She knew she was to jump into the water and swim the short distance to the beach.

She whirled around in a last desperate attempt to save herself. "You call yourselves men? None of you were man enough to challenge me in combat? Pathetic, the lot of you!" she spat.

Purcy only smiled. "As I said to you, this isn't personal, it's divine. It's the will of the gods."

"You want this pathetic, cowardly worm, as your captain?" she asked, pointing a finger at Purcy. "A man who clearly wants to be captain but wasn't brave enough to fight a woman over it?"

"We haven't decided on a captain yet," Purcy smirked. "All in due time. Now, Evonne, time to swim."

Evonne's heart felt like it was about to burst from her chest. Abandoning her on that island was in every sense a death sentence. "What? You won't even give me some clothes? My boots? Not even a dagger?"

"Bromm," was all Purcy said.

The tip of Bromm's sword forced Evonne off the plank and into the icy water of the sea. Then a new worry overtook her. She was going to die on that island anyway but she would rather not get eaten by a shark or a sea troll along the way.

The Grinning Kraken lifted its anchor from the water

and unfurled its sails. As the ship moved away from the island, Evonne noticed Dragon standing near the railing. He looked about, cautiously, then dropped a small sack over the side. He saluted Evonne and then wiped a tear from his eye. She looked to the sack that floated in the water then back up to the ship. Dragon was gone.

Expecting teeth to sink into her legs at any moment, Evonne swam as quickly as she could. First to retrieve the sack and then towards the beach. She managed to eventually reach the beach without incident and collapsed with exhaustion. The Grinning Kraken was now just a small dot in the distance.

She opened the small sack to find a half-empty water skin, along with some fruit and water-logged bread. She might last a week with that, she figured, maybe a little longer. When her strength returned, she paced back and forth on the beach, seething with anger. Why would Grim turn his back on her? Did he disapprove so strongly about her letting those prisoners go? And what about Zack? Did he hate her so much that he did not care that they had just left her to die? Fools, all of them. Purcy had them all under his influence. He would be named captain, she knew it. Well, to the Abyss with them. They deserved him.

Evonne turned to regard the thick jungle that lay about two hundred yards from the beach. There could be fruit in there, and possibly some fresh water, but many were the tales of pirates who went into these uncharted jungles and never came out.

CHAPTER 18

It should have been mid-afternoon but the sky was black. A storm was brewing, Vrawg knew, and a bad one at that. He had been rowing for two days now and had lost all sense of direction. There was no landmarks; nothing to focus on. Just water in every direction he looked.

His stomach growled, angrily. Vrawg had not brought any food or water with him since his foolish idea was made in such haste. Several times he was tempted to drink the sea water in desperation but resisted when he recalled the horrible salty taste. He never believed that it would take this long to row the boat to the end of the world. It seemed now that this sea stretched on forever. But how was that possible? he wondered. The world had to end somewhere.

At times the waves were quite high and threatened to overturn his boat and toss him into the sea. All he could do was hang on with all his strength to remain inside the boat. He had been spun around so many times that he could actually be rowing back to where he had started from, for all he knew. And now, Vrawg figured, that was not such a bad thought at all. The more he pondered his current predicament, the more he wished he was back in his cave, back on dry land. He allowed a moment of weakness to throw away his life. A life that his mother had done so much to protect. In a way, she had given her own life because of him. This mad decision to end his life would shame his mother and her memory.

Vrawg hung his head in sorrow as the first drops of rain began to fall.

*   *   *   *

The boat suddenly jolted and Vrawg's eyes flew open. He had fallen asleep from sheer exhaustion. The rain had been coming down so hard that his boat was beginning to fill up with water. He spent hours attempting to remove the water without flipping the boat over. The only good part of the storm was that it provided Vrawg with water he could drink. When the storm finally decided to let up a little, Vrawg passed out. But something had just hit his boat. It did not feel like a wave; it was something solid.

The sky was still black with thick storm clouds but the rain was only falling down in a fine mist. Vrawg scanned the water for anything unusual but saw nothing. The sea was fairly calm at the moment so he knew that it was not a wave that had awakened him.

Just as he allowed himself to relax, he saw it, and sucked in his breath. A large snake peeked over the right side of his rowboat. It was dark orange in color and thicker than the oars on his boat. As he was frozen in place, he made the realization that there were no eyes, in fact, there was no head. It was not a snake after all, it was a tentacle. A moment later, several others snaked their way out of the water to feel the boat. With tentacles that long and that thick, Vrawg could not imagine what they belonged to, but he had a dreadful feeling he was about to find out.

With no other weapon at hand, Vrawg picked up one of the oars in both hands and slammed it into the closest tentacle. The tentacle pulled away and bubbles rose to the surface of the water. Vrawg's eyes widened as a pointed, cone-shaped head, appeared next to his boat. A giant yellow eye blinked and that eye was as large as the half-ogre's head. A sharp beak jutted out from the cone-shaped head. Vrawg had never seen or even heard tell of krakens before. It was a hideous-looking beast straight out of a nightmare.

The kraken was young and fairly small, though it struck pure fear into the large half-ogre. The sea monster's head moved in and the beak snapped at Vrawg. He narrowly avoided the bite and nearly lost his balance. He managed to keep from tumbling into the water and broke the oar on the side of the kraken's head. It screeched and its tentacles waved about violently.

Vrawg snatched up the remaining oar but before he could strike with it, another tentacle rose from the water behind him and grabbed him by the waist. Circular suction cups lined the full length of each tentacle, allowing it to latch onto the half-ogre with an iron grip. It squeezed tightly and Vrawg smashed the oar into the tentacle, hoping to force it to release him.

The second oar broke in half and Vrawg was still a prisoner of the kraken. Demonstrating immense strength, the kraken lifted the half-ogre into the air with little effort at all. Vrawg looked down at the open beak and did the only thing he could. He leaned over and sunk his teeth into the tentacle that held him. His teeth managed to penetrate the tough rubbery-skin of the kraken and it screeched once more, dropping Vrawg into the icy water.

Vrawg knew he was now completely defenseless in the water and at the mercy of the sea monster. Something brushed against his leg which brought his feeling of panic to a whole new level. The kraken screeched again, only this time, Vrawg had not touched it. The water surrounding the beast turned red with blood. The kraken's head disappeared below the surface and its tentacles thrashed about. It appeared that its attention was now drawn elsewhere.

Vrawg used its distraction to swim back to his boat. It was not easy for the half-ogre to drag his bulk back aboard but he somehow managed. He sat in the boat, panting breathlessly, watching several large fins break the surface of the water and circle the kraken. These fish were enormous; much bigger than any Vrawg had ever seen before. It seemed as though they were attacking the sea monster from below.

Soon, the tentacled-beast vanished from Vrawg's sight and the large fish sped away from the boat in apparent pursuit. Vrawg noticed a trail of blood leading further and further away. He allowed himself to exhale as he slumped his shoulders in exhaustion. He was not naïve enough to believe that these fish had somehow come to his rescue; he just figured the sea monster looked more delicious than he had.

Vrawg knew then that he was not yet prepared to die. He had rowed out to sea with the intention of ending his miserable life but when faced with the threat of the kraken, he fought very hard to remain alive. But the situation was grim. During the brief battle, Vrawg had broken both the oars of the rowboat and was now at the complete mercy of the sea. He could only go where the waves would guide him, and by the look of things, there was nowhere to go. He had not seen land in days.

It took several hours before Vrawg could relax and was satisfied that the sea monster and the large fish had gone. He lay down in the boat as heavy rain, again, began to fall. He watched lightning dance about in the dark sky and cursed himself for his foolish decision.

CHAPTER 19

The rain came down hard and Evonne sat huddled with her knees to her chest on the open beach. Several days had passed and she had not yet found the courage to enter the jungle, so she had no shelter from the storm. She at least felt some small satisfaction that these terrible storms had not stopped after her removal from The Grinning Kraken. Evonne hoped that some of the crew felt like fools for believing Purcy's mad tale of angry gods.

What little food Dragon was able to throw overboard was now gone, along with the water. Evonne would be able to drink some collected rain water but if she wanted to survive a little longer, she would have to consider searching the jungle for food. She dreaded that idea. She wore very little clothing and felt completely naked without any weapons. If she ran into any trouble at all, she had no way of defending herself.

Despite her dire situation, Evonne did not give in to despair. She was left on this island to die but she would not cry or give up. She felt like that is what was expected of her. Breaking down would mean that Purcy had really defeated her. Her anger played a large part in remaining composed. She passed most of time away by pacing back and forth in the sand, imagining all the types of revenge she would enact on Purcy and his followers if given the chance.

When she thought of Grim, though, she was deeply conflicted. She loved Grim as the father she never had and considered him her first true friend. Why did he not at least warn her? Like Dragon, she imagined that siding with her meant a death sentence, so the dwarf just chose self-preservation. In some way she understood that. She did not fault Dragon at all for his decision and she clearly saw the sorrow in the man's exotic eyes. Maybe she was angrier with Grim because he had not had the courage to even face her. Then again, she felt her and Grim had more of a connection. Were the roles reversed, Evonne would have given her life to stand and fight with him. That is what true friends should do. Perhaps the dwarf never really viewed her in the same way. That thought hurt more than being left to die on an island by her crew. Hurt more than being betrayed by her own brother, even.

The weather finally cleared on the following day and Evonne's empty stomach voiced its displeasure with her. She paused at the edge of the jungle and stared into the thick greenery. Exotic birds sang and insects chirped. It was the things she could not hear that worried her the most. What else lived in the jungle but remained silent, waiting for an unfortunate explorer? Grim had told Evonne that many dwarves had left his homeland to explore uncharted regions of the sea. They were seeking treasures on the islands that others rarely visited. None of those dwarves had ever returned.

Evonne knew, though, that fruit generally grew in abundance on some of these islands. Or at the very least, she could find a sharp stick and possibly spear herself some fish, or even a bird. She also fantasized about finding a spring or a pond, so she would not have to drink rain water she collected by digging holes in the sand.

But, as hungry as she was, her mind always wandered back to the dangers of the jungle. She had no weapons to defend herself or even boots to protect her from possible snake bites. Many a pirate had fallen to snake venom by unknowingly stepping on one of the sleeping serpents.

Once again, fear won over and Evonne turned and walked back down the beach. She knew the longer she waited to search for food, the weaker she would get. The future looked bleak, indeed.

*   *   *   *

Evonne dreamed she was back aboard the Kraken, drinking and gambling with the others. Life was back to normal. It was not until Grim approached her, to refill her nearly empty flagon, that she felt something was off. It was only a dream but Evonne was suddenly filled with intense anger at the sight of the dwarf.

Grim leaned in close to whisper into her ear. "You didn't really expect me to give my life for yours, did you?"

Evonne's eyes shot open and then she screamed in horror. Instead of the dwarf leaning over her, something else loomed above her, something very large. Still disoriented from sleep, she scrambled away in the sand as best she could. She had to wonder if she was still dreaming; she had to be.

Standing on the beach, merely a few feet away, was a seven-foot monstrosity. The heavily-muscled man, or beast, or whatever it was, had greyish skin, with a bald head. It wore tattered-leather clothing but she could see no visible weapons, though, this thing clearly would not need a weapon. She imagined it could rip her in half with just its bare hands.

Evonne's heart thumped rapidly as she began to realize this was no longer a dream. She was now fairly positive that she was truly awake and this thing was really standing before. She was certain that it was some race of monster she had never seen before, but there was something about its eyes, something almost human. The thing stared at her with curiosity. It made no sudden movement, and in fact, held its hands out in front in a gesture to signify it held no weapons and meant her no harm.

For several long moments, the pair stood frozen, eyes locked. Evonne got her breathing back under control as it appeared the thing was not intending to attack her. Not yet, anyway.

"By Azark's beard, where in the Abyss did you come from?" she finally dared to speak.

The newcomer tilted its head and then sat down, cross-legged, in the sand. Whatever it was, it suddenly seemed very weary.

"Are you a giant? Must be a giant. Grim spoke of giants in the mountains of his homeland. You can't be a man, of that I am certain."

Evonne cautiously approached the seated giant.

"I will have you know I am the captain of a pirate

ship. My crew is searching the jungle right now for food so attacking me would be very unwise. I just wanted to make that very clear."

The thing sighed and slumped its shoulders. For something so large and obviously powerful, it seemed weak, along with weary. Perhaps it was sick, or like herself, starving.

"I am Evonne."

It looked her over from top to bottom.

Evonne pointed to her chest. "My name is Evonne. E-vonne. That's me. I come from Tauros. T-auros. It is a land east of here." She pointed east. "E-ast. East of here. That way. Ummm," she began drawing lines in the sand to indicate water and land. "This is the sea," she pointed to the water. "You know, water? The Western Sea. I come from way over here, across the water. I came on a boat. B-oat." She did her best to draw a boat. "See, it floats in the water. Humans travel across the water on boats."

When Evonne got no response, she wiped out the drawings with her foot. "Oh, forget it. How would you ever understand a word I am saying?"

"I have boat," it spoke, with a very deep voice.

Evonne stared at the thing, stunned. Her face went red and she picked up a small stone and threw it at the stranger.

"You understood me and let me stand here and make a fool of myself this whole time? Why didn't you say something earlier?"

It shrugged its massive shoulders.

"You have a boat?" Evonne asked. "Where? Are there more of you?"

"Only me," it replied, struggling to stand.

It pointed to a spot on the beach and Evonne saw it. It appeared to be a small rowboat. She ran towards it and the stranger lumbered behind her. The young woman was awash with excitement. She might actually have a way off this dreadful island.

She knelt in the sand beside the boat and hugged the side. It was not very big, nor in the greatest of shape, but it was a boat. It appeared to have been battered by the recent storms. She noticed something else, then, and stood to look around. It was a rowboat but there were no oars in sight. What use was a rowboat without oars?

"Where are your oars?" Evonne asked, when the stranger finally caught up.

It looked at her but shrugged, seemingly unfamiliar with that word.

"Oars. Paddles. The things you use to row the boat," she said, while making rowing motions with her hands.

"Gone."

"Gone? How did you get here then if you can't row?"

"Storm bring me. Oars gone."

Evonne sighed. "So you are useless to me then. Useless."

It tilted its head, quizzically.

She pointed at its chest. "You. You are useless."

"No. I am Vrawg."

*   *   *   *

"Well that was quite a tale," Evonne said, lounging on the beach not far from Vrawg's rowboat. "It would seem we both have had our share of family issues. I have heard of ogres actually. They used to say, don't go into the mountains or the ogres will get you."

Vrawg frowned. It was those stories that haunted him everywhere he went.

"Not sure that I believed there really were ogres, though. Actually, I never really gave it much consideration, to be honest. Wow, a real life ogre."

"Half ogre."

"Oh yeah, sorry. Half ogre."

Evonne found that part of Vrawg's story the most interesting; that a human would have actually mated with an ogre. The thought repulsed her. This Vrawg was a hideous giant and he was only half an ogre. She could only imagine what ogre females looked like. But Vrawg seemed harmless enough. If he had meant her any harm, he would have done something by now. He was a lost soul without anyone in his life, just like her. She had felt it was safe enough to tell Vrawg that she was stranded here alone and there was no crew scouring the jungle. They abandoned her.

"Oh, and for your information, the world is round and not flat. You were going to sail off the edge of the world? How ridiculous."

She thought back to the time when Grim informed her that the world was round and not flat, but Vrawg did not need to know she had thought the same thing.

"Well, your foolish plan got you stranded on the same island as me. Now I won't have to die alone, so thanks for that."

"Boat," Vrawg said, pointing to it.

"Yeah, that's a boat, I get it. But it's a rowboat that you can't row. The waves would just push us back here again. We could have probably carved us some new oars from a tree, only neither of us has a blade of any kind."

"I hungry."

"Yeah, same here. There is probably fruit of some kind in that jungle. The best thing for you to do is go in there and look for some. Don't worry, I will wait here for you and guard our boat."

Vrawg stood and marched towards the jungle. Evonne thought to warn the half-ogre of potential dangers, but then she did not want to dissuade him from going in. She was beyond starving and she hoped that whatever horrors lurked inside the jungle, might find Vrawg as equally terrifying.

*   *   *   *

Hours had passed and just when Evonne thought Vrawg was most likely not going to return, he emerged from the jungle, and with an armful of various fruit, no less. As weak as she was, she ran to greet him with a sudden surge of energy.

"You actually made it. I take it all back, you might be useful after all."

The half-ogre smiled, obviously proud of himself. But more importantly to Vrawg, here was a human that was not running away from him in fear.

"Good, good," Evonne commented, excitedly, taking some fruit from Vrawg. "These orange ones and red ones are perfect. These ones with the shells are useless, we have nothing to open them with."

Vrawg looked around, then smashed one of the shells against a rock and cracked it open, revealing a juicy white fruit inside.

"Impressive. Remind me not to anger you. I don't even want to know what you could do with my head."

The pair took a seat in the sand and ravenously attacked the fruit. It did not take long before every piece was devoured and their stomachs were silenced, for the time being.

It was then that Evonne noticed some blood on Vrawg's legs and crawled closer to inspect. She found small puncture wounds on both his legs, just above his boots. Snake bites.

"By Zalara's black heart, you have been bitten by snakes."

Vrawg casually glanced down to regard the bites that he had not previously noticed. He was not overly concerned. There were many venomous snakes that lived in the Grey Ash Mountains and the ogres had developed an immunity to their poison over the centuries.

"Do they hurt?" Evonne wondered. "How do you feel? Are you dizzy at all?"

Vrawg just shrugged his massive shoulders. He felt fine. Especially after getting some food into his belly.

"Hmm, I suppose being a half-ogre has its advantages then. You are on permanent fruit duty from now on. And we need to find a source of fresh water. The animals on this island can't drink the sea water, so there has to be something drinkable around here. That's as important as the fruit. But, my friend, if we really want to survive, we are going to have to find some makeshift oars for your boat and attempt to row out of here."

Vrawg tilted his head. He focused on only one part of that conversation. "Friend?"

"Yeah, friend. Well it was a figure of speech but sure,

yeah, we are friends. Right?"

Evonne noticed the strange way that the half-ogre's face seemed to light up with joy. He smiled and repeated, "Friend."

The former pirate smiled back and punched him playfully on the arm. "Yeah, friends."

* * * *

"No, these are no good. Too flimsy. We need thicker sticks."

Vrawg had made several trips into the jungle, returning with more fruit and tree branches. Evonne was hoping they could find the perfect branches to act as oars, if they were to have any chance of escaping their island tomb.

"How about water? Any luck?"

Vrawg frowned and shook his head. That had Evonne the most worried. They needed fresh water. And soon.

"Alright, come here. Turn around. Bite check."

Vrawg held out his arms and slowly spun in place so that Evonne could inspect him for snake bites or any other wounds he may not have noticed.

"You are good. Maybe the snakes have determined that ogres taste awful. Back to the jungle with you. And focus on finding water."

Vrawg nodded and turned to head back to the jungle to continue his search. About halfway across the beach, something caught the corner of his eye. Something dark was floating in the water near the shore.

"EE-Vonne," he shouted, stressing the first part of

her name, as she had when she first told him.

When he had her attention, he pointed to what he saw. Evonne squinted her eyes and then ran towards the mysterious object. Vrawg jogged over to join her.

As Evonne got closer, she realized it was a body floating in the water. The tide had washed it to their island. She scanned the horizon but saw no ships in view. If she was correct about their location, very few ships ever came into this region of the sea. She could not imagine where this body would have come from.

Closer inspection revealed it was a short body and Evonne sucked in her breath. She really did not wish to find the body of a child floating in the water. Then something struck her as odd. She felt like the red shirt the corpse wore seemed familiar.

Evonne waded knee-deep into the water and then her heart stopped. Her legs suddenly felt weak and threatened to give out on her. She did recognize that shirt and the black hair. The body floated face down but she knew immediately that the face would have a distinctive, braided black beard. It was Grim.

Somehow she found the courage to turn the body over and she yelped as her fears were confirmed.

"No, no, no, no, no, no, no, no, no, no…"

She dragged the body of the dead dwarf onto the beach next to where Vrawg now stood. The half-ogre watched her curiously. It was evident to him that she had known this person.

Evonne continued to repeat, "no", while she inspected Grim's body for evidence of what happened to him. She gasped when she turned him on his side to look at his back a little more closely. Several stab wounds were found on his back. Grim never had a chance. His murderer, or murderers, had apparently attacked him from behind. The gutless cowards.

Evonne's lower lip quivered as she came to the realization as to why Grim was not present on the deck the day she was banished. Purcy, or more likely someone acting on Purcy's orders, had killed Grim prior to that. They knew Grim would not sit by and allow them to strip Evonne of her captaincy. So he had been murdered and dumped overboard.

Evonne felt completely ashamed of herself for ever doubting Grim. She could not believe that she allowed herself to think that he had simply hid, not having the courage to face her that day. She knew Grim's heart and he was her first true friend.

Something grabbed her attention and she managed a faint smile. She pulled a sharp dagger from the top of the dwarf's right boot.

"Even in death you continue to help me, my old friend."

Emotions finally got the better of her and Evonne broke down and wept. Even when she believed that she would die alone on this island, she had not cried. Anger had kept the tears at bay. And while she was even angrier now, she could not control herself. Tears flowed freely down her face.

Vrawg felt her pain. His new friend was clearly distraught by the death of whoever this little person was. Ogres did not cry so he watched her curiously but understood that this was a human reaction to sadness. Ogres very rarely showed any kind of affection but Vrawg's half human side nagged at him to do something.

Instinctively, he wrapped a gigantic arm around her. Evonne welcomed the gesture and did her best to hug the half-ogre's waist, burying her head in his rock-hard chest. Evonne cried until there were no more tears left to fall.

CHAPTER 20

Evonne held up her newly-carved oar and nodded with satisfaction. Grim's dagger was exactly what she had needed. Vrawg had managed to find two branches of perfect size and Evonne, with limited skills, did her best to carve the ends into makeshift paddles.

"This might actually work," she commented to the half-ogre. "Although, this does not guarantee our survival. The odds are in favor that we will die at sea quicker than we would on this island, but we have to try. Right? Do you agree?"

Vrawg nodded in agreement. He would go along with any plan that Evonne came up with. He had quickly learned that this little human was quite clever. She was smaller than most humans, so therefore, Vrawg considered her weak and frail, and would need to depend on her brains. He felt sorry for her as well, seeing as how she was so unattractive. She was so different from a muscular and strong ogre female, and her skin was so pale. But she was his friend; she had said so. Her looks mattered little to him. Vrawg had a purpose to his life now, to keep this little human safe.

"Before we decide to leave this island, we need to search deeper into that jungle for water. This time I am coming with you."

Evonne's mouth was parched. She had exerted much energy in digging a grave for Grim on the beach. Vrawg had lent a hand but she needed to be a part of it. She owed Grim that much. They were out of dirty rain water and if they did not find a water source their trip was going to be a short one.

* * * *

The jungle was hot and humid. The air felt so thick Evonne thought she could cut it with her dagger. It was not long before what little clothing she wore was drenched with sweat. The beach was hot but a nice breeze blew in from the sea. There was no breeze in the jungle.

The former pirate captain also noticed that the jungle had gone eerily silent since the pair had entered. No birds, no monkeys. Evonne was undecided as to whether that was a good thing or not.

Proving to his tiny friend that he was not just all brawn, Vrawg had picked up Evonne and placed her on his shoulders. This was so she could avoid accidentally stepping on and disturbing any serpents. She thought the idea was brilliant and marveled at how he had lifted her like she was a mere child.

Riding high up on the half-ogre's shoulders did have its setbacks, though. Several times she brushed against hanging vines and Evonne's heart nearly stopped, thinking they were snakes. She hated snakes.

The vegetation was thick and made for poor visibility. Spotting a particularly tall tree gave Evonne an idea.

"Vrawg, that tree over there. Take me there. If I climb up I could have a much better view of the island."

The trunk was tall and fairly small around, allowing Evonne an easy climb. Her worst fear was running into some kind of snake while being that high up, but fortunately for her, there was none.

The jungle was thick, and despite the great height of the tree, Evonne was not afforded the greatest of views. She could see that the island they were on was quite large and stretched for several miles. As she scanned the tree tops, something of interest did catch her eye. She squinted to make out what she believed was the top of a keep's battlements. About a half mile's distance from their location, appeared to be a stone structure jutting out slightly above the trees.

Evonne ran through all the possibilities in her mind. A pirate outpost? An ancient ruin? She figured pirates would not have built a structure so deep into the jungle, thinking that remaining closer to the beach would be more practical. Unless they wanted to remain hidden from passing ships. Whatever it was, it deserved a closer look. Whoever built it might have done so close to a source of water.

Evonne slid slowly down the tree to rejoin with Vrawg. "I saw something interesting but we are going to have to trek deeper into this accursed jungle. It's possible we are not alone here, so let's try and use a little stealth, huh? Alright, my large friend, that way."

Evonne winced as Vrawg's attempt at stealth still

sounded as if a large bear was crashing through the trees.

"I think they will hear us coming on a neighboring island," she commented.

Vrawg shrugged and continued along with Evonne clinging to his shoulders. At one point, the former pirate nearly fell from her perch with fright, as she spotted a snake nearly as thick around as the half-ogre's leg. Luckily for them, it slithered off in the opposite direction. Being out of sight, though, did not mean out of mind for Evonne. She constantly glanced behind with panic, expecting the serpent to pursue them.

In about an hour's time, the pair reached their destination. The jungle opened into a clearing, where sat a stone fortress built into the side of a large hill. The fortress was overgrown with vegetation and appeared in disrepair. Double doors once barred the entrance to this keep but one door was now missing and the other hung barely in place by a set of hinges. Two towers rose up from the main structure but only one, the one that Evonne had spotted from the tree, was still entirely intact. The second tower had crumbled into ruin and was only half the height of the other.

Evonne leaped down off of Vrawg. "I don't think the original inhabitants still dwell here by the look of this place. But that doesn't mean that *something* doesn't live here. Let's get a closer look but stay alert."

Vrawg nodded and picked up a fallen branch, holding it in both hands like a club. Evonne crept forward with Grim's dagger in hand. As they got closer, Evonne made an interesting observation. The doors to the keep were fairly short in height. It was perfect for her, or perhaps a dwarf. Her mind reeled at the possibility that this was an old dwarven stronghold at one time. Maybe even built by the dwarven explorers that Grim had told her about. Then she also recalled the part of the story that said those dwarves were never heard from again. She attempted to shake those thoughts from her head. The place appeared devoid of life and she could find no footprints in the immediate area.

Suddenly, a sight made her smile and all her immediate worries were pushed aside. Just to the right of the keep sat a large pool of water ringed with a stone border. Someone had built a pond, long ago.

Evonne smacked Vrawg in the leg and then raced over to the pond, unceremoniously dunking her head into it. It felt so refreshing, and most importantly, it was fresh water. It was about two feet deep and fairly clean. Evonne wasted no time in drinking her fill. Vrawg quickly joined her and slurped up mouthfuls of the liquid joy.

"Now we have to find a way to bring some water with us when we leave," Evonne commented to her new friend. "I was thinking of hollowing out some of the kabaranut shells. Could probably plug the holes with some leaves to keep them from spilling."

Vrawg nodded. This little human was clever indeed.

Evonne lay down next to the pond and turned her attention back to the overgrown fortress. "Or...there could be something useful in there," she wondered, aloud.

Vrawg frowned and shook his head. He did not like that idea. The doors to the fortress were too small and he would be unable to accompany her inside. Vrawg liked this little woman and he did not wish to lose his new friend so quickly after meeting her.

Evonne stood and decided to have a look around.

She gripped her dagger tightly and was mindful of slithering creatures. She inspected the stonemanship of the fortress walls while keeping her distance from the entrance. She was no expert by any means but she could tell that much skill went into the construction of this place. Grim had told her that dwarves were the masters of stonework.

Something in the distance, amid a tangle of creeping vines, caught Evonne's eye. It was definitely stone and was situated several yards from the fortress. She figured it was a piece of the ruined tower but walked over for a closer look.

"I was right," she whispered to herself. "Dwarves."

Evonne moved some thick vines and vegetation aside to reveal a toppled stone statue. There was no mistaking that the statue was carved in the likeness of a dwarf but the statue stood tall, much taller than any dwarf, or human for that matter. The giant, bearded, stone dwarf lay on his left side, while gripping a most curious war hammer in his right hand. Oddly, the hammer was not made of stone, but was actually forged with real metal. It was enormous and the craftsmanship was truly amazing.

She then took note of some symbols that were carved into the base of the statue. Many nights she had peered over Grim's shoulder to look at various books he was reading and some bore similar symbols. It was dwarven writing. She even recognized one particular symbol that Grim had told her represented the dwarven god, Horgar.

"You are gazing upon a dwarven god," she told Vrawg when he joined her. "A fallen god, though, quite literally."

"Dwarven?" he asked, unfamiliar with the word.

"Yeah, a dwarf. You know my friend that we buried on the beach? Grim was a dwarf. Smaller than most humans but hardier and stronger. Incredible craftsmen and weaponsmiths. They come from western side of the sea. If you sail straight west, you do not fall off the end of the world, like you foolishly thought, you would eventually hit land again. I have never been but Grim told me all about it."

Vrawg nodded. The person they buried had just looked like a short human to him. Although he did appear hairier than the average human. The world was much vaster than he could have possibly imagined. If he and Evonne were successful in escaping from the island, perhaps they could explore it more together. But escaping was not going to be easy.

"I think I am going in there for a look around," Evonne stated, pointing to the fortress entrance.

Vrawg grabbed her shoulder gently and shook his head.

"There could be useful stuff in there. Maybe a sword or even some armor. Well, something that would fit me at least. Don't worry, I will be careful and I won't be long."

The half-ogre gave her a concerned look but let her go. "Quick," he said.

Evonne smiled. It was a nice feeling again to have someone worry about her well-being. Even if that someone was a giant, seven-foot, monstrosity. Well, she figured, who better to look after her? She could only imagine what Vrawg was capable of in a fight. He could definitely be worth keeping around.

The former pirate took a deep breath, steeling her courage, then cautiously stepped through the archway into the dark fortress. The jungle was hot and humid but the fortress offered some immediate relief. She felt a cool breeze and there was a slight chill to the stone beneath her feet. Enough sunlight trickled in to illuminate the first room she entered. There were no surprises, as the inside of the fortress was in the same state of disrepair as the outside. Vines and weeds crept their way through every available crevice. This place must have been abandoned for quite some time, she thought.

The room was devoid of any furnishings or any objects at all. A crumbling stairwell led upwards toward the ruined tower and two hallways branched off from this room. She peered down the halls but could see very little in the gloom. The cool breeze came from the hallway that led deeper into the fortress, towards the hill that it was built upon. She wondered how deep underground this fortress went. From Grim's tales, she knew that dwarves were great miners and preferred being underground. Without a source of light, though, her exploration would have to end. She doubted now that there was anything of value left in here. She also had to consider what had caused the dwarves to abandon this place. And what were they looking for deep within the hill?

Before Evonne turned to leave, a sparkle caught the corner of her eye. It was about midway down the darker of the two hallways. Stone debris littered the floor but something shiny, something that was not stone, reflected back the last of the sunlight.

The hallway appeared empty enough so curiosity got the better of her and Evonne crept her way down. Her knuckles were white from the tight grip she had on the dagger's handle. Reaching her destination, she knelt down and scooped up a bright red gemstone. The stone was uncut and was the size of her palm. Her eyes lit up. She could not even imagine what a stone this size would be worth. Now, she figured, she knew what the dwarves were after here. They must have been mining gemstones from within the island. But how could someone have left behind such a large and clearly valuable stone? Unless…it was dropped. Perhaps someone was in a great hurry to leave here.

A chill ran down Evonne's spine at that thought and she quickened her pace back towards the fortress entrance. Before she reached the first room, she heard it. Not from any one particular direction but from everywhere at once. A scraping sound. The sound of something being dragged along a stone floor. She glanced behind her but saw nothing in the gloomy hallway. She sprinted for the room and a horrific sight awaited her there.

Evonne gasped out loud and froze in place. From out of the second hallway, slithered something from her deepest, darkest, nightmares. It resembled a giant serpent but was much more than that. A thick and long, scaled tail, extended back into the shadows of the hallway. But this serpent had a humanoid torso, with four arms. Four! Each arm ended with a hand that gripped a finely crafted sword, dwarven-made, most likely. Its head was humanoid in shape, with distinctive, serpentine eyes. A forked tongue shot out of scaled lips and Evonne screamed.

*　　*　　*　　*

Vrawg paced back and forth, sweating in the humid jungle. He did not like the idea of Evonne alone inside that ruined fortress at all. This region of the world may be unfamiliar to him but he knew that danger lurked everywhere. He wondered if trolls and wraggoth also made their home underground here as well.

Vrawg did not have faith in the gods above. Surely Blaggrath never had his best interests in mind. But something brought him to this remote island. He was at the storm's mercy, and out of all the places he could have landed, his boat landed here. Evonne had little chance of surviving here on her own. Their survival was still not a sure thing but the little human felt they had a chance. She was familiar with the sea and Vrawg trusted in her to get them to safety with his stolen rowboat.

Despite his heritage and intimidating appearance, Evonne had taken to him and called him friend. That word meant the world to Vrawg. He knew that from this point forward, he would do anything to keep his friend safe.

Vrawg walked back over to the statue of the dwarven god. Dwarves were supposed to be small so he did not understand why this statue was so large. Perhaps the gods were bigger than normal mortals. He regarded the hammer in the god's hand and made the same observation that Evonne had; the hammer was real and made of actual metal, not stone. He admired the superior craftsmanship. He had never seen such a beautiful weapon before. Ogres and wraggoth were poor craftsmen and their weapons were crudely-made.

He also took note that the hammer, forged to fit into the hand of the large statue, would have been the perfect size for his hands.

A scream from inside the fortress gave the half-ogre a start. Evonne was in trouble. He ran towards the entrance but knew he could never get inside unless he was on his hands and knees. What use would he be then?

An idea struck Vrawg and he turned back towards the statue. He placed a booted-foot on the stone god and using every ounce of strength he could muster, he tore the hammer from Horgar's hand. The hand, and a portion of its arm, crumbled to pieces. For a brief moment, Vrawg lamented the damage he had done to such a magnificent piece of work, but Evonne was in trouble.

Hammer in hand, he ran to the fortress entrance and smashed the top of the door's archway. If the entrance was too small, well, he would just have to make it bigger.

*   *   *   *

Evonne ducked under the first sword-swing and rolled to the side, avoiding the second and third attack. All four arms worked in unison and the former pirate had no idea how to face such a foe. She held her dagger but the blade was far too short to match the serpent-man's blades. Its tongue flicked with excitement as it pursued the female human around the room.

The creature maneuvered itself in order block Evonne's path to the entrance. A loud *boom* echoed through the room she occupied. It felt as though the entire fortress shook. She wondered if Vrawg had anything to do with that. The sound continued but Evonne's attention was brought back to the dire situation at hand. She hated snakes to begin with and this serpentine nightmare made her skin crawl with revulsion.

It provided her with no time to think as it moved in once more to attack. Four arms swinging four swords. She backpedaled into the wall and then at the last possible moment, ducked under an attack. Sparks flew as two of the swords connected hard with the stone wall. Evonne side-stepped the third blade, taking a minor nick on her left forearm.

She sprinted for the entrance but knew the creature was already in pursuit. Thinking that she would be unable to outrun the serpent-man, she turned and threw her dagger with a loud grunt. Evonne had practiced throwing blades with Dragon for years and that practice paid off. The dagger spun with deadly accuracy and the blade buried itself into the forehead of the serpent-man. It crashed to the floor, lifeless.

Evonne did not even think to retrieve her dagger or scoop up one of the dwarven swords. She turned and ran. Evonne nearly collided with Vrawg who stood in front of the entrance, slamming the dwarven hammer into the archway. Stone chunks rained down but Evonne made it outside unharmed, aside from the cut on her arm.

Vrawg looked at her with concern as she panted with exhaustion. Her eyes suddenly widened but she lacked the energy to shout a warning. From behind the half-ogre, a second serpent-man slithered out of the fortress, with four swords held in its four hands.

Vrawg turned in time, following Evonne's gaze. He roared and swung his mighty hammer. The serpent-man's head exploded and showered the fortress with blood and gore.

Evonne shook her head in amazement. "By Azark's beard." She then turned and ran back into the jungle. "Forget the water, Vrawg. Come on, we are leaving."

CHAPTER 21

Fortunately, the sky was clear and the sea was not as rough as it could be. Evonne and Vrawg, mostly Vrawg, had been rowing for the better part of a day. The island had long ago vanished from sight and now they were just surrounded by the open sea.

Evonne knew their general whereabouts but that did little to help improve her mood. She knew there was no land to be found for days, or even weeks, given their current rate of travel. In their haste to leave the island, they had only taken a small amount of fruit along with them and they had no water. Unless it rained and they could drink the rain water from the boat, they would die of thirst before ever reaching another island. Evonne had also brought the large gemstone she found in the fortress, which, despite its value, was useless to them while lost at sea.

The former pirate cursed their luck. They had found a pond near the dwarven fortress but she refused to remain on that island one moment longer. She had no idea how many of those serpent-men called that island their home. She imagined it was quite a few to have chased away or killed all the dwarves. Vrawg was strong, there was no doubt about it, but she did not think that even he could fight them all.

She sighed as she watched her heavily-muscled friend row the boat in the direction that she had indicated. Using the sun by day and stars by night for navigation, Evonne was hoping they were traveling in the direction of the next closest island but she could not be entirely sure.

She did not like being out on the open sea with only a small rowboat. She felt very vulnerable and found it hard to relax. Although, as much as she hated the boat, she would have swam off that island if necessary. She did take some small comfort in the fact that she was not alone. A smile came to her face when she thought back to Vrawg, attempting to smash his way into the fortress to save her. He hardly knew her but was ready to risk his life for her. Evonne knew from this point forward, she too, would do anything to keep her new friend safe. All they had now was each other.

*   *   *   *

"Alright, alright, enough. Don't you ever sleep?" Evonne asked, annoyingly. "Most of the time you don't say a word and now when I want to sleep you won't shut up."

Vrawg smiled and shrugged.

"You rowed almost the entire day. Take a break and close your eyes. We got a long a way to go yet, my big friend."

"Friend," Vrawg repeated.

"Yes, yes, we are friends. We established this already. Unfortunately for you, you have no choice but to be my friend. You are stuck with me now."

Vrawg picked up his new hammer and admired the way it reflected the moonlight. Despite its size, it felt much lighter than it should have been. It did not appear to have been forged from iron. It was a metal he had never seen before.

"A fine weapon," Evonne commented. "It was forged for a dwarven god. And you weren't struck with a lightning bolt when you took it, so that's good. Grim would be rolling over in his grave if he knew it was in the hands of an ogre."

"Half."

"Right, half ogre. That's still about the oddest tale I have ever heard but if you say it's true…" Evonne lay back down, staring up at the stars. "Do you ever miss your home?"

"No."

"Nothing about it at all?"

Vrawg paused. "Miss Gurtha."

"Your mother?"

"Yes."

"I don't miss my mother and I certainly don't give a damn about my father. I have no fond memories of home. None."

"Now you make."

"Huh? Make what?"

"Good memories."

"Yeah, sure. If we don't die in this boat. Which is a very distinct possibility. My last memories of this world is going to be floating in the middle of nowhere with a half-ogre."

"No. With friend."

Evonne sighed. "I am sorry, you are right. Floating in the middle of nowhere, with a friend. Now I have had about enough of your chatter tonight. Get some sleep, you big oaf."

Evonne closed her eyes and Vrawg smiled an ogre-sized smile. He was exhausted but he decided to watch his little friend sleep for a while longer.

*　　*　　*　　*

Three days at sea had put Evonne in a most sour mood. There was not a cloud in the sky and the sun beat down on the pair relentlessly. Vrawg was kind enough to give his little friend his tattered leather vest so Evonne could shield herself as best she could from the sun. Both of their mouths were parched and there appeared to be no rain in the immediate future.

Strong waves had also pushed them way off course, despite Vrawg's attempt to keep rowing them in the right direction. The sea was just too powerful and they were at its complete mercy.

Later that afternoon, on the third day, Vrawg spotted something off in the distance. He said nothing at first, thinking it a trick of the sun, until the object drew closer and he was sure of what he saw. He nudged Evonne, who had managed to drift back asleep.

"What do you want?"

"Boat."

"Yeah, this is a boat. Our floating grave."

"Boat coming."

Evonne sat up. "Huh?"

Vrawg pointed in the direction of the approaching ship. It was quite large with four massive sails. It was now close enough to make out many men moving about the deck.

"We saved."

Evonne shook her head. She was not so sure about that. The only ships that would be out in this region of the sea would be pirates. This situation could now be worse than slowly dying of thirst. Much worse.

It appeared the ship had spotted them and was making their way towards them at a decent speed. Soon enough, Evonne could read the name of the ship, but she was unfamiliar with the Siren's Call. She knew they were pirates, though, and knew her and Vrawg were in real trouble.

Evonne's mind worked at a furious pace until she had an idea. "Vrawg, do not say a word, let me handle this. No matter what I do, or what I say, you just stand there and don't do a thing. Got it?"

Vrawg looked at her curiously.

"Just nod your head, yes. Don't do or say a thing unless they attack us. If they attack us, feel free to crush as many as you can before we die. And hide this in your belt," she said, handing Vrawg the gemstone.

Vrawg nodded. Evonne's stomach was in knots. She had no weapon and was scantily clad. That was not a good combination for climbing aboard a ship of pirates. A quick death would be desirable in comparison to what could happen.

The Siren's Call came alongside their rowboat and

dropped a rope ladder. Many men peered down at the two
lost strangers but did not say a word. Evonne motioned
for Vrawg to go first and then she quickly followed him up
the ladder. She heard a gasp from the crew as Vrawg went
over the railing and onto the deck. Once she joined her
friend, all eyes were on her. Hungry eyes.

Evonne glanced around, nervously, sizing up the
crew. There appeared to be roughly fifty men above deck,
with possibly more below. It was a fight they could never
win, no matter how big and how strong Vrawg was. The
majority of the men had the bronze skin of southerners.
Zalhandrians. Evonne's desperate idea banked on the
thought that these southerners would have no clue what an
ogre was.

"Well, well, well, what do we have here?" a man
asked, as he swaggered over to stand before the two
strangers.

This man was clearly the captain, Evonne knew. His
bare chest sported several tattoos and a nasty scar ran
from his left ear to his jaw. His black hair and facial
stubble had hints of grey and a jewel-hilted sword hung
from his belt.

"What in the world is that?" he inquired, indicating
Vrawg.

Evonne smiled inwardly as the crew, along with their
captain, seemed completely befuddled by the half-ogre.
Vrawg stood as still as a statue, his war hammer held in
both hands. He was an intimidating sight.

"I am, Yalara, and this is my master, Zog," Evonne
finally spoke, adding a purposeful quiver to her voice.

"Well, Yalara, I am Captain Volos," his eyes scanned
her up and down. "I think I am going to enjoy your

company aboard my ship. What are you doing out here in a rowboat?"

"My master's ship was battered in a recent storm and went down. We are the only two survivors."

"What do you have to say, Zog?" Captain Volos asked. "And pray tell, what are you?"

"Master Zog is a kralex."

"I am speaking to Zog, woman."

"Master Zog does not speak like you or I. My master communicates directly into my mind, like all kralex," Evonne said, referring to a creature she had heard tales of that took human slaves by using mind control.

The captain looked unconvinced. "Speaks into your mind, does he?"

"Yes," Evonne replied, purposefully nervous. "You m-must obey the will of a kralex, or they can d-destroy your mind with only a thought."

"You expect me to…"

"Argggghhhhhhh!" Evonne interrupted the captain with a horrible scream, falling to her knees with her hands pressed against her head.

The captain and the crew each took a step back, watching the spectacle with a hint of concern.

"Please, Master Zog, I was only informing these men of your brilliance. Arggghh, do not punish me, I beg."

Evonne rolled around the deck in apparent agony. Vrawg was confused but did as Evonne had instructed and stood emotionless.

A few moments later, Evonne panted and then got onto her hands and knees. "Master Zog demands safe passage to the nearest port. Be happy that he has plans elsewhere and will not enslave you and your entire crew."

"I don't think that…"

"Arggggh!" Evonne screamed again. "P-please, Master Zog, I told him your wishes. Please torture the Captain instead, not me. I-I am your faithful slave."

Captain Volos visibly paled at that remark. One of the crewmen, a grey-bearded man who had seen many years, approached the captain and whispered something into his ear. Volos appeared shaken. Evonne guessed that the older pirate had also heard tales of the kralex and had imparted some of his knowledge onto his captain.

Volos cleared his throat. "Ah, there will be no need for any hostilities here. We can offer you safe passage, ah, Zog, but our destination is Trollport."

Evonne had to contain her smile. She stood up, rubbing her temples. "Master Zog says that will suffice. We will part ways in Trollport. Oh, and my master demands water."

"Mister Landron, fetch our guests some water."

CHAPTER 22

Purciful Tannis strode into the Dark Mistress tavern with purpose. The main taproom was crowded as usual with pirates and scallywags of all sizes and not an empty seat could be found. Purcy was unconcerned about the lack of seating; he was not here looking for a table to drink at.

He stood in the center of the room and scanned all of the faces. He was disappointed not to find the one person he came seeking.

"You bony, good-for-nothing, wretch. Where is your entourage of bodyguards?"

Purcy turned to face a particularly ugly individual, nearly twice the size of himself. The brute was bald with a bushy black beard and the tattoo of a woman on the left side of his neck.

"Ah, Garrus, I see Captain Riley has let you out of your cage for the evening?"

"Careful, Purcy, I don't see Bromm or your other lackeys around to protect you. How about you hand over the fifty gold pieces you owe me."

"You weren't happy with that crate of weapons? We had a deal."

"There was nothing in that crate but broken and useless weapons. You thought you could swindle me and get away with it?"

"You inspected the swords yourself before making the purchase. It's not my fault that you are not happy with the quality."

"I saw two swords and the two you showed me were not even in that crate. Captain Riley nearly had my head for that."

"I can't imagine anyone wanting that unsightly head of yours, my friend."

Garrus scowled. "You are gonna give me the gold you owe me, after I knock out your rotten teeth."

"You wouldn't dare strike a captain."

"I ain't gonna. I am gonna strike you, you lying dog."

"And I am Captain Purciful, Captain of The Grinning Kraken."

"Liar. Captain Krayne would flay you alive for making that claim."

"Krayne is dead. The Kraken is mine now so you should choose your next words carefully."

Fights in Trollport were a common occurrence. A fist was thrown almost as often as a mug was raised, but to strike a captain brought on serious consequences. Pirate captains were placed above the average man, naturally, and were essentially untouchable.

"You would say anything to get out of a fight. You have always been a coward," Garrus accused.

"Is there a problem here?" a feminine voice interrupted.

"Good evening, Dark Mistress," Purcy said. "Just the person I was looking for."

"I have already had to clean up after six fights this evening, I am not in the mood for another," replied Nagar, the sorceress who owned the tavern.

"Then please inform this awful beast that he threatens a captain in Trollport. A very unwise course of action."

Garrus gave a nod to Nagar. "Dark Mistress, I don't mean to disrespect your establishment but this scrawny dog is claiming he is a captain."

"My sources have confirmed that it is indeed true, Garrus. Captain Krayne is dead and Captain Purciful now commands The Grinning Kraken."

"How did you pull that off? Poison him in his sleep?"

"That is of little consequence. Now if you will excuse us, I have some business with the Dark Mistress."

Garrus pointed a finger towards Purcy's face. "This isn't over between me and you. You owe me."

The large pirate begrudgingly walked away and Purcy turned to the little dark-haired woman. "Good riddance to him and my apologies for making a scene."

"What do you want Pur…Captain Purcy?"

"I was coming by to tell you the good news but I see nothing escapes the ears of the Dark Mistress. I should have known that you would have already been informed."

"How did Captain Krayne die?"

"Does it matter? He was a tyrant that was unfit to command. The Kraken is mine and that is all that matters. The crew supports me."

"Alright, well you have told me your news. I will get back to work, it's a busy night as you can see."

"Let's share a drink in the back to celebrate."

"I am very busy, Captain."

"You never gave me the time of day, Dark Mistress, ever. You told me once to come back and see you when I am a captain. Well, now I am a captain and I want to share a drink with the most beautiful woman in Trollport."

"I am happy for you and flattered but I was not lying, I am quite busy."

"You should never be too busy for a captain. Think of the benefits to allying with the most feared ship in the Western Sea." Purcy looked her over, hungrily. "Give me what I want and I will make you rich and powerful."

Purcy knew that every woman in Trollport fantasized about becoming the favored pet of a successful pirate captain. It meant no more slaving away in a tavern or brothel. They would be respected and wealthy. He knew the Dark Mistress was already greatly respected, and fairly wealthy, but there was room for more. There always was. He knew women were just as greedy as men.

Nagar was silent, processing Purcy's words. The pirate captain grinned, he knew he had her. He, like every other man in Trollport, lusted after the tattooed woman.

"Drinks are on me," he winked. "Your staff can do without you for an hour or so. Let's go in the back."

Nagar slowly nodded and gave him a sly smile. "Alright, Captain. Just an hour, though."

Purcy beamed with excitement and followed the sorceress through a door behind the bar.

Nagar paused in the hallway. "Oh, what did you want to drink?"

"Surprise me. Two of your best bottles."

"Alright. Second door on your left. Get comfortable

and I will join you in a moment."

Purcy was already unbuttoning his shirt as he entered the dark room that the woman had indicated. He could barely see in the pitch darkness when the door closed. Cursing, he fumbled around for an oil lamp.

To his surprise, the room lit up and a familiar voice came from behind him. "Purcy. What a pleasure to see you again."

"You!? How did you get off that island??"

"So, how is my ship? How is Grim doing?"

*   *   *   *

Evonne descended the stairs and joined Nagar and Vrawg in the cellar of the Dark Mistress tavern. "I apologize for the mess in that room," she said, holding a bloodied sabre in her hand.

"No bother at all," Nagar replied. "Where did you find this charming fellow?"

"It's a long story."

"And one I would love to hear."

"Umm, about Purcy…"

"Don't worry about him," the sorceress said, running a finger over the tattoo of the spider on her left forearm. "Ingrid will take care of the body."

"I hope I haven't caused you too much trouble. People did see him here and talking to you."

"People can say what they want. If there is no body there is no crime."

Evonne nodded. "Thank you. That was more for Grim than it was for me."

"I understand. I will miss that dwarf."

"Vrawg, give her the stone."

Vrawg pulled the large gemstone from his belt and handed it to Nagar.

"Can you change that into coins for me?" Evonne asked.

Nagar's eyes widened. "Where did you get this?"

"It's part of that long story."

"I am afraid I don't have easy access to the amount of gold that this would be worth. The man I could deal with won't be back in port for a few weeks, if you can wait."

"We can't wait that long. Just give me what you can and keep the rest."

"The rest would be too much."

"I don't care, you have done a lot for me. And I will need to ask you one more favor."

"Anything."

"Vrawg and I need safe passage out of here. Are there any captains you trust?"

"Where are you going?"

Evonne thought for a moment. "Tauros, I suppose. I don't think I can handle the heat in Zalhandria this time of year. Someone going to Port Bayswater would be ideal."

"Captain Bryce and Captain Cade both owe me a favor and I trust them. Well, as much as you can trust any pirate captain. But they would be your best bet. I will speak with them."

"Thank you. And thanks for this set of clothes but I will need more. Also, Vrawg and I are going to need some weapons and armor. Recommend anyone?"

"The best smithy in port is Bartleby. His shop is over on Crimson Way. Give me an hour and I can have some gold for you. But you owe me a story."

"We will have to hide out here for about a week so you will hear that story." Evonne turned to Vrawg. "But I wouldn't be here right now if it wasn't for his foolishness."

"When I return with your gold, I will bring a few bottles of my finest. Can't wait to hear this."

*   *   *   *

Evonne and Vrawg moved through the busy streets of Trollport in search of the smithy's shop. Evonne wore a dark cloak with the hood concealing her face. She did not wish to be recognized. There was nothing that could make Vrawg less obvious and people stared. The benefit to walking with the huge half-ogre was that crowds parted for them. Folk scrambled to get out of the way of the marching giant. Trollport had its share of large men but Vrawg dwarfed them all.

They turned onto Crimson Way and found Bartleby's place in short order. Evonne entered and bells that were hung on the door chimed to announce their arrival. Vrawg had to bend down and turn sideways to squeeze himself into the shop.

Bartleby walked up to a desk from a back room and Evonne stood in place, her jaw hanging open.

"I said, can I help you two with something?" Bartleby asked for the second time.

Evonne shook her head to clear it. "Sorry, yes. You just reminded me of someone."

Bartleby was a short and stout dwarf with a long black beard and bushy black eyebrows. When he first emerged from the back room, Evonne thought she had seen a ghost. Upon closer inspection, Bartleby and Grim were distinctly different but her mind flooded with memories.

"Are you looking for a new weapon, perhaps? I have plenty to choose from on the wall over there." the dwarf asked.

"Ah, actually we wanted some custom work done. Weapons and armor."

The dwarf eyed Vrawg. "I have nothing that will fit the ogre."

"That's why I said custom work. And he is only half an ogre."

"Well, to outfit the ogre half of him won't be cheap."

Evonne motioned to her friend to present the chest he carried. Vrawg dropped a heavy chest onto the desk in front of the dwarf and opened the lid. Bartleby's eyes sparkled.

"And we need everything within a week."

"A week?" the dwarf snorted. "Custom work takes time."

"Which we don't have. We are leaving in exactly seven days. Is it possible?"

"Perhaps if I didn't sleep for a week."

"I suppose you can do without sleep for one week. We can always take that chest to someone else."

"No, no, I will do it. Follow me into the back, please. I will need to take some measurements from you and your, ah, large friend here."

"Friend," Vrawg repeated with a smile.

Evonne punched him in the thigh. "Don't act foolish. Come on, let's make you look more frightening than you already are."

*   *   *   *

"You two look like a couple of gladiators," Nagar commented.

Evonne and Vrawg, fully outfitted in their new gear, stood in the cellar of the Dark Mistress tavern.

"Why doesn't anything match? On second thought, it looks like you robbed a couple of gladiators."

"I think it looks good," Evonne replied. "Bartleby was short on time so he had to mix and match pieces of armor. Keep in mind he had to custom-make everything. Vrawg was too big for anything he already had and I was too small."

Evonne was not used to wearing armor as pirates rarely did. Someone did not wish to fall overboard while wearing armor and sink straight to the bottom. Since her life as a pirate was now over, she figured she should get used to it.

She did not overdue it, though. Evonne wore a chainmail vest and tasset, with a steel pauldron on her right shoulder. Her left shoulder and arms were bare except for two black bracers and she wore steel greaves on both legs. On her left hip hung a razor-sharp sabre and across her chest were five throwing knives. Slung over her back was a custom-made crossbow which was a little smaller than the average crossbow. A pouch of ammunition sat on her right hip.

Vrawg was a truly intimidating sight. Even more so than usual. He wore spiked pauldrons on both shoulders which ran down to his elbows. Black leather armor covered his chest and thighs, while black, steel greaves protected both shins. He wore a black leather girdle with a skull etched into the front.

"Cost you a small fortune, did it?" the sorceress wondered.

"The entire chest. Bartleby's eyes nearly popped out of his skull when he spied Vrawg's hammer. He offered us enough gold to buy our own warship for the hammer but this giant oaf wouldn't part with it."

Nagar stared at Vrawg with surprise but the half-ogre just shrugged his shoulders.

"He said it has sentimental value. The hammer brings him fond memories of when we first met. I told him I would buy him a hundred hammers but he wouldn't hear of it, the fool."

Nagar laughed. The half-ogre was an interesting character to be sure. She did not think she needed to worry about Evonne with Vrawg by her side.

"So what about this Captain Bryce, we can trust him?" Evonne asked.

"He is still a pirate, of course, but yes I trust him. He owes me. He is traveling straight to Tauros from here and knows to leave you and Vrawg alone. He won't ask any questions. He is expecting you at the first hint of dawn."

"Thank you, again. You have been a tremendous help. I don't know what I would have done without you."

"Oh, you would have thought of something, Evonne. You are definitely a survivor. What will you do now?"

"I don't really know. I just know that I have had my fill of boats, for now. We will need a job of some sort, I suppose. I can only imagine how expensive it is going to be to keep this one fed," Evonne pointed to Vrawg.

"Well, I am going to miss having you both around. Especially Vrawg with his stories," Vrawg smiled. "You should reconsider my offer and stay. You can run the place with me and Vrawg can keep the peace upstairs."

"I appreciate the offer, I really do, but I have had enough of pirates. You can keep them all to yourself."

Evonne had considered paying a visit to The Grinning Kraken before they left. She thought she would like to see Dragon and let him know that she was alright, and to even laugh in her brother's face that she had survived. But she changed her mind. It was far too risky given the amount of supporters that Purcy had aboard the ship. If the crew knew that Evonne was alive, it would not take them very long to link her with the disappearance of their new captain. It was just better for everyone if she was believed dead and they left as quickly as possible.

As the sun began to rise, Evonne and Vrawg, escorted by Nagar, approached the docks and the awaiting Red Reaver. The ship was not nearly the size of the Kraken but it would be faster. The quicker they reached Tauros, the better.

"Farewell, Nagar."

"Farewell, Evonne. Perhaps our paths will cross again someday."

"Perhaps they will."

The sorceress turned to Vrawg. "You take good care of her, you hear?"

Evonne rolled her eyes. "Oh, please, this fool thought the world was flat and he could just row off the end of it. I am gonna have to look after him."

Nagar laughed as she watched the two cross the gangplank to be greeted by Captain Bryce. The sorceress imagined that a road filled with adventure awaited them both.

CHAPTER 23

True to Nagar's word, Captain Bryce and the rest of his crew left Evonne and Vrawg well enough alone. The voyage would be several weeks long, so to eliminate boredom, Evonne had been tempted to help out around the ship. She thought better of it, though, not willing to reveal herself. During the day she kept the hood of her cloak tight about her face. Instead, she passed most of the time by attempting to teach Vrawg games of dice and how to play cards. Dice was simple enough for the half-ogre to learn but he had difficulty understanding the rules of the various card games.

One breezy evening, after giving up at cards, the pair stood by the bow of the boat, watching the stars above.

"No, I don't know the names of all the stars, who could know them all? What do I look like, a scholar from the Ivory Citadel?"

Vrawg looked at her questioningly, unfamiliar with the reference.

"Oh, forget it. What do you care what the stars are

called anyway? Just enjoy the view."

"Where we go?" Vrawg asked, after a moment of silence.

"To Tauros. How many times have you heard that?"

"Then where?"

"Then? I really have no idea. Port Bayswater is a fair-sized city, we could find work there. Though, I don't know what either of us is qualified to do, other than fight."

They stood in silence again while Evonne considered her large friend. She had to imagine that his goals in life were not to just follow some human around.

"You know, Vrawg, you can always go anywhere you want."

He gave her a puzzled look.

"I mean, you are not stuck with me. When we reach Tauros you are free to go anywhere you want. You don't have to follow me around. I will understand if you wish to follow your own path."

Vrawg shook his head and placed a hand gently on Evonne's head. "Friends."

"I know we are friends, you remind me constantly."

"I go with you. Anywhere."

"Alright, big guy, alright. I just wanted to be sure you wanted to stick around with me. I am not always so sweet, just so you know."

"Evonne funny."

The former pirate rolled her eyes. "When we get to port we are gonna have to figure things out fairly quickly. That sack of gold Nagar gave us before we left won't last forever. If you had just sold that silly hammer we wouldn't have to worry about gold at all."

Vrawg held up the massive dwarven hammer. "Good

memories."

"Good memories? I was almost killed by a four-armed snake. That place was a nightmare."

"Evonne island."

"Evonne island? What, you are naming that island after me?"

Vrawg nodded.

"Well, aren't you Mister Creativity. That soft heart of yours will only lead to trouble, mark my words."

Vrawg chuckled. He knew all the tough talk was not the real Evonne. He figured all the bravado was to compensate for her size. She must have had a difficult time being a female, and a small female, trying to survive in a world of pirates. But she had. And she not only survived, but rose to the top. It would take an extraordinary woman to accomplish that.

* * * *

Evonne had known they were in Taurosian waters but it was not until she saw the first buildings of the port in the distance, that she knew exactly where they were. She immediately rushed to the side of the Red Reaver's captain.

"Where are we going? That's not Port Bayswater."

"You are correct, Miss, that is not. We have had a change of plans. This is as far north as we go. We will let you off in Guildburg and then we head south."

"I can't go there."

"Then you can travel to Zalhandria with us, if you have the gold to pay for your meals. Your large friend eats like a horse."

"I was told you would take us to Port Bayswater."

"I said I would take you to Tauros. Guildburg is in Tauros, so I have fulfilled by obligation to the Dark Mistress."

Evonne gazed out at the approaching docks of Guildburg. A flood of awful memories ran through her mind and her heart raced in panic. She never wanted to step foot in that city ever again. They did not have the gold to waste on traveling to Zalhandria and she really had no desire to visit the desert-dominated lands of the south.

Vrawg joined his friend on deck and immediately noticed the change in her demeanor. She looked pale. Well, paler than usual, for a human. He gave her a quizzical look but she ignored him.

As the ship docked and the gangplank was dropped, Captain Bryce approached Evonne. "I am sorry this isn't to your liking, Captain Evonne, but we have urgent business elsewhere. So, this will have to do."

Evonne shot the man a suspicious stare. She had not told him her real name. "My name is Yalara."

"Call yourself whatever you like, now, but I will always know you as Captain Evonne. I recognized you the moment you came on board. Word travels quickly in Trollport. I had heard the whispers that you killed Captain Krayne after challenging him to combat. An impressive feat, if entirely true."

Evonne nodded.

"I always hated Krayne. He sank my first ship many years ago, before you had joined on. So you have my gratitude and respect for that. No matter what that weasel-of-a-man Purcy did to take over, you cannot be stripped of the title, Captain. Nobody will know where you have gone by my lips, have no worry."

Evonne and Vrawg: Bounty Hunters

Evonne shook the man's hand. "My thanks, Captain Bryce. Farewell. Come on, Vrawg, let's go."

*　　*　　*　　*

As much as Evonne hated being back in Guildburg, she was dying for a decent hot meal. The problem was finding a tavern that she had never worked at before. She had bounced around from job to job so much there were not many taverns that had not employed her at one time.

She was surprised at how well she navigated the narrow streets of the port city. Everything looked pretty much as it had when she left. Nothing really changed, except for the faces that passed her by. And those faces were thoroughly transfixed on the giant half-ogre that walked closely behind her. It was not long before a group of five guardsmen approached the pair, hands resting on the hilts of their swords.

"Is there a problem?" Evonne inquired.

"The ogre is with you, is he?" asked the tallest of the guards.

"He is only half an ogre. And yes he is."

"Where are the two of you going, exactly?"

"To find a place to get a hot meal if you wouldn't mind stepping aside."

"Ogres aren't supposed to be in the city."

"Since when? Where are the signs telling ogres to stay away?"

"We don't need signs. The beasts can't read, anyhow."

"You know as well as I do that there is no such rule. Now, this half-ogre has gold to spend and he wishes to spend it in this city. You let every pirate in the Western Sea slink into port against the explicit orders of The Purple King, so I think you can overlook one honest half-ogre."

The five guards exchanged glances with one another. Evonne spied a tavern behind the guards with a name that she did not recognize.

"There. We are going to eat our fill at The Crowded House. You can come watch us if you are so concerned."

"Stay out of trouble," the guard said, pointing a finger at Evonne.

The five men parted to let the strangers through, never taking their eyes off the half-ogre. They did, however, follow the pair to the tavern to wait outside, just in case.

It was around lunch time in the city so the tavern was not as crowded as it might have been in the evening. The folk that were there quickly moved to the far side of the room in a panic as Vrawg entered behind Evonne.

"Alright, everyone can relax. We are only here to eat, same as all of you," Evonne shouted. "Haven't you seen a half-ogre before?" She grabbed a chair at an empty table and grumbled to herself. "Of course you haven't. None of you have ever left this rat-infested city."

It was not until Vrawg took a seat and paid everyone no mind, that they slowly made their way back to their tables and their half-eaten meals. The owner of the establishment somehow found the courage to approach the pair and take their order.

"This is going to be a problem everywhere we go," Evonne said, after downing a mouthful of ale. "Folk just aren't used to seeing your kind wandering around city streets. If they only knew what a softy you really were like I do."

Vrawg put on a mean scowl.

"Oh yeah, real scary. You don't fool me."

Their meals arrived and the pair dug in like a couple of half-starved animals. For the last several weeks they had only eaten the slop that the Red Reaver tried to pass off as food. They sat in silence until both their plates were completely clean.

"Change of plans, big fella. We can't stay here. After our meals digest we are leaving this city."

"Job?"

"Not here. I won't stay here."

"Where go?"

"East, I suppose, or north-east. Tauros is fairly big, there are plenty of other towns and cities to visit. I have never been to any but I vaguely recall the layout of the land."

"Why leave?"

"Too many bad memories."

*   *   *   *

Evonne led Vrawg through a labyrinth of narrow streets. The sights and familiar smells had Evonne feeling like a little girl again, skipping through the streets to find her friends. Only there were no friends to be found. Not here.

Without conscious thought, Evonne took a series of turns until she stopped dead in her tracks, facing a familiar door to a familiar house. She had no intentions of returning here and yet here she stood. Her breathing quickened and her heart pounded inside her chest. The front door to her house looked exactly the same, aside from some further paint peeling off. She could perfectly envision everything beyond that door as if it was only yesterday that she had left.

Vrawg stared at his little friend, noticing her apparent distress. He had wondered why Evonne wanted to leave this city so quickly after only arriving. Now, he had a pretty good guess as to why that was.

The door to the house opened and Evonne sucked in her breath. Her first instinct was to turn and run in the opposite direction but something kept her feet firmly planted in place. A young man exited the home and closed the door behind him. He was tall, much taller than Evonne, but she knew that face immediately. Harlon. Her younger brother did not look so young anymore.

Evonne was about to shout his name but some invisible force held her tongue. She opened her mouth but nothing came out. She realized, then, that she was trembling. She watched Harlon's back as he walked in the direction of the docks. She took note of his clothes, which were well-worn, with a few holes. He appeared in good health but it would seem her family was still in the same financial situation. She imagined Harlon working hard all day at some grueling job, only to bring home his pay to support their father's drinking habit.

When Harlon disappeared from sight, Evonne exhaled a giant breath of air. She turned to her friend. "Come on, let's get out of here."

*   *   *   *

Like most young men in Guildburg, Harlon worked

at the docks, loading and unloading cargo from ships.
Whether it was for legitimate merchants or whether it was
for pirates, it did not matter. Harlon never questioned. He
worked from dawn until dusk, ate dinner, went to sleep,
and then repeated the same routine the following day. He
worked seven days a week. There was no choice in the
matter. With all his siblings gone, he had to support his
mother and lazy father.

This day he was carrying heavy crates from a
merchant vessel to a nearby warehouse. He had just
returned to work from a very brief lunch break. During his
third trip back to the warehouse, he exited through a
doorway in an alley, only to have a strong a hand grab his
shoulder and push him up against a wall.

"What is this…?"

His sentence got caught in his throat as he looked up
at a seven-foot, grey-skinned monster, smiling down at
him. Because of his father, Harlon did not drink, so he was
positive that he was not hallucinating. The creature before
him looked like some gladiator from the fighting pits of
Valdrow.

Vrawg grabbed one of Harlon's arms and then placed
a small but heavy sack into his hand.

"From Evonne," he said in his deep voice.

"W-what did y-you say? Evonne? My s-sister
Evonne? You know Evonne?"

"Friends."

"Is she h-here? Evonne is here in the city?"

"From Evonne," Vrawg repeated, pointing to the
sack.

The half-ogre turned and marched away. Harlon had
so many questions but could not bring himself to chase

after the monstrous stranger. When Vrawg had vanished around a corner, Harlon finally opened the sack to peer inside. His heart skipped a beat. It was filled with gold. By his estimate, there was several months' worth of his salary sitting inside that sack.

"T-thank you," he shouted, but he was alone in the alley.

CHAPTER 24

It was summer in Tauros and it was a perfect day. There was not a cloud in the sky and there was a comfortable, cool breeze. Evonne and Vrawg traveled a road east of Guildburg. The pair could not afford horses, and Vrawg could not ride one anyway, so they walked. They had purchased a small wagon to carry their meager supplies, which Vrawg pulled behind him. Evonne offered to help, though of course, she was glad when Vrawg refused.

Evonne pointed to a farm that sat off in the distance. "Maybe we could work on a farm. What do you think? I am sure any farmer would welcome someone with your strength. And my brains," she added.

Vrawg just shrugged his shoulders. He did not know the first thing about working on a farm.

"We are almost broke so we can't be too picky. We will follow this road to the town of Goldfield. Should only take us a couple of days. If we get desperate enough we can go north and fight in the pits of Valdrow. Good coin in that, if we can survive long enough to spend it, that is.

Or, I may just wait until you fall asleep one night and then sell your hammer for a king's ransom."

Vrawg scowled.

"Oh, don't cry. I can't even lift the bloody thing. But let's not take that option off the table. It's gonna get dark in a couple of hours so we should find a good spot to rest for the night. Don't you whine again about how we should have stayed at an inn tonight. There wouldn't have been a bed to fit you so you would have slept on the floor, anyhow."

Vrawg frowned.

"Yeah, just keep it quiet. No more whining from you."

*   *   *   *

"Hmm, it's a decent-sized town. We could find some work here, you never know. At the very least we can get another hot meal and I will have a bed for the night. You will have the floor most likely but that's better than the ground we have been sleeping on the last few days."

The journey to the town of Goldfield was uneventful. They had not even passed any other travelers along the way. Evonne was dying for a mug of ale and a home-cooked meal. She had also never walked so far in her entire life. Her legs were quite angry with her.

Evonne paused a fair distance from the town's entrance. "Perhaps I should check out the town first and then come back for you. I bet this place is full of country bumpkins. You might not receive the warmest of welcomes. Let me get a feel for the folk."

Vrawg shook his head. He did not like the idea.

"Don't worry about me. I may have lived at sea for a long time but I am still Taurosian. I won't eat without you, in case that is what you are afraid of. I will take a stroll around and come back for you. I doubt The Purple King has any troops stationed here so they probably have their own little militia to keep the peace. Local militias in towns like this don't see a lot of action so they stir up trouble when they shouldn't. And that is usually directed at unwanted strangers. We just gotta be careful."

Vrawg knew he could not argue with Evonne so just shrugged his shoulders. She was clever and did know how to handle herself. He pointed to a large tree just off the road, indicating that he would sit there and wait for her.

The sun was getting ready to set when Evonne walked into the town of Goldfield. She imagined the town got its name from the numerous wheat fields that dominated this area. She spotted a market where merchants were beginning to close their stalls for the evening. Folk milled about the streets and flashed surprised looks Evonne's way. She realized that a woman decked out in armor and armed as she was, was probably not a very common sight in these parts. It was not unheard of but it was rare. Still, people looked and then went back about their business. She did not draw the same attention that Vrawg would.

She passed a few merchants who were packing away their goods for the day and decided to get some useful information about Goldfield, along with the neighboring towns and cities. Evonne learned that Goldfield was a largely agricultural town with not much else going on. Unless she and Vrawg did wish to work on a farm, there would not be many other employment opportunities here.

Once the sun had set, Evonne realized she had been talking longer than she had originally planned. She figured Vrawg would be getting worried so it was time to go find him. As she set off in Vrawg's direction, another merchant stopped her.

"Hello, Miss? I couldn't help overhearing your conversations with the other merchants. You are looking for work, are you?"

"I am. For me and my friend."

"Well, I am headed to Valdrow in two days and could use some help along the road."

"Help?"

"Well, yes, protection. I have five wagons and seven horses. I hired five men to escort me here from Beldover but three of them have since gone to Guildburg, leaving me a little short. Bandits operate on the roads in this region. You look, well, ah, you look as though you can handle yourself. Though, I am not sure about your friend."

"Oh, don't worry about my friend, he can handle himself quite well. How many days to Valdrow?"

"About five, without trouble and with cooperating weather."

"And the pay?"

"I can pay you and your friend twenty pieces of gold each, for a successful trip."

Evonne rubbed her chin. It was not really a lot of gold but her and Vrawg needed to make an earning somehow. She figured escorting this merchant to Valdrow was easy enough and she could not imagine bandits willing to rob them after getting a good look at Vrawg. Also, Valdrow was a larger city where they could find other employment opportunities.

"Meals are included?" she asked.

"Naturally."

"Deal."

"Excellent, my dear, ah…"

"Evonne."

"Excellent, Evonne. If you will just meet me here in the market at dawn in two days' time, we will begin our little journey."

Evonne nodded and walked away, feeling quite pleased with herself for finding them work so quickly. She could not wait to tell Vrawg of her success.

She spotted a man exiting a tavern with a mug of what had to be ale. The man downed the drink and tossed the mug aside, reminding Evonne as to how thirsty she was. Licking her lips, she thought that one quick drink would not hurt. Vrawg could wait a little longer.

Evonne entered the tavern which was fairly quiet, given that there were quite a few people inside. As expected, all activity ceased as all eyes turned to regard her. She just shook her head and approached the bar.

"Mug of ale, if you don't mind."

The barkeep filled a mug and slid it towards the former pirate. She eagerly grabbed it with both hands but paused before taking her first sip, sensing someone standing behind her.

"You gonna tell me what you want, or you gonna stand there and stare at the back of my head?"

"I'd rather be staring into your pretty eyes, lass," a gruff voice responded.

Evonne sighed. "Look, I am going to drink this ale and leave. I am not here for company."

"You are gonna enjoy my company and if you are

good, I might even pay for that ale."

Evonne turned to face a large man. Not Vrawg large but large for a human. His head was bald and his nose was flat. He was quite unattractive but obviously did not feel that way. A curious thing Evonne took note of was the way the patrons in the tavern were frozen. There was a nervousness in the air that was palpable. She quickly determined that this man must have been the local bully. She had seen his kind many times, living among pirates for as long as she had.

The man took a seat next to her.

"I thought I told you I am not here for company?"

"You haven't had the chance to get to know me yet," he replied with a hideous grin.

"I am only going to tell you one last time. Leave me alone."

With speed that Evonne was not expecting, the man grabbed her by the back of her head and slammed her face into the bar.

"I like the feisty ones," he laughed.

Evonne's vision blurred and she felt the blood flowing from her nose. She thought she was falling off her stool but then realized the man had ahold of her and dragged her to the floor. Evonne attempted to grab one of her knives but her hand was not ready to cooperate. She was dragged across the floor of the tavern until the man kicked open a back door.

She could not make out the details of her surrounding but she felt the coolness of the air and knew that they were outside. Her eyes could still not focus and she still fumbled clumsily in an attempt to arm herself. She cursed herself for being in this situation. She just really did not expect the man to strike out at her as he did in front of so many others.

"What the…? Who in the Abyss are you?" the man suddenly said.

Evonne heard a sickening crunch of bones and something heavy landed on the ground beside her. She shook her head and rubbed her eyes. Finally pulling a knife from its sheath, she attempted to rise, only to stumble back down. She swung the knife wildly but soon realized her attacker was lying motionless on the ground.

As her vision slowly returned, she saw the man's face was a bloody mess. Several of his teeth lay on the ground around his head. She looked up and smiled weakly as Vrawg looked back at her, his face a mask of concern.

"Sorry, big guy. The gods punished me for trying to have a drink without you. I was just so thirsty."

"Evonne, ok?"

"I have had worse injuries."

Evonne finally stood but wobbled on unsteady legs. Vrawg growled and turned his attention back to the prone man. Voices could be heard approaching and Evonne smacked Vrawg in the leg.

"Don't bother with him. If it's the militia, they are gonna want to toss you in a cell for assault. Just let me do all the talking."

Two men came into view. One was wearing armor and a sword, a member of the militia as Evonne had expected. The other she recognized from inside the tavern. Both men suddenly froze in place at the sight of Vrawg.

"Holy Mother Belandria!" the armored man said. "What is that?"

"That is Vrawg," Evonne answered. "He is a half-ogre and he is with me. We don't want any trouble here."

He passed Vrawg with caution to inspect the man lying unconscious on the ground. "Well I'll be damned. Graydon Fink." He turned back to Evonne. "I am Captain Hillsboro of the Goldfield militia. If I can ask for your friend's help here in dragging this scum to a cell, I can see to your reward."

"Reward?"

"Yeah, the bounty on this man's head. I am assuming you two are bounty hunters, no?"

"Ahh…yeah of course we are. Why else would we be here? So how much was this guy worth again?"

"Five hundred pieces of gold to bring him in alive. He has had everyone in this town terrified to raise a hand against him, admittedly, even the militia. Help me get him locked in a cell and I will be more than happy to process your reward this evening."

Evonne smiled ear to ear. "Vrawg, help the good Captain, would you?"

*   *   *   *

Back at Captain Hillsboro's office, Evonne held a bloodied rag to her nose as she scanned the wanted posters on the wall. One face she found particularly interesting due to the one thousand gold-piece price attached to it.

"Who is Tobram Janx?"

"Janx is a rotten piece of filth. He is the leader of the Janx Gang. They are bandits that operate on the roads north of here."

"And these four men here, they are his gang

members?"

"Yes. They are each worth one hundred gold, alive. Janx is the one we really want the most."

Evonne rubbed her chin. "Any idea as to where they could be hiding?"

"Somewhere in the Hadfell Hills, would be my guess. Bandit territory."

"Interesting."

Suddenly, Evonne did not feel like guarding a merchant for a measly twenty gold pieces. Rounding up wanted men seemed much more profitable. Sure, there was danger involved but life as a pirate had prepared her for danger.

Captain Hillsboro placed a small wooden chest on the table in front of Evonne and opened the lid. "Five hundred gold pieces. You can count it if you like."

"Nah, I trust you."

The captain said something else but Evonne was too distracted to hear him. The wheels were turning in her mind as she considered her new career.

* * * *

On the appointed morning, Evonne met with the merchant she had spoken with days before.

"Ah, Evonne, you made it. And where is this friend of yours?"

Evonne pointed in the direction of Vrawg, who was approaching while pulling their wagon behind him. The merchant went pale and nearly fainted.

"You feeling alright?" she asked.

"Is t-that an o-ogre?"

"Nah. Just half an ogre. That's not going to be a problem, is it?"

"Is he…is he civilized?"

"What kind of question is that? Most humans I have encountered aren't civilized. I was in this stinking town for an hour and nearly got my nose broken. You can trust him not to eat you, if that's what you are really worried about."

"I don't see a problem then."

"But, there is a change of plans."

"How so?"

"We are only accompanying you as far as Silvertree Road."

"But I am going to Valdrow."

"I know but we ain't. You don't have to pay us anymore we will just share the road together until that point. Then my friend here and I are heading into the Hadfell Hills."

"The Hadfell Hills? Are you mad? That's bandit country."

Evonne smiled. "It sure is."

CHAPTER 25

"Would you quit your whining already? Where else can we earn that much gold so quickly? You tell me."

Vrawg sighed.

"Look, I understand your concern for me but trust me, you ain't the only one of us who can fight." Evonne rubbed her nose. "Those five hundred gold pieces made the pain in my nose vanish fairly quickly. I will gladly trade a broken nose for that much gold any day of the week."

The pair sat together in a large wagon pulled by two horses, a short distance behind the merchant in his own wagon. Up ahead rode two other men who were hired protection. They had received word that the Janx Gang had struck again only two days ride north of Goldfield. That was just about the point where Evonne and Vrawg would part ways with the merchant and venture off the road.

Vrawg was not thrilled by the idea. He was no coward but he worried about the safety of his petite friend. He had encountered bandits in the past and they were a nasty lot.

Vrawg knew that Evonne could talk tough but he had yet to see her in action. He was unaware of her skills with a blade or crossbow. He just recalled the shape she was in when he happened to stumble across her and Graydon Fink behind that tavern. Evonne had taken too long to return from the town so Vrawg had gone looking for her. Fortunately for her, he arrived when he did.

"It's a thousand gold pieces if we bring in this Janx fellow. Do you know how much that is? Of course not, look who I am talking to, you can't count. Well it's a lot. This bounty hunting could be even more profitable than piracy."

"How?"

"How, what?"

"How we find Janx?"

"Don't worry about that. He is going to find us."

*   *   *   *

Evonne sat huddled alone by the fire to keep warm. The sun had disappeared hours ago and despite it being summer, there was a chilly breeze this night. Behind her sat a large covered wagon. She was a good two-hour trek from the main road into the region known as the Hadfell Hills. The merchant called her mad one more time before they parted but he was appreciative for their free company this far.

Crickets and night owls provided the only soundtrack this night, along with the crackle of the fire. Evonne tossed another piece of wood into the flames to keep it going. She wanted the fire as big as possible, in order to get noticed.

The terrain here was very hilly with a thickly wooded area not too far from Evonne's campsite. She was hoping the glow from the fire would travel a far distance. Just as her patience was wearing thin, a voice spoke from the darkness.

"Raise your hands above your head, woman, and stand up."

"Who do you think you are to tell me what to do?" she answered back, scanning the darkness but could see nothing.

An arrow lodged into the ground, directly in front of her feet. "I hold your fate in my hands so I would do as I was told if I were you. Unbuckle that sword belt and drop it to the ground."

Evonne did as she was instructed and dropped her sword on the ground.

"Now slowly remove those knives from across your chest and drop them too. Then the one from your right boot. Then the one from your back."

Evonne sighed but one by one, removed each weapon and dropped it.

"Good, now take ten steps forward."

She did. A lanky man holding a sword stepped from the shadows to her right. His voice was different from the other.

"Well, well, what brings such a delicious sight into these hills? Are you lost, little girl?"

"I ain't little."

"Excuse me," he laughed. "Where is the rest of your group?"

"It's just me."

"And what would just you be doing in these parts,

huh?"

"That's none of your business."

"I am making it my business."

Evonne just spat on the ground.

The bandit frowned. "Erlick."

Another arrow landed a mere inch from Evonne's left foot and she correctly guessed that Erlick was the hidden archer.

"Erlick here can hit a fly on a tree from a hundred yards away. Unless you want to be short an eye, little woman, start talking."

"I am looking for bandits."

"Found some, you did. Why?"

"I want to join a gang."

The man laughed. "You? A little woman?"

"I told you, I am not little."

"Just because you dress the part, doesn't make you a bandit. Why do you want to become a bandit?"

"I've run afoul of the law. I need to hide somewhere but I also still need to make a living."

"What's in the wagon?"

"None of your business."

"Erlick…"

"Alright, alright. Some blankets and alcohol. I robbed a merchant on the way to Valdrow."

"Not bad. Well, little woman, that wagon and your weapons are now ours. Run along."

"No."

"No?"

"That's what I said, no. I didn't do all that work to hand this over to just anyone."

"Well, you don't have a choice in the matter."

"Fine. But just know that you will be stealing from Tobram Janx."

"Stealing from Tobram Janx? And how do you figure that?"

"Because I want to join the Janx Gang. This wagon here is a gift for Janx. So, by my reckoning, if you steal this wagon from me, you are also stealing it from Janx."

Another man stepped from the shadows. "I like her. She's got courage, I'll give her that. So, you are giving this wagon to Tobram Janx, are you?"

"That was my plan."

"Well, you are looking at him."

"Tobram Janx?"

"In the flesh."

"I have heard so much about you. I am honored."

Erlick, the archer, finally stepped from the shadows as well and lowered his bow. The three men approached Evonne to look her over.

"Your armor looks expensive. Your weapons too," Janx commented.

"I was a sellsword until I assaulted some guards in Valdrow."

"A sellsword? What did people hire you for, little woman?" the other bandit asked.

Evonne narrowed her eyes. "Looks can be deceiving. You would be surprised."

"Don't mind Cobin," Janx said. "He is always mouthy. So, this wagon is mine, is it?"

"All yours."

"And there is drinks in there?"

"Thirty bottles of Taurosian whiskey."

"Well then, let's have a look and crack one open, shall

we?"

Tobram Janx grabbed the tarp that covered the wagon and threw it aside. To his surprise, he did not find thirty bottles of Taurosian whiskey, all he found inside the wagon was an angry half-ogre.

Vrawg growled and punched Janx in the face, breaking his nose and knocking out several teeth. The bandit leader fell to the ground unconscious. Cobin shrieked at the sight of Vrawg and stumbled backwards, falling. Erlick had enough sense to turn and run.

Evonne grabbed her loaded crossbow from inside the wagon and took aim. She pulled the trigger and Erlick cried out. It was a perfect shot to the back of his right leg, sending the bandit to the ground where he rolled about in pain.

Vrawg climbed out of the wagon and approached Cobin, who cowered on the ground.

"Vrawg, go see to the archer. Leave this one to me." Evonne picked up her sword and pointed it at the bandit. "Come on, Cobin, stand up. If you can beat this little woman, you can go free."

Cobin looked, nervously, between Evonne and Vrawg.

"Don't worry about him. This is just between you and me."

Cobin rose, slowly, with his sword in hand. He glanced once more at Vrawg, and when he was satisfied that that monstrosity was occupied with Erlick, he smiled. He figured he could run this mouthy little woman through and make a break for the woods.

The bandit lunged forward, hoping to drive his blade straight through Evonne's stomach. Evonne stepped to the right, avoiding the attack and countering with her own, slashing the man across his left thigh. Before he regrouped, she skipped behind him and slashed the back of the same leg. Cobin spun around with a clumsy strike and received a nasty gash to his right leg. Unable to stand any longer, he crumpled to the ground with an angry grunt.

Evonne smacked the weapon from his hand and pressed the tip of her sword against Cobin's throat. "Looks like you just got beat by a little woman. I guess you don't go free."

*   *   *   *

Merchants and townsfolk, alike, gathered in the streets of Goldfield to watch two bounty hunters pulling a wagon full of wanted bandits. Their jaws hung open in astonishment at the large one who was pulling the wagon. Some folk recognized these two as the pair who captured Graydon Fink and others were seeing them for the first time. Rumors sped through the town as to who these bounty hunters were and where they had come from. They were a complete mystery. As frightening as the ogre was, the townsfolk viewed him as a hero. Ridding them of Fink and Janx just earned him their respect and admiration.

It did not take long for folk to set aside their fears and approach the two bounty hunters, thanking them and offering to buy them drinks. Evonne looked up to find Vrawg smiling. She knew the big oaf was excited to have humans actually happy to see him. This bounty hunting may just be their calling, she thought.

They stopped in front of Captain Hillsboro's office and the captain came out to greet them. "Evonne, I thought you were honestly joking when you said you were going into the hills to get Janx."

She smiled. "Tobram Janx. Cobin Larratt. Erlick the Archer. I believe that's twelve hundred gold pieces?"

"Yes, that is correct."

"Erwall Shant was not with them at the time. My apologies."

"That's quite alright. Shant and some of the others are nothing without Janx. Now, it is going to take me a few days to process this and get your reward. I hope you both are alright with waiting?"

Evonne glanced around at all the eager townsfolk who were willing to buy them meals and drinks. She figured a few days of waiting would not hurt.

*　　*　　*　　*

Later that same day, Evonne and Vrawg had eaten and drank their fill at one of the taverns in town. The tavern was filled near to capacity with folk wishing to meet the two bounty hunters. The women in the town were especially interested in seeing Evonne. Word had spread quickly that one of the bounty hunters was a female and as tough as any man in town.

After hours of dull conversations and endless questions, the pair found a rare moment alone. "See, I told you this was a good idea. Do you realize how hard it is to earn that much gold? Damn near impossible. But we did it within a matter of days. Think of how much we could make in a year."

Vrawg nodded. He knew Evonne was clever and now he knew she was also a skilled fighter. He had watched her handle that bandit as if he was a child and she had also used that crossbow of hers with amazing accuracy. Vrawg learned that Evonne was just as tough as she said she was. Perhaps they could make a good living from hunting down wanted criminals. He certainly enjoyed the attention and admiration he was getting from the humans in this town. For once people were not running in fear or threatening him with weapons. If Evonne wanted them to be bounty hunters, then they would be bounty hunters. He would follow her anywhere.

"Now, Captain Hillsboro does not have any other bounties worth pursuing here," Evonne continued. "But he assured me every city and town in Tauros would have some wanted posters up. As soon as we get paid we head for Valdrow and see what's up there for us. Sound alright with you?"

A group of children had finally gotten the courage to approach the half-ogre and poke at him. Evonne had pushed some of the annoying little buggers away but Vrawg was in his glory. He nodded to his friend. It sounded like a great idea to him.

CHAPTER 26

The icy wind swept in and bit at the skin of Evonne's exposed face. She pulled her white fur cloak tight around her body to keep the wind at bay as best she could. She knew that being this high up on the mountain was going to be cold, only she did not think it was going to be as cold as it was. Up ahead, Vrawg marched on, seemingly unconcerned. Many portions of his grey skin were exposed to the elements but the cold had little effect on the half-ogre who had grown up in similar conditions.

The path they followed was narrow and each time Evonne hazarded a glance over the side, her stomach rose up into her throat. She did not do well with heights. If it was not for her armor and thick cloak weighing her down, she figured the wind would have carried her over side long ago. Vrawg, on the other hand, had no such worries.

The pair wound their way up the side of the mountain for another hour before the path they followed ended with the entrance to a cave. Evonne signaled for Vrawg to stop and keep his distance from the entrance.

"I have to rest a moment and catch my breath. We don't all have an ogre's endurance here."

The pair stood in silence, watching the cave entrance, intently, until Evonne felt she had adequately recovered from their long trek.

"Let's hope the information we got from that wanderer is correct. I would hate to think we came all this way for nothing. Stay alert, big fella, you ready?"

Vrawg nodded and pulled the war hammer off his back to hold in both hands. Evonne held her crossbow at the ready and followed Vrawg into the cave. She did not bother carrying a lantern as they noticed torchlight coming from within. Evonne was pleased that the cave was tall enough for Vrawg to enter as she had no real desire to go inside alone.

The floor of the large cave was covered in various animal furs, such as bears and wolves. The skulls of many small animals hung from the ceiling, all tied together, swaying in the wind, clinking together like some macabre wind chimes. Three torches were mounted on the wall with their flames flickering.

The torches were not the only source of light, though. A fire burned in the center of the cave, upon which sat a large black cauldron. Behind the cauldron stood a small cloaked individual, stirring the contents of the pot with a large wooden spoon. The cave's inhabitant looked up to regard the arrival of the bounty hunters and Evonne cringed from the face that peered at them from within the hood of the tattered black cloak.

The hag was every bit as hideous as the reports had said. Her long crooked nose had many warts and she smiled with blackened teeth. Her eyes were milky-white and sent shivers down Evonne's spine. Evonne had seen many strange things in her life so she did not take it lightly that this woman was said to be a witch with terrible powers. She would never have bothered to hunt down a witch living high up in a mountain, if it were not for the five thousand gold-piece price on her head.

The hag was said to be a jealous and vindictive old crone, taking out some misplaced anger on the beautiful women in the region around the mountain. Some women had been poisoned and others had been cursed, causing their faces to become blistered and disfigured. When the wife of the nearby town's mayor became the hag's next target, the large bounty was posted on her head. It was said a few bounty hunters had thought to collect but were never heard from again.

Evonne aimed her crossbow at the old hag while Vrawg slowly circled to her left. He tossed a pair of iron shackles that landed beside the woman.

"Pick up those shackles and put them on. You are going for a little walk," Evonne commanded.

The hag cackled and sent a new wave of shivers down Evonne's spine.

"We can do this the easy way or we can do this the hard way. The choice is yours."

"You've got a pretty face," the woman said, with a raspy voice; a grotesque smile widening from within her hood.

"I will only say it one more time. Pick up the shackles and put them on."

The woman only cackled some more, so Evonne aimed her crossbow at one of her legs and pulled the trigger. The hag vanished in a puff of black smoke and

Evonne's bolt struck some furs on the floor.

"Where did she go? Vrawg, do you see her?"

The hag reappeared behind Evonne and grabbed the bounty hunter, spinning her around with supernatural strength. "Give me that pretty face of yours."

A withered hand, with long black nails like talons, reached for Evonne's face. The bounty hunter panicked and kicked the old crone but it had little effect. Vrawg roared and threw his hammer, causing the witch to vanish again with a puff of smoke. His hammer bounced off the cave wall.

Evonne breathed a sigh of relief and quickly reloaded her crossbow, turning in circles in search of the hag. The woman was suddenly standing behind her cauldron once more. Evonne raised her crossbow and the hag opened her cloak. She cackled as a swarm of black bats flew from the folds of her cloak. Evonne yelped as the bats crashed into her, flapping wings striking her in the face. The bounty hunter stumbled backwards, attempting to swat them away.

Vrawg ran at the hag. He reached for her head but his hand closed over nothing as she vanished again. This time she reappeared on the half-ogre's right shoulder and dug her talon-like nails into the exposed flesh of his neck. Vrawg reached for her but she was gone. The half-ogre tripped on some furs and tumbled away as the hag stood behind the cauldron once again.

The bats had all scattered and flew out through the cave entrance. Evonne thought she noticed a pattern and formulated a quick plan.

"Vrawg, by the cauldron! Grab her!" she yelled.

Vrawg stood and dove at the hag, but as Evonne

expected, she vanished. Evonne looked about frantically until she spotted the cackling old crone standing in a far corner. She raised her crossbow and took aim.

"Now I got you."

Only, Evonne did not pull the trigger at that moment. The hag vanished again and Evonne quickly aimed her weapon towards the cauldron. She waited a brief moment and then pulled the trigger. As the witch reappeared behind the cauldron, Evonne's bolt struck her in the shoulder and she fell back with a shriek. Evonne noticed that each time the hag appeared somewhere else in the room, she returned back to the cauldron the very next time. The bounty hunter gambled that she would reappear behind the cauldron once more and she had been correct.

Evonne reloaded and approached the hag who lay on the floor, screeching. "Vrawg, chain her and gag her."

* * * *

"Damn it, Drew, you are cheating again, I know it," Kris accused.

"To the Abyss with you, I am not."

Kris threw his cards on the table and stood. "I refuse to play one more round with this cheater."

"You just don't like losing. You are a sore loser."

"I don't like losing when someone is always cheating me out of my coins."

Neville shook his head in frustration. "Will the two of you just shut up? Kris, sit your ass back in that chair and let's finish this game."

"No, I am done playing with him."

Drew threw his cards on the table. "Fine, game's

over. Happy now, you child?"

Kris inched his hand towards the handle of a dagger he wore on his belt. "Careful. I don't take kindly to being cheated or being called names from that cheater."

"What do you plan on doing about it?"

The door to the small dwelling opened and another man entered, closing the door quickly behind him.

"Thank the gods you are back," Neville said. "These two are driving me nuts and are about ready to kill each other."

"I hope you weren't followed," Kris added.

"I leave for a few hours and you all can't get along?" Raylon answered.

Kris threw up his hands in frustration. "How long do we have to stay here for? I am getting mighty sick of only seeing your ugly mugs every day."

"Maybe another couple days. Four max," Raylon replied. "We just have to be completely sure the heat is off before we try and leave this city."

"What's it like out there? Folk still talking about the robbery?" Drew wondered.

Raylon nodded. "You bet they are. The city has been crawling with patrols and they even have the dogs out, sniffing every alley. This is the best place for us, they will never find us here."

"They better not. I have a lot of plans for my share of that gold," Kris said.

"Well, if you would stop accusing everyone of cheating and just sit tight for a few more days you will have your chance to spend that gold," Neville commented.

"I won't have any gold left to spend if that bastard right there keeps cheating me out of it," Kris pointed to

Drew.

"Boys! Boys! You gotta…"

A loud knock at the door cut Raylon off in mid-sentence. In fact, it sounded as if the door was about to collapse. Three of the men pulled daggers and the fourth, Kris, retrieved a sword that was leaning against a wall.

"Who in the Abyss would that be?" Neville dared to whisper.

"Alright, gentlemen, exit that house with your hands raised in the air, real slow like," a female voice shouted from outside.

"Curse you, you were followed," Kris accused Raylon.

Raylon ran to the window and peeked around the drawn curtain. "Ulshaba save us. It's Evonne and Vrawg."

"What?"

"Are you sure?"

"Can you see them?"

"I can see Evonne. She is in the middle of the street behind an overturned wagon. Her crossbow is aimed at the door."

"And Vrawg? What about Vrawg? Can you see him?" Drew asked, panic evident in his voice.

"I can't see Vrawg but who do you think nearly bashed that damn door down?"

Neville turned pale. "I feel sick. We have to give up."

Kris did not agree. "Give up? You coward. You wanna just throw away all this gold we are sitting on? There is four of us and only two of them."

Raylon turned away from the window. "Maybe you didn't hear me. I said it's Evonne and Vrawg."

"I heard you. And that is still four against two."

"That bloody ogre is worth four men at the least."

"We have to give up," Neville repeated. "Look, we never killed nobody. We will get what? Six months in a cell? Maybe a year? That sounds a whole lot better than having all my bones broken by that ogre."

"I'm with him," Drew agreed.

Raylon stood in silence while weighing their options. There was no backdoor to this place which meant they would have to go out the front and fight their way to freedom. That meant getting past a giant ogre while trying to avoid getting shot by that wicked wench and her crossbow. The odds were stacked heavily against them.

Raylon dropped his dagger and his shoulders sagged in defeat. "We have to give up unless you want to live as a cripple for the rest of your life. Or wind up dead. I, for one, wish to remain in one piece."

"I am only going to say it one more time," Evonne shouted from outside.

"Alright, you evil harpy. We heard you," Raylon answered. "We are coming out."

"No weapons and your hands where I can see them."

"Yeah, yeah."

Neville and Drew dropped their weapons and followed Raylon, slowly, out the front door. Kris hesitated, but for only a moment. He had heard tales of Evonne and Vrawg and had no desire to test his luck on his own. The gold they acquired from the robbery was supposed to change his life. Kris never wanted to return to his job of patrolling streets and telling people where they could and could not park their wagons and horses. But that gold would do him no good if he was dead. He threw down his sword and followed the others.

CHAPTER 27

Evonne and Vrawg walked through the streets of Ironcliffe in awe. Ironcliffe was the largest city in Tauros and the capital. It was the seat of power for The Purple King and his magnificent castle sat up high on a rocky hill, overlooking the immense city. Neither of the two bounty hunters had ever seen a city this size.

For the last couple of years, the pair traveled and worked all over Tauros but avoided the capital. Nothing good was ever said about The Purple King. Folk said he was mad. A raving lunatic. More people were hung in the capital than in any other town or city in Tauros, combined. Evonne had always just thought it was best to avoid Ironcliffe and its politics. Now, though, they had been summoned.

Evonne took in the sights and smells of the city. It was nothing like Guildburg at all. Most notably, there was no smell of fish in the air. Vrawg even appeared smaller, if that was possible, against the backdrop of the impressive city. Buildings here were so much taller. The architecture was unparalleled anywhere in Tauros and the castle was breathtaking to behold.

Knights in gleaming plate armor patrolled the busy streets in groups. Evonne and Vrawg even had their own escort. Evonne was not entirely sure if the escort was for the sole courtesy of guiding them to their meeting, or to keep a close eye on Vrawg. The half-ogre was widely accepted in places around Tauros but was still watched with a cautious eye.

Vrawg loved visiting different cities. It was so obviously different from the mountain caves that the ogres lived in. He found it hard to believe that humans could be capable of building such giant structures to dwell in. Nothing was built to his size, though, which made visiting various inns and taverns a challenge for the giant half-ogre, but he never once complained.

Evonne had made the right decision when she suggested the two of them become bounty hunters. It allowed Vrawg to gain the trust of the common people. They were not popular with criminals, for obvious reasons, but Vrawg could not care any less about them. They made their choices in life and he never regretted dragging any of them in to face justice. Folk still stared and he knew that would never change. He learned to ignore it and just go about his business.

The two bounty hunters followed their armored escort through the winding streets of Ironcliffe until they reached a building that sat at the bottom of the hill which housed the castle. It was clearly a government building and many more of the city's knights were stationed around it.

They were directed to enter the building and two knights guided them into a small office, where they stood guard inside the door while Evonne and Vrawg took a seat at a desk. The seat groaned underneath Vrawg's weight and threatened to collapse. The half-ogre elected to stand.

They did not have to wait long before a thin, expensively-dressed, middle-aged man, strolled into the room and took a seat opposite them at the desk. His black hair was perfectly combed and his thin black beard was neatly trimmed.

"Good day, I am Falvo, representative of the King. Please, ah, Vrawg, have a seat."

"He doesn't wanna break the chair and end up on his big behind," Evonne answered. "So what does The Purple King want with us?"

Falvo shook his head, disapprovingly. "We don't say, The Purple King, here. He is, the King."

Evonne had forgotten that little tidbit of information. The King had a real name, of course, everyone did, but it was not used or even widely known. When the man took power he just called himself the King. The Purple part of the name was just a nickname given by folk for the King's penchant for wearing purple.

"My apologies, what does the King want with us?"

"The two of you have quite the reputation at being good at what you do. Your work has not gone unnoticed. We wish to enlist your aid in eliminating an unscrupulous individual for us."

"Eliminating?"

"Yes. We wish for this person to cease existing."

"Vrawg and I are not assassins. We do not eliminate people."

The man looked confused. "Are you not bounty hunters?"

"Yes, we are. We bring in people alive to face justice."

"What's the difference if we hang him or if you just shot him in the head with your crossbow?"

"Because hanging him is on you. I am not a judge to say whether he is guilty or not. We will bring him in so a judge can decide his fate."

"Fine. Whatever. Bring this person here and we will remove his head."

"Who is he?"

"They call him The Collector. A wicked moneylender who has a practice of asking for unreasonable terms when lending money. More often than not, customers are tortured and murdered when payments cannot be made on time. The Collector then holds family members responsible for the debt or they too receive the same fate."

"What makes this person so hard to find?"

"We don't have a name or even a face. He wears a featureless white mask when dealing with anyone. He operates throughout the entire city and we have been unable to pinpoint any type of hideout or base of operations. All efforts to locate this man have so far failed."

"What's he worth?"

"Ten thousand gold pieces."

Evonne whistled. "Nice. But seems like a lot of investigative work. We could end up wasting a lot of time here."

"We will even be willing to remove the price on your head."

"Excuse me?"

"Are you not the same Evonne who served under Captain Krayne aboard The Grinning Kraken? A pirate and outlaw? Scourge of the Western Sea?"

Evonne was speechless.

"That's what I thought. If you ever visit Port Bayswater or Denbrannon, you could find a wanted poster with your lovely face on it. Now, your work throughout Tauros has been commendable which has caused us to turn a blind eye to your past. But if you want it permanently erased, then bring us The Collector. Or, you may find yourself on trial."

*   *   *   *

Evonne sat at the bar, stewing. Two weeks had gone by and they were no closer to finding this Collector than they were when they first arrived in Ironcliffe. It was almost like he was a myth. Just a rumor whispered through the streets. Watch out or The Collector will get you. She and Vrawg had tried all of their usual information gathering techniques to no avail. If there really was a Collector, nobody was giving him up.

Evonne knew from the beginning that this was not going to be an easy job. Under normal circumstances, she would not have accepted, but Falvo had her over a barrel. In the past, she had often wondered if there had been a price on her head. She knew, undoubtedly, there was one on Krayne's head. He was one of the most sought-after pirates in history. So, it made sense that his crew would all have prices on their heads. Evonne wondered what the drawing of her face would look like on a wanted poster. She was curious about how accurate it would have been. She just figured that enough time had passed that all that would have been forgotten. But it would seem The Purple

King did not forget.

"Is that *the* Evonne sitting at that bar? The famous Evonne?"

She did not recognize the voice so turned to face the speaker. She may not have recognized his voice but that face was fairly well known. Skald was a bounty hunter with quite the reputation as well, though he tended to operate only within Ironcliffe and the surrounding areas. Many deep scars criss-crossed his face but it was a particularly deep one in the top of his bald head that made him so readily recognizable. At some point in the man's life, someone had attempted to cleave his head in two with an axe, but unfortunately for them, Skald had not died. Evonne imagined that the axe-wielder was made to regret not killing the bounty hunter. He was tall, a few inches over the six-foot mark, and generally was never seen without his giant dog, Brandy. Brandy was not permitted in this particular tavern, so Skald stood alone.

Evonne nodded. "You know it is, Skald."

"I don't believe we have ever formally met."

"No, I don't believe we have."

"What brings you to Ironcliffe?"

"Ah, you know, just wandering through. Between jobs at the moment."

"Do you usually spend two weeks in a place you are just wandering through?"

Evonne snickered. "Needed a break. This city has everything. Lots of places to drink."

"You won't find The Collector in here."

"The who?"

"Don't play me for a fool. I know why you are here. I've tried to find him myself with no luck. Ten thousand gold is a lot of coin. Just give up while you can. If I couldn't catch him what chance does a tiny woman have?"

"I thought they didn't allow dogs in here?"

"They don't."

"Then why I am talking to Brandy's pet and not with Brandy herself?"

"Speaking of pets, where is this pet ogre of yours? I wanna see if this big bad Vrawg is as big as everyone says he is."

"See for yourself," Evonne smiled as Vrawg chose the perfect time to return to the tavern.

Skald turned and visibly paled as he had to look up to see Vrawg's grinning face. The half-ogre was every bit as big and frightening as everyone said he was. Skald nodded to him and excused himself from the tavern. Vrawg fixed his partner with a curious look.

"Ah, forget about him. Big-headed bounty hunter is all. What we do have to worry about, though, is how to find this Collector. I am thinking we need a change of tactics. I believe some undercover work is necessary."

Vrawg tilted his head.

"Not for you, you big oaf. The only thing you could disguise yourself as is a building. Our usual tactics are never going to work here. Nobody is going to willingly talk. So, I have an idea."

*   *   *   *

Evonne moved through the rowdy crowd and immediately second-guessed her decision to be there. The secret underground den was a host to Ironcliffe's criminal class. Even though she wore a black wig and kept the hood of her cloak pulled tightly around her face, she worried about being recognized. She had already spotted several men with smaller bounties on their heads and if anyone ever did recognize her as a bounty hunter, she knew this crowd would tear her to pieces.

The location of this den was not widely known and entry was granted by invitation only. Evonne had spent the better part of two weeks, undercover as Yalara, before her patience had paid off. She had to go it alone and that was what made this mission quite dangerous. She had seen very little of Vrawg these last two weeks as she needed to make her role as the lonely widow, Yalara, believable. Vrawg was strongly against her coming to this place alone but Evonne had told him that she was only going to scout it out. She could not have told him what she really had planned.

To receive an invitation, Evonne had to feign some interest in a particularly greasy individual. His presence made her skin crawl and she was always forced to suppress her urge to vomit. But he had been easily manipulated with only a few winks and smiles. She only hoped that he was going to live up to the promise he had made her. If she had to spend any more time around him she was going to be forced to remove several of his teeth.

This dimly-lit place, located underneath the streets of Ironcliffe's poorer quarter, was a haven for gamblers. It hosted games of every kind. If something could be wagered upon, it was found here. Evonne moved towards a crowd of cheering people to find that they stood above a fighting pit. Below, a slim, short-haired woman, had just entered the pit to a chorus of cheers.

"Who is that?" Evonne asked a hawk-nosed man beside her.

"Who is that? That's Bareknuckle Heather, that's who."

"Bareknuckle Heather?"

"Yeah, the toughest female pit fighter in Tauros."

"Are there really that many female pit fighters in Tauros?"

"No, there isn't. Which is why Bareknuckle Heather fights men most of the time. And still wins."

Evonne was impressed. That took a lot of guts and no small amount of skill. There is no way she would be jumping into any pit without a sword in her hand.

Someone tapped Evonne on the shoulder. "Yalara?"

It was a short man with shifty eyes, not much taller than Evonne. "Yes, that's me."

"Follow me," the man said, then turned and walked away.

Evonne was slightly disappointed by the man's timing. She was hoping to catch the fight but she was here on business and had already wasted far too much time. Evonne followed the man through the crowd and passed several gaming tables. Card and dice games appeared to be the most popular.

She was led into a small dark room with a table and two chairs. The room had a second door by which to enter. The small man left her there and when nearly an hour had passed, Evonne was about ready to get up and leave. The other door opened then and a large man in a chain mail vest entered first, followed by a cloaked individual wearing a featureless white mask. The Collector. The Collector casually took a seat opposite Evonne while his imposing bodyguard, a brute of a man, stood directly behind him with his muscled-arms folded across his chest.

Evonne's heart beat rapidly. She had heard many tales of The Collector in the month her and Vrawg had been in Ironcliffe. If even half of them were true, then he was indeed a monster. He lent coins to those in dire need and with nowhere else to turn. Those that never paid their debts, and the ridiculous interest he added on top, met their end in skin-shivering fashion.

"Good evening, Yalara," he said, in a most disarming soft voice.

"Good evening," Evonne answered.

"Virgo tells me you are in need of some financial aid?"

"Ah, y-yes, I am."

"I understand your husband just passed?"

"Yes he did."

"And you are looking to start your own business?"

"Yes, a tavern. I am a good cook, the best some say. I have only enough gold to cover half of my starting cost. But I know if I could open my own place, I could make all that gold back in no time. I used to work in a tavern in Valdrow and folk came from all over just for my chicken stew."

"Must have been delicious, indeed."

"That's what I am told."

"Did you have a location in mind?"

"Yes, of course. The owner of the Raven's Roost is looking to sell. I think it would make for a fine location with so much foot traffic near there."

"I think I may just be able to help you out, young lady."

"Oh, brilliant. That is wonderful news."

"I will lend you the gold to get started."

"I cannot thank you enough. I know I will be able to pay you back once everything is up and running. I am very confident."

Evonne imagined a most sinister smile behind that mask. "Oh, I trust that you will, my dear. I am not worried about that at all."

"So, how does it work? Where do we go from here?"

"You will leave me with the total that you require and it will take me a few days to have it ready. You will be contacted when I have the appropriate amount of coins and I will have it delivered to you."

Evonne extended her hand towards the masked man. "Thank you, so much."

The Collector stood and shook Evonne's hand, only Evonne did not let go. She held his hand firmly and yanked him across the table towards her. No weapons were permitted in the gambling den but Evonne had smuggled in a knife hidden underneath the bracer she wore on her right wrist. Holding the knife in her left hand, she pressed the tip under The Collector's chin. The bodyguard lunged forward but Evonne shook her head.

"I would stand still, if I were you. Any further movement and I will cut your employer's throat."

The large man stood his ground.

"What madness is this?" The Collector growled. "Do you realize who I am?"

"Ah, obviously, or I would not be here holding a knife to your throat. A throat that is attached to a head that is worth ten thousand gold."

"You are a filthy bounty hunter?"

"Bounty hunter, yes, filthy, no. I bathed just before coming here."

"You think you will get out of here alive?"

"Well, if I don't, then you don't."

"I will peel the skin from your body while your eyes are pinned open and forced to watch."

"A real charmer, you are. I bet you say that to all the ladies."

"Drop the knife and I am sure we can come to some mutual agreement."

"I get the strange feeling that it would not be mutual."

"You said my head is worth ten thousand? I will give you fifteen to walk out of here."

"I can't spend that without my skin attached to my body."

"Don't be a fool, woman."

"Here is what's gonna happen…"

Evonne was unable to finish her sentence as The Collector suddenly broke free. He took the gamble that this bounty hunter was not actually prepared to cut his throat and was correct. Evonne hesitated and that was enough.

"Get her, Marko, but keep her alive," The Collector shouted.

Marko came forward and Evonne did the only thing she could under the circumstances. She threw her knife at the bodyguard, the only weapon she possessed, and silently prayed her aim was true. Time seemed to slow down as she watched the blade spin end over end through the distance between them.

The knife caught Marko in the throat and he stumbled backwards, gurgling and choking on his own blood. Evonne glanced over to The Collector just in time.

He had produced a dagger and stabbed at her. Evonne's reflexes were spot on. She twisted her body and knocked the weapon aside by slamming her wrist into his. Then wrapped her fingers around his wrist and used his momentum against him, jerking his arm down. She held the wicked moneylender in an arm bar and slammed his head into the table, knocking the mask from his face and forcing him to relinquish his weapon.

He was quite an unremarkable looking man. Without the mask, The Collector was invisible in Ironcliffe, drawing no attention to himself. You would have passed him on the street, or sat next to him in a tavern, having no idea what a monster he truly was.

"When we walk out that door, you won't get ten paces before that crowd descends upon you," he threatened.

"We aren't going out the door I came through, we are going through the one you came through. I am willing to wager you don't walk around this place wearing that mask for all to see. So I would imagine that door is a secret way out of here that only you and a select few others know about."

The Collector growled and Evonne knew she guessed correctly.

"You have no idea what you have just gotten yourself into, wench. Pull my shirt down."

"This isn't the time or the place for that."

"You fool, look at my heart."

Evonne grabbed his dagger and repositioned herself into a choke hold, once again pressing a blade to his throat. "Try to break free again and this time I will cut your throat, don't you doubt."

Evonne meant it this time and The Collector believed her threat. Marko had collapsed to the floor and ceased moving. The Collector had no immediate help so figured his reputation may be his only hope.

"Pull your own shirt down, slowly" she commanded.

The Collector pulled down the top of his black shirt far enough to expose the left side of his chest. There, above his heart, was a tattoo that Evonne immediately recognized. A memory flashed in her mind and she recalled Grim using the name, the Sundered Sons. They were a far-reaching criminal organization operating throughout Tauros. Their name was spoken of in fear. She and Vrawg had somehow managed to avoid crossing paths with any of their members to date, or none that they were aware of.

While this revelation made The Collector a much more dangerous man to deal with, it did not change Evonne's mind. The tattoo did not have the man's desired effect on the bounty hunter.

"Open the door, we are leaving."

"You are making a huge mistake. You will never live long enough to spend a coin of your bounty money. My brothers in the Sundered Sons will see to that."

"I think I am going to impose a no talking rule, starting now."

"You stupid…argghhh."

Evonne drew a thin line of blood under her captive's chin. "No. More. Talking. Now pick up your silly mask and let's go."

CHAPTER 28

"Alright, alright, enough with the lectures. Yes, I was clearly mad to have done what I did but it all worked out in the end. So you can stop now, please? My head hurts."

Evonne rubbed her temples but Vrawg continued to glare at her with anger. She was only to scout out that gambling den so they could formulate a plan together. She was not supposed to go after The Collector on her own. But as she explained to her giant friend, it had worked out in the end.

Falvo upheld his end of the bargain, rewarding them with ten thousand gold pieces and promising that Evonne's past as a pirate would be forgotten. He had also been delighted by the news that Captain Krayne was now dead, by Evonne's own hand, and The Grinning Kraken was essentially no more. Falvo even accommodated one of Evonne's last minute requests. The bounty hunter looked over to a small table next to her bed at the inn and smiled at the drawing of her own face on an old wanted poster. "You sexy devil," she whispered to herself, impressed by her likeness the artist had captured on the parchment. Her head had been worth five hundred gold pieces, dead or alive.

Evonne had spent the last several days depositing much of their gold into an Ironcliffe bank and converting some of it into small gemstones that were more easily transportable than bulky chests of gold. She and Vrawg were wanderers and it was not wise to travel with so much gold. They tried to carry as little as possible and had stashes of coins buried in secret spots all over Tauros. They were not as wealthy as some of the lords and ladies of Tauros but they were well off. They never went cheap when looking for an inn and generally stayed at whichever establishment was considered the best.

They could even afford separate rooms. "Maybe it's time for you to go back to your own room, eh?" Evonne suggested, after Vrawg continued to stare. "Besides, you need some sleep. I have to run out and do a few things today and it's much easier to accomplish stuff without everyone following us around to stare at you."

Vrawg reluctantly returned to his own room and Evonne headed out into the busy midday streets of Ironcliffe. She wanted to see about buying them a new and larger wagon, along with a couple of horses. Their wagons never seemed to last too long after having to support Vrawg's weight over long journeys. She was hoping to find a much stronger one this time. Ironcliffe boasted the best of the best in Tauros, for whatever it was that you were seeking. And Evonne enjoyed the feeling of having enough gold to buy the things they needed without having to worry overly-much about costs. Of course, she still haggled merchants down as much as she could, just because she just enjoyed it.

After spending hours in the market quarter, Evonne was satisfied with her accomplishments this day and started looking for a tavern to quench her thirst. A familiar and quite unappealing face greeted her in the middle of the street.

Evonne looked down and addressed the man's dog. "Good day, Brandy, and how are you doing?"

The large hunting dog with a spiked collar barked a reply.

"I have to say I am impressed," Skald admitted. "I heard stories about you and your pet ogre but most often stories are just that...stories. Too bad The Collector won't hang. Though, I suppose the bounty on his head will now double at least."

"What do you mean he won't hang?"

"You haven't heard?"

"I wouldn't be asking if I had."

"He escaped from his cell two nights ago."

"How does he escape from a cell here in Ironcliffe?"

"Never underestimate the power and influence of the Sundered Sons. They have agents everywhere, even within the city guard and the castle. The right amount of gold can buy you anything, even a ticket out of the dungeon."

"Incredible."

"Well, you still cashed in but tread carefully if you want to be able to spend those coins."

"I am not too worried about a gang of thieves."

"The Sundered Sons are more than just a gang of thieves. From one bounty hunter to another, I am advising you to watch your back. They ain't a very forgiving lot."

Evonne thanked Skald for the news and moved on.

She passed several inviting taverns but decided she was no longer in the mood to drink in public. There were a few bottles of expensive rum back in her room at the inn. She figured she would just down one of those and crash for the rest of the night.

She passed by Vrawg's room at the inn and considered knocking on his door and asking him to join her. The half-ogre could be heard snoring loudly from behind his door so Evonne smiled and decided to let him sleep. She knew Vrawg had worried a lot lately and had not been getting any rest as a result. He deserved a good night's sleep.

Evonne entered her dark room and locked the door behind her. As she turned, something hard struck her in the stomach, stealing her breath and sending her back to slam against the thick door. She struggled to take in air and was struck in the nose, snapping her head back in an explosion of lights.

She clumsily reached for her sword but strong hands grabbed her and flipped her onto her back. Evonne landed hard with her head bouncing on the floor. Her body ached and she had not yet been able to make out her attacker in the dark. She groaned and now noticed a dark form circling around her. Her attacker was not very big and made not a sound on the floor of her room.

Evonne's eyes focused enough to realize this intruder was dressed head to toe in black, including a black mask. She thought to call out for Vrawg when a foot came down onto her stomach, again stealing the wind from her lungs.

Evonne rolled onto her side and struggled to stand but an elbow to the back of her head sent her sprawling again to the floor. This time she decided to lay still and not move at all. She could not hear the assassin walking but knew he was circling her again. A toe nudged her in the side but she continued to lay still.

The assassin rolled her onto her back and then produced a dagger while leaning over to inspect the bounty hunter's face. With the speed of a cat, Evonne grabbed the assassin by the front of his shirt and pulled him downwards. Evonne shot her head forward and head-butted him square in the nose, eliciting a squeal.

She pushed him off and managed to get to her feet, drawing a dagger of her own from her boot. The assassin spun in the air and kicked Evonne, catching her in the chest and sending her stumbling back. Before Evonne fully recovered, she was kicked again in the leg and nearly lost her footing. She stabbed with her dagger but received a palm-strike to her chin instead. Another kick sent her into a wall.

The assassin rushed forward and Evonne gasped as the blade of a dagger entered her right side. The bounty hunter grunted when the assassin twisted the blade inside her. Evonne dropped her own weapon, unable to do anything in response.

Evonne was roughly grabbed by the front of her chain mail vest and thrown across the room where she fell and slid up against the side of her bed. Blood flowed from her nose and dagger wound. Evonne pushed herself up into a sitting position when her elbow knocked into the loaded crossbow she always kept propped up against the bed.

The assassin watched Evonne grab the loaded weapon and sprinted towards her. The bounty hunter pulled the trigger as the assassin leaped into the air to avoid the attack. The bolt struck the mysterious person in the right leg and a most curious feminine voice cried out with pain.

The assassin landed with a thump and rolled about on the floor. Evonne rose and drew her sword, walking over to disarm her attacker. She pressed the tip of her sword into the throat of the assassin and leaned over, placing more weight onto it, drawing blood. Again, it was a feminine voice that cried out. That gave Evonne pause.

She slid her sword-tip under the black mask and sliced it off the assassin's face. Evonne was surprised to find a woman staring back at her. She had long dark hair that was hidden within the mask, and exotic-looking eyes, much like Dragon's from the Far East. Memories of her old friend and mentor flooded into her mind.

"What is your name?" Evonne asked, once again placing her blade against the woman's throat.

There was no answer.

"Tell me your name," she asked again, this time drawing another trickle of blood.

"Kandyce."

"Who sent you, Kandyce?"

"Do you even need to ask that? The Sundered Sons will see you dead."

Evonne had figured as much. Skald had not been kidding when he warned her. If this was any other assassin, Evonne would have gladly cut their throat and tossed their body out the window. But Evonne had never killed another woman before and was not about to start now. She was not exactly sure why that thought bothered her so much but it did. This woman did just try to kill her and Evonne generally took offense to that. Something stayed her hand, though.

"This is your lucky day, Kandyce. I don't kill women and you happen to remind me of someone I once knew. You can leave with your life and tell your employers that anyone else that comes after me will be returning to them in pieces. You included."

The assassin struggled to her feet and meant to exit through the door. "No, not that way," Evonne said.

The bounty hunter grabbed Kandyce and threw her out the third-story window. The woman went through the glass with a loud crash and landed on the street below. Evonne reloaded her crossbow and when she returned to the window, the woman was gone. A trail of blood led to a nearby alley.

Evonne hobbled over and collapsed onto her bed. Blood still flowed freely from the wound in her side. She pulled off a boot and threw it against the wall that separated her room from Vrawg's.

"Vrawg!" she shouted. "Vrawg, wake up, you big oaf! Vrawg!"

*   *   *   *

Evonne and Vrawg sat in a sturdy wagon pulled by two strong horses. They traveled a road heading east, away from Ironcliffe. Evonne got stitched up and the pair left Ironcliffe the day after the encounter with the assassin. They were no cowards but decided that putting some distance between them and the capital might be a good idea. The Sundered Sons were everywhere, it was said, but Evonne hoped they could avoid more assassins by traveling somewhere quiet for a time.

She and Vrawg were successful bounty hunters and she was confident they could find work to keep them busy no matter where they went. The world was full of evil-doers with prices on their heads. Evonne wished that Grim could see her now. The dwarf was always against her becoming a pirate and she imagined he would be quite proud of what she had made with her life.

Her mind drifted to her brother, Zack, and she briefly wondered where he was today. She thought of all of her brothers, in fact. She wondered if any of them had heard of the famous bounty hunter, Evonne, and put the connection together. She also hoped that Dragon was still alive and well. With the death of Purcy, and so many of the Kraken's senior crew members, she had no idea what would have become of the ship. She did not feel that anyone else would have had the charisma or support to claim the captaincy. If the remaining crew was smart, they would have sold the Kraken and went about their separate ways.

Those thoughts led Evonne to think of Nagar, the Dark Mistress. She too, would have been proud to see Evonne today. Evonne wished there was some way to get word to her friend that she was doing well. She figured the next time her and Vrawg were near the coast, she would have a message sent to Trollport.

The pair of bounty hunters stayed a night in the village of Gorn before continuing east. They passed several small towns and villages but Evonne preferred that they put a little more distance between them and Ironcliffe.

They traveled through the thickly-wooded Darbyvale Forest, before eventually arriving in the town of Darbyvale, itself. It was a quiet town but just large enough for Evonne's taste. It was surrounded by a thick forest and ringed by large, wooded hills. Evonne and Vrawg enjoyed the change in scenery.

On their second day in Darbyvale, the bounty hunters had caught wind of some recent murders, and grisly ones at that. Not much was left of the victims aside from their bloodied clothes. It would appear that they had been eaten.

Evonne and Vrawg entered the local militia's office and studied a wanted poster on the wall. The face on the poster was worth five thousand gold pieces.

"Who is Devon Klurk?" Evonne inquired.

EPILOGUE

"So, we captured Devon Klurk, the werewolf, and you approached us shortly thereafter, wishing to hear all about our lives. Then we spent an entire day in this cramped cabin until my throat ached from telling stories."

Evonne downed a mouthful of warm ale in an attempt to soothe her sore throat. She could not remember ever talking so much in her entire life.

She glanced over at her partner, who was searching around for any crumbs of food that may have escaped him earlier. "Hey, piggy, did I leave anything out? Anything you want to add?"

Vrawg just shrugged his shoulders, having long since lost interest in talking to the old scribe from the Ivory Citadel. Hornoglio never looked up at the pair and continued to scribble things down on a piece of parchment spread out before him.

"So, ah, that's it, I suppose," Evonne said, turning her attention back to the scribe. "I think you got everything you wanted and then some."

Hornoglio paid her no mind.

"Hey, I think we are done here. Vrawg and I are gonna leave now. If I don't get this big oaf fed a proper meal you may end up on the menu."

When Hornoglio did not acknowledge her, Evonne stood up and walked around the table. The bounty hunter's jaw hung open as she looked down to regard the parchment the scribe had been writing on. She saw no words written, only tiny drawings and scribbles all over the page.

"What the…"

Evonne reached over and grabbed the piece of parchment to inspect the others beneath it. They were all the same; filled with drawings and nonsensical scribbles. Hornoglio jumped, having been pulled from his daydreaming.

"This is what you have been doing the entire day? Did you hear a single word we told you?"

"I-I-I…," Hornoglio stammered.

Just then there was a loud knock at the cabin door. Evonne spun to find the head of an arrow that had penetrated the thick wood.

"Evonne and Vrawg," a voice called from outside. "Please exit the cabin, slowly."

Evonne drew her sword and pointed it at Hornoglio. "What in the Abyss is going on here? Talk!"

"I-I had n-no choice."

"No choice in what? Speak quickly, old man."

"They said they would kill me and my family."

"Who are they?"

Frustrated by his slow response, Evonne ran to a window. "Vrawg, watch him."

Evonne peered around a curtain and could see that the sun had nearly disappeared behind a hill. It appeared the cabin was surrounded by men in dark cloaks, each wearing a featureless white mask. The Sundered Sons. Evonne counted six men from this vantage point and ran to another window to find another three. She imagined that at least fifteen men stood outside, all waiting to skin them alive.

"Curse me for a fool. I should have known that the Ivory Citadel wouldn't give a damn about us."

"They might," Hornoglio said.

"What do you mean, they might?"

"I don't work for the Citadel. I have never even been there."

Evonne shook her head in disgust. She allowed herself and Vrawg to walk straight into a trap. And a good trap it was. She sheathed her sword and picked up her crossbow. Her first instinct was to start picking them off, one by one, but there was too many. She had not come prepared for battle and carried very little ammunition. This was not looking good.

The voice from outside shouted again. "Trapped like a little rat, are you? You will regret the day you crossed the Sundered Sons, Evonne. There is no place for you to hide where we cannot find you. Our interest is in you, alone, the ogre may go free. Hand over Evonne, Vrawg, and you can leave here unharmed. You have our word on it." When no immediate answer came, the man was heard saying, "Viztigo, how about you coax them out."

Evonne watched from the window as one of the cloaked men began tracing symbols in the air with his finger while chanting. When he finished, a ball of fire sprang to life within his right hand. Evonne smashed the glass of the window and fired her crossbow at the wizard. The bolt bounced harmlessly off of some invisible barrier that surrounded the man. The wizard smiled and hurled the fireball at the cabin, igniting the roof.

"We are running out of time," she said to Vrawg. "Look, they only want me for catching The Collector. You go. There is no sense in both of us dying."

Vrawg fixed her with an angry stare. He could not believe what he was hearing. "Friend," he said.

"Alright, I was just letting you know that you had options here. For us to have any chance of surviving this, I have to get to that wizard."

*　　*　　*　　*

Viztigo, a wizard of the Sundered Sons, watched with pleasure as the cabin went up in flames. It was only a matter of time now before the two bounty hunters would be forced to exit, or die from smoke inhalation. Their orders had been explicit; bring Evonne back to Ironcliffe alive. The Collector had something special in mind for her. But Viztigo knew how dangerous she and the ogre truly were, so if they happened to die, then so be it. They were to kill the ogre anyway, so the easier the method, the better.

Everyone tensed up as the cabin door opened. Three of the cloaked men took aim with their bows. Vrawg stepped outside, coughing, with his hands raised in the air.

Tanor, the group's spokesman, clapped with joy. "Ah, the mighty Vrawg has come to his senses. Come forward, Vrawg, slowly. When we have Evonne in custody, you are free to go on your merry way."

Vrawg moved slowly but cut the distance in half between him and the group. The men waited impatiently for any sign of Evonne.

"That's close enough, ogre. How about dropping that hammer of yours, strapped to your back. Slowly."

Vrawg reached behind his back, slowly, as instructed, only he did not grab his hammer. Viztigo's eyes widened as Vrawg produced Evonne from behind his back and then proceeded to throw her in his direction. The wizard did not have time to get off a spell before the small bounty hunter crashed into him, sending them both to the ground in a tangle.

Evonne recovered quickly and climbed onto the wizard's chest; a knife in her hand. "You know, they used to call me, Evonne the Wizard-Slayer."

Evonne slit the wizard's throat and then launched the knife at the closest archer, catching him in the shoulder and forcing him to drop his bow. She drew her sword and advanced on another man who held a sword of his own.

The remaining two archers paused from the sudden chaos that erupted. One of them regained his wits quickly and let loose his arrow, striking Vrawg in his left thigh. The second archer followed suit but his aim was off as the angry half-ogre charged straight for him. The arrow whizzed by Vrawg's head and he roared, grabbing the hammer from his back and crushing the archer's skull in one fluid motion.

More cloaked men ran from around the other side of the cabin. Several carried swords, while two carried large harpoons, brought especially for the half-ogre.

Evonne parried a strike and then dodged the next.

She slid her sword into the belly of the man she was fighting, only to duck under the attack of another. Growling, she pulled her blade free just in time to deflect the next strike. She risked a glance over at Vrawg to watch her partner take a second arrow in his back. Evonne had to trust in Vrawg to handle himself, as she was hard-pressed with her own problems.

Tanor watched the she-devil engage one of the other men and decided to take advantage of her distraction. He was a thief and not a true warrior. He had no reserves about stabbing someone in the back, not even a woman. The thief raised his sword above his head and chopped downwards towards Evonne's back. The bounty hunter somehow sensed the attack and slipped to the side, avoiding the deadly slash. Tanor felt a sharp pain and looked down to watch Evonne's sword exit his chest. She did not even give him a second glance as she returned to face the other attacker. Tanor collapsed and choked on his own blood.

Vrawg felt the sting of the second arrow and spun to face the last of the archers. The man visibly paled as the half-ogre fixed him with a murderous stare. He took a step forward but found his way suddenly blocked by three of the cloaked men. One of them launched a heavy harpoon which penetrated Vrawg's left thigh, right below the shaft of the arrow. A rope was attached to the harpoon with the other end tied to a large rock. A second, similar harpoon, flew at Vrawg from the side but missed its target.

The half-ogre realized they were attempting to impede his movement so grabbed the shaft of the harpoon, thinking to tear it free. The head of the weapon was barbed and searing pain shot through Vrawg's leg, causing him to abandon that idea. So, he decided to change his tactic.

With his free hand, Vrawg grabbed ahold of the rope and started to spin. His immense strength, combined with his momentum, lifted the rock from the ground and it became a deadly weapon, flying through the air. Vrawg used it, much like a ball and chain, and three men were flung in different directions, battered and broken.

Evonne ducked in time, as the body of one of the men sailed past her to strike a tree. He fell to the ground in a bloody heap and drew his last breath. She battled two men, while the others were attempting to bring down Vrawg. She knew these men were originally attempting to capture her alive. Now, with the deaths of several comrades, they would be just as happy to drag her corpse back to Ironcliffe.

Evonne danced back and then skipped to her right side; a sword narrowly missed her midsection. Sparks flew as she parried another attack and then skipped to her left. She was desperately trying to keep both men in front of her and prevent them from surrounding her. So far it had been easy, as she possessed the superior footwork.

The sun had completely vanished but the burning cabin illuminated the field of battle. Fortunately, for Evonne, one of her attackers tripped over a fallen comrade and stumbled forward. Evonne stabbed at him and punctured his chest. She withdrew her sword and slashed across the knee of the second attacker. The cloaked man gasped and paused a moment to rethink his next attack. That pause was all the bounty hunter needed. She ran him through and then kicked him to the ground, freeing her red-stained weapon.

Evonne panted with exhaustion as she watched four men surround Vrawg. Two arrows and a harpoon attached to a rock, stuck out from his body but the half-ogre showed no sign of slowing. Evonne noticed that the rock on the ground was limiting Vrawg's movement as he swung his hammer wildly at one of the men.

She found the energy to race over and roll between two of the attackers. The bounty hunter came back to her feet just in front of Vrawg and severed the rope between the harpoon and the rock. That was when she spotted the remaining archer and his bow was aimed in her direction. Before she could dive to the side the archer fired; his arrow catching Evonne in the left shoulder. The head of the arrow passed straight through to stick out the other side.

Evonne swooned from the sudden pain and was forced to take a knee. One of the Sons leaped at Evonne to take advantage of her distress. She rolled aside but was not quick enough. His sword still tore a nasty gash across her scalp. Evonne laid on her back, her face a bloody mask. Ah well, she thought, at least she would die a warrior's death.

Vrawg watched the arrow strike Evonne and then witnessed one of the men nearly take her head off. When his dear friend collapsed onto her back, something in Vrawg's mind snapped. His roar shook the trees and sent sleeping birds flying into the night sky. With a two-handed grip on his hammer, he swatted the man who last struck Evonne. He caved-in the man's chest and sent him flying several feet through the air. His next target lost his head in an explosion of gore.

The remaining two swordsmen stumbled back in a

panic. Vrawg took that moment's reprieve to switch his hammer to his left hand and grabbed the end of the harpoon in his right. He was in a full berserker frenzy and felt not a thing as he tore the barbed harpoon from his thigh. He threw it like a spear and impaled the archer, pinning him to a tree.

The last two men were now in full flight. Vrawg hurled his hammer at one and was rewarded with a crunch of bones. Now weaponless, the half-ogre looked about for something to throw but curiously the last man fell, a throwing knife lodged into the back of his neck.

Vrawg turned to find Evonne standing on unsteady legs with a smile spread across her bloodied face. Then she fainted.

* * * *

When Evonne regained consciousness, she had found that Vrawg had done a decent enough job of keeping her from bleeding to death. He was no healer but had patched her up enough to keep her alive. Now, it was her turn to patch him up. Her friend had some fairly deep wounds, but surprisingly, showed no sign of distress. He sat there, silently, while she did her best job to stitch the wounds with her limited supplies.

"The gods were with us today, my friend," she commented.

Vrawg gave her a disappointed look.

"Spare me your speech about the gods, I have heard it too many times before. Look, it was a figure of speech, alright? Happy?"

Vrawg pointed to what was left of the burnt cabin.

"Old man?"

"Ah, forget about him. He had that coming. He had every opportunity to warn us about this trap and didn't. That was almost the end of us."

When Evonne had done all she could for Vrawg, she walked around and inspected the bodies of the dead. Each man wore the tattoo of the Sundered Sons above his heart. Evonne realized some of the men had escaped, no doubt to run straight back to Ironcliffe to inform them of what happened. This would not sit well with the Sons, she knew.

"Perhaps we should leave Tauros for a while. Just until things cool down, huh?"

Vrawg just shrugged. He did not care where they went.

"We could head south and escape the winter in Zalhandria. Or continue east. They got wanted criminals all over the world. Finding work won't be any trouble at all."

Evonne surveyed the battle scene around them one last time and nodded. They had defied the odds and came out victorious. But how many more assassins would the Sundered Sons send after them? It did not matter, she thought, they would send them all running. A change in scenery, however, would do her and Vrawg some good.

"Don't forget your hammer. Let's go."

*　　*　　*　　*

Evonne and Vrawg sat by a large fire they had built, just off the road heading east out of Tauros. Night had fallen and the pair of bounty hunters had decided to stop and rest until morning.

"By Zalara's black heart, you call that singing?" Evonne covered her ears. "Please stop, I can't take any more of it."

"Who Zalara?"

"Zalara is the wicked queen of the deep, who collects the souls of drowned sailors."

Vrawg shook his head.

"Yeah, I know, silly gods."

The pair sat in silence for a time, hypnotized by the flames of the fire, before Evonne spoke again.

"I am glad Hornoglio turned out to be a fake. We don't need the whole world knowing everything about us, right?"

Vrawg shrugged his indifference.

"The past is best left in the past, I say. There is a reason why stuff is left in the past, because we have moved on from that. Am I right?"

Vrawg shrugged again.

"You are just a real bundle of joy to be with tonight, aren't you?"

A twig snapped behind Evonne and she stood in a flash; loaded crossbow in hand. Vrawg growled.

"Step out where I can see you or I will just start shooting," she called into the darkness.

"I don't mean you any harm. I am Doran, a merchant from Stonewood."

"Come forward then, Doran, stop skulking in the shadows."

A heavy brown-bearded man stepped into the firelight with his hands raised above his head.

"Myself and two colleagues saw your fire from the

road and wondered if we might share it with you. We are exhausted and need some rest. I am unarmed."

"There are three of you, you say?"

"Yes, Novak and Bildar are back on the road. We have three wagons and five horses. I came here alone to seek your permission to join you."

"You have no problem sharing a fire with a half-ogre?"

"We would share a fire with a troll right now, if we had to."

"Take your shirt off."

"I beg your pardon?"

"I said take your shirt off."

"It isn't worth much, it…"

"I am not stealing your shirt. Take it off for a moment and then you can put it back on."

The merchant wore a puzzled expression but did as he was told. Evonne nodded when there was no tattoo of the Sundered Sons above his heart.

"Alright, put it back on. Your friends can join us after they, too, remove their shirts. You will also leave all your weapons over here beside Vrawg."

Doran agreed and soon the three merchants sat around the warm fire, opposite the two bounty hunters.

"You are mercenaries?" Novak asked.

"Bounty hunters," Evonne replied. "Where are you three off to?"

"Anywhere, we don't care," Doran answered. "We just want to get as far away from Stonewood as possible."

"Stonewood, that's a pretty big city, ain't it? From what I heard tell."

"Twice the size of Ironcliffe, if you can believe that."

"Then I would imagine that's the place to be, if you are a merchant? No?"

"Not in recent times. The Thieves Guild in that city has always been a problem but the situation there has gotten much worse. There is some dreadful cult of demon-worshipers operating in the city and the Thieves Guild is waging a war against them. The streets are not safe for honest merchants to ply their trade, I regret to say."

"It would be the perfect destination for the two of you, however," Bildar added.

"How so?" Evonne wondered.

"King Stonewood has posted hefty bounties on the heads of Guild members. A good bounty hunter could make a small fortune there."

Evonne rubbed her chin in thought. She knew very little of the Stonewood lands but figured it was far enough from Tauros to give them some breathing room from assassins.

She turned to Vrawg. "So, let's head over to Stonewood. How difficult could it be to round up a bunch of thieves?"

The adventures of Evonne and Vrawg continue in the second book of The Stonewood Trilogy, The Demon of Stonewood.

The Dark Mistress

Bonus sketch by Joseph Garcia

ABOUT THE AUTHOR

Jeremy was born in Scarborough, Ontario, Canada. He started creating his own characters and writing his own stories by the age of 9. He is a boxing fanatic having been an amateur boxer and is now a professional boxing judge. In his spare time when not watching boxing, or reruns of Lost in Space and Rocket Robin Hood, Jeremy tries to find time to write some of the many stories floating around in his head.